In this Life
and the Next

In this *Life* and the *Next*

A Story of Love's True Powers

ALBERT HUGGINS JR.

IN THIS LIFE AND THE NEXT
A STORY OF LOVE'S TRUE POWERS

iUniverse books may be ordered through booksellers or by contacting:

iUniverse
1663 Liberty Drive
Bloomington, IN 47403
www.iuniverse.com
1-800-Authors (1-800-288-4677)

ISBN: 978-1-5320-8390-7 (sc)
ISBN: 978-1-5320-8391-4 (e)

Library of Congress Control Number: 2019914858

Print information available on the last page.

iUniverse rev. date: 09/27/2019

Prologue

H AVE YOU EVER known that you had something great inside of you? Not the potential for greatness, but that you had the power to feel so deeply that it made you stronger physically? The power that love wields is greater than any force in this life or the next. As humans, some feel the potential for the depths of love. We know that people are willing to kill for it, steal for it, live for it, cry for it, or even die for it.

Love is a boundless power. It is the connection that binds the entire universe together. Love allows beings like me to see past my own self into the lives of others. I can also see events that have already happened. I've harnessed love's energy in the physical form one time on Earth. But I could always feel it coursing through my veins.

We'd met one time as kids.

The year was 2000 and I was a husky twelve-year-old. I was about five feet four inches and my skin was dark brown. I usually wore some type of oversized jersey because I thought it would make it harder to tell my weight. I'd always looked younger than my age but was more mature than my peers. It was the year before I started swimming competitively so most people would have called me chubby.

My parents, my brother, and I were on our traditional Memorial Day picnic in Eagle Creek State Park located on the far west side of Indianapolis. Deer and rabbits moved among the trees, which were thick with green leaves that lined the dirt bicycle trails. I remember the smell of grilled burgers and hot dogs as my dad would cook the first round of food. My dad was a master griller or at least I thought so. He always brought his own grill because the park's grills were too small and rusty.

This particular year, I saw a young girl riding her bike down one of the paths in the park. She looked to be about my age or a year younger. I can't say why I felt so drawn to her. *She was just a girl*, I remembered thinking. She had peach colored skin that had a slight tan from the summer months. Her bright golden hair stretched slightly past her shoulders. Her blue-gray eyes seemed to glitter when the sun hit her face in just the right way. I don't remember noticing a girl's features so much before that day.

Her pink Schwinn bike had matching pink and white streamers flowing from the end of each handlebar and a banana seat with a flower or butterfly design on it. Like most boys my age, I didn't care too much for girls back then. At least, not until that day. She seemed so carefree with her hair blowing in the wind as she glided up and down the hilly trails.

As I continued to watch the girl ride her bicycle around the park, she glanced over at me. I quickly looked down at my feet. "Maybe she didn't see me," I said to myself. I looked back up and there she was, much closer than I had realized. The girl was heading towards me. Strangely, she was smiling.

"Hey there. Do you want to play?" she asked. The sound of her voice made me feel strange.

"Uh, yeah sure," I replied.

"Do you know how to slide?" the little girl asked.

Nervously, I asked, "You mean as in baseball?"

"No silly! It's like patty cake but you want to see how high you can count up to without messing up. Here, I'll show you," she said as she grabbed my hands.

She placed her soft hands on either side of mine. My body started to tingle. I felt warm and at home. I had never held a girls hand before unless you count my mother's. But holding mom's hand was different from what I was feeling.

Interrupting my thoughts she said, "Now put your other hand on mine."

"Uh, okay," I said, placing my hand on hers.

"First we will go slow... until you get the hang of it," she said coaching me through the game. Next, she slowly pulled her hands away prompting me to do the same. As she pulled, she said almost singingly, "Sliiiide." Unhurriedly saying the words in rhythm to her pulling away. Then she clapped her hand and I clapped mine.

She held up her right hand. "You hold up your right hand," she said tenderly. The girl slapped my hand as one does in patty cake. "Now your other hand," she said, still moving at a slow and steady pace. After that, she held up both of her hands. Again, I followed. We high fived our front palms, then the back of our hands, and we clapped our hands together.

"Alright!" she said with a smile and a hint of excitement.

I let out a nervous laugh.

"Now we do it again but this time, twice." She said ready to pick up the pace.

"Ok!" I replied like an eager pupil. We must have played that game for an hour. I got better with each attempt. We would laugh out loud every time one of us messed up.

After about an hour had passed, her father called her away from me. "Coming dad... Well, I have to go," she said.

"My name... it's... Sam," I said in a timid voice.

She giggled as she started back toward her father then said, "Ok, Sam. I had fun playing with you."

"What's yours?" I yelled at the back of her head as she rode away on her bike.

At first, I didn't think she heard me but then she looked back and shouted Carrie or Carol. I could not make it out. But she gave me her name and I decided to just call her "Carrie". Not that I'd ever see her again but it seemed proper to remember just in case.

My dad had already grilled the second round of meat, which was ribs and chicken quarters. My mom had the sides and plates laid out on a park bench for our family picnic. I quickly grabbed my favorite foods from the spread and sat at a bench table that faced the bike trails so that I could see if Carrie rode past. She did.

As she rode her bike, she had made it to a bend in the path. At the same time, I noticed a car cruising down the same path from the opposite end. This was not just any car. It was a baby blue and white 1972 Chrysler Imperial LeBaron. Carrie saw the car only a split second before it was about to hit her. I was frozen in fear and couldn't yell at her to look out.

The driver of the car was my Grandfather. He had come to join us for our picnic. He saw the little girl at the last second and jammed on his breaks as quickly as he could. The car was so big and huge that it took time to make a complete stop. Carrie just barely escaped by jumping off her bike into the gravel road. She lied on the ground crying. Her bike was crushed by the metal beast. The front wheel frame had been practically bent in half. The frame of the bicycle was twisted and the back wheel continued to spin as if a rider was still atop it.

Finally unfrozen, I rushed to her. "Are you ok?" I asked. The girl looked up at me and did not respond with words. Her gaze was familiar but I couldn't understand why. She was stunned, I think.

At the same moment, a tall, older man appeared and nudged me out of the way. It was her father. He was an adult after all and likely knew what he was doing more than me. I watched as he brushed away the girl's tears and comforted his little princess. Soon her cries turned to laughter as he eased her pain by tickling her. Carrie was going to be okay.

My grandfather was also there surveying the scene to see if he could do anything to help with the nearly fatal accident. He saw that she was alright and apologized for the bike. He offered to pay for the damages but her father refused to take any money. Eventually, they were able to come to a settlement of the matter. The old man's conscience was eased enough when Carrie's father accepted a ride back to their car. Her dad threw her broken bike in my grandfather's trunk, helped Carrie into the car, then they drove away.

That moment would stick in my mind until that same girl ten years later would walk back into my world. This is not to say that I looked for her but I never forgot her. The energy that we eventually shared was pure magic. It was impossible to explain except to say that we fell in love very quickly and this is part of our story.

Chapter 1
Here's to Honor

ONE DAY IN my college dorm room, Ted, my roommate, asked me to go to one of those shallow Pi Gamma Iota frat parties.

"Ah man! Those parties are full of d-bags and drunk freshman girls with daddy issues," I said.

"My point exactly! Bro, you have to lighten up! You need to just let yourself go for a few hours." Ted was great in these types of moments. He could be very animated and usually convinced or conned people into doing whatever he wanted.

Ted was a handsome six foot tall former high school backup quarterback. He had a frat boy attitude and a slim build that attracted young women to him. He had sandy brown hair that always seemed to stay in place. Looks were very important to him. His clothes were always stylish and he would never leave his room until he looked perfect.

"We are in the prime of our lives! We will be working stiffs for the next fifty years, retire for ten and die," Ted explained.

At this point, he was in full salesmen mode and there was no stopping him.

"What stories will you have to pass down to your kids' man? That we stayed in the dorms, turned down chance after chance to meet smoking hot sorority girls?"

"Come on Ted!" I said, hoping that he was done.

"No, seriously Bro! One party, one epic night, one chance to meet the girl of your dreams!"

Ted could be very dramatic when the situation called for it. The selling point for me was how he said that I had a chance to meet the girl of my dreams. I mean, how could he possibly know this? Furthermore, why would he choose that day to say those words in the way that he said them?

Ted knew that he had cracked me. I looked up at him in that moment. I caught myself. I looked back down and then away. It was too late. Ted was locked in and saw me caving.

"Oh, I get it," Ted said.

"Ted, you don't get it."

"No, no, Bro I do," he replied.

I gave him a look that said, "Yeah right."

"I do," he said in a more sincere voice.

"You're looking for... the ONE," he held his hand to his heart in a joking manner but still taking the comment seriously.

Ted shifted from the party idea to a different subject. Flipping through a small black book, he found the page he wanted. Then he jumped on his computer. "Boom! Here it is! This is the girl I was telling you about, Sam."

"What are you talking about?"

"The girl from Biology class. Look, come over here and check it out," he said.

Only because I was curious I walked over to the computer to look and see what he was rambling about.

"Remember that weird hippie chick I was telling you about?" Ted asked.

I gave him a questioning look.

"The hippie! The hippie girl that would only give me her name and email!" said Ted. He was very excited at this point and disappointed that I couldn't recall one of his many strikeouts with the members of the female persuasion.

"Oh, the hippie girl, yes!" I said, finally remembering.

Ted had met this girl but he didn't get very far with her. He said that she was really weird and always talked about the power of love. She had all of these new-aged thinking ideas. He said that she would go on and on about meeting the right guy and that he was clearly not the right person for her.

"In short Ted, she wouldn't sleep with you. So, you forgot all about her until now."

"Look Bro, I'm trying to help you here. She would be great for you. You're always talking about love and the mushy stuff that girls are in to," said Ted.

"That only felt slightly backhanded. I'm sure you meant that as a compliment," I replied.

"Just check out her pics on Snap Book. Tell me she's not cute."

I had to say that the picture I saw was of a very beautiful girl.

"Why would a girl like her want to date me?" I asked, feeling a little insecure.

"Bro, I know she's out of your league but I can get you a shot. Just talk to her about… her. Chicks dig that kind of crap. It'll be like a double date so no pressure. I've been on a few dates with one of her friends after we decided that we weren't a match."

"And you don't find anything odd about that?" I asked.

"Relax, Hippie Chick is the one that set us up. All I have to do is call her friend and make sure we are good to go."

After a few moments of deliberation, I agreed to go on the date. I asked Ted her name.

"Caroline," he said.

At the time, it was just a name. Now, I know that she would be the love of my life and the impetus I needed to unleash my abilities. You see, within the powers of love, one can find motivation. Love performs the role of the engine to the heart's desires.

The phone rang a few times as Ted made the call.

"Hello Sara, yeah it's Ted. I was just hanging here with my bro Sam and uh wanted to see if you were free tonight... Oh, sure uh your hair... uh, I guess Friday night is as good a night as any to wash your hair... Well, that's a bummer because I was really trying to set up Caroline with my main bud Sam but I guess... Oh, what's that? What does he look like? Well, I guess he's kinda handsome. I mean... well, he's good looking for sure. He's black and uh clean cut. I don't know Sara... Okay, seriously though he's about six-two. He was a swimmer in high school and he is still very fit. Uh, he has dreamy brown eyes. Come on Sara... he's nice. Caroline would really like him, I think. Is she seeing anyone right now? No? Great! Well... like I said, it's a bummer you are washing your hair tonight... oh, you'll wash it tomorrow... Tonight? You and Caroline want to meet tonight? Absolutely! Yep. I know where that is... Late dinner sure, sure. Okay. See you soon. Bye."

And just like that, we had a date set for that night.

Sara was Caroline's closest friend. They met freshman year of college and hit it off. Outside of classes, it was not hard to find the one if you knew where the other was. They did not like the cattiness and drama that came along with being friends with large groups of women. So, they decided by sophomore year to become roommates and stay clear of the cliques.

"So, Care, whacha doin' tonight?" Sara asked.

"Nothing, I think I'm going to wash my hair."

"Seriously?" Sarah asked in a judging way.

"Well, it's not like I have anything better to do," Caroline said, defensively.

"You do now."

"I do? What?" Caroline asked.

"You and I have a double date with Ted and his friend Sam."

"Come on Sara! These blind dates never work out for me."

"That may be, but you know Ted. You guys went out on a date before. You thought we would be great for each other and so far so good. Now we found a guy that might work out for you. What's the worst that could happen?" Sara asked.

"Do you really want me to answer that Sara?"

"Okay, David was a bad set up but how was I supposed to know that he was so into his mother that he'd bring her with him on the date."

"I still have the picture of his mother cutting his steak for him in my head. At least she paid for dinner," Caroline commented.

"Let's look Sam up on Snap Book. I'm connected to Ted. He said that Sam was a good guy. How many guys named Sam can he be connected with?" Sara asked.

"Alright," Caroline said, reluctantly. Sara sat down at her desk and pulled up her social media website. She found Ted's page and searched for his connected friends. She found two Sams. Me and an old girlfriend of Ted's from high school.

"I'm assuming that the guy is the one we want. Okay, Sam Connelly," said Sara. They scrolled through a few pictures, scrutinizing and judging the different photos and posts on my profile. I wasn't a big picture taker. But there was one picture that they stopped on with me and Ted standing near the deck of our high school's swimming pool. Ted was fully clothed. I had just won a race and was only in swim jammers, swim cap, and my shirt was off.

"Very nice!" said Sara.

"Wow, he's cute. I wonder if he still has those abs," Caroline said.

"Let's see. Oh, this one looks recent. Wow, his muscles are bigger in this one and his arms are really toned. If you aren't interested, I'll dump Ted and give him a shot."

"That won't be necessary Sara. I'll do it for you," Caroline interjected.

"Yeah right, for me. Okay well, I already said yes. It's a good thing you are coming."

The girls took turns in the shower and Sara helped Caroline with her makeup.

"You are going to blow Sam away," Sara said.

"You look pretty good yourself," said Caroline.

"Let's go have a good time."

It was time for the big date. I do not remember what I wore but I do remember what she had on, but I'll get to that in a minute. It was a cool Indiana spring evening. I had clammy palms because I didn't have much experience with the ladies. Most of my time was spent in the pool at swim practices and meets. Getting a scholarship meant putting off girls for a while.

Ted's voice startled my thought process as he said, "Relax Bro, you'll do fine. Just be yourself." I started to feel calmer. After a few beats, two girls appeared from around the corner.

It felt like forever but it was only a few seconds before they were in plain sight. Both girls were attractive by most standards. Ted's date, Sara, was five-foot nine, thin build, with black hair. Caroline wore a white flowing sundress with flower prints all over it and a navy blue cardigan. She was about five-foot eight with Golden Blonde hair. Her eyes were a grayish blue. She had the kind of gaze that locks you in and only lets you go when she had decided it was time. She was a classic beauty. One you would see in a black and white movie. Her figure was like a Monroe or Mansfield but she was shy about showing it off. Caroline seemed anxious too. This made me feel less nervous.

"Hey Ted," Caroline said.

"Hey, Caroline," Ted responded.

"Hello there Sara. This is my friend Sam," Ted announced.

Sara nodded and shook my hand.

"Caroline," she said with a smile. She placed her soft hand in mine to shake it. Her smile was so inviting. I found comfort in it. The world seemed to stop when she smiled.

Collectively we had decided on a nearby restaurant. Indiana, while not known for its fine cuisine, had a few gems here and there. The one we chose was a nice, quiet place. The lights were dimmed to set the mood for romance. At the center of each table a dimly lit battery powered candle illuminated the white linen table cloths upon which they sat. Each chair was paired with a burgundy red cloth napkin that had the silverware wrapped inside.

We all sat at the table and chatted together. Soon Ted and Sara, having already been on a few dates, started a more private and intimate conversation with each other.

I was smitten right away with Caroline but I couldn't say why. She was gorgeous, yes. But I'd seen a lot of pretty girls. There was something different about her. I wanted to impress her. I wanted her to like me. I, awkwardly, attempted to start a conversation of my own with her.

"So, where are you from?"

"I'm from here and there and all around," she said.

I gave her a curious look hoping to gain more information from her response.

"Oh, I'm sorry. I was born in northern Indiana and I lived in various states and cities. My dad's job moved us around a lot," she said, seeming almost shy talking about it.

"Oh, okay. I didn't mean to pry."

"No, you're fine," she replied.

After a few minutes of awkward pauses and nervous smiles, I tried again by asking, "Have you seen any cool movies?" I was not a smooth guy and I felt I was already striking out. Ted gave me a shot and he was right - she was way out of my league.

"I'm not too much of a movie person. I'd rather be out in nature. I like to listen to old school R&B when I'm out on a trail. I just put my earbuds in and disappear into myself."

I smiled at her in a judging way. She looked at me and noticed my reaction.

Caroline asked, "Why are you looking at me that way?"

"What do you know about R&B?" I asked her skeptically.

There it was again, her smile. It was even brighter now. "I know plenty!" she said, with a slightly flirtatious tone.

It was around this part of the conversation that Ted and Sara joined back in.

"Care is always walking around singing old songs I've never heard of," Sara explained.

"Oh yeah, well my Bro Sam here can sing like every song that Caroline knows and then two more that she doesn't." Ted had been known to include me in dares and challenges even though I had no intention to participate and sometimes no idea that it was about to happen.

"Ted," I said in a *please don't* tone.

"I've got this Bro!" That only meant that I had no choice but to go along with it and I would actually possibly enjoy it more if I didn't fight it. "Let's do it Sam!" Ted demanded.

"Ah geez Ted."

He gave me a look with one eyebrow up. "Sam..."

"Alright." I looked at Caroline and Sara. I could tell that they were up for whatever the challenge was. Caroline seemed a little nervous but she was trying to hide it.

"Let's go to Kip's Pub and get the Karaoke train going!" Ted said. He was in full Ted challenge mode.

"Kips it is," Sara responded with a look that said, *You've lost and you have no clue!*

We arrived a short time later after walking a few blocks. Kip's was a nice little hole in the wall joint on the north-east side of town. It had its regulars that sat in their normal seats and the standard pool tables and jukebox. The servers were cute in a plain sort of way. They were also the type of ladies that knew how to handle a guy that got too handsy. We'd frequented Kips from time to time if we felt the urge to sing. Normally, I was in an inebriated state before I was really up for singing. There was a small platform near the back of the bar. It was just big enough for a small band to play. That night, the stage was set up for a karaoke DJ and singers.

The DJ booth had a sound board and computer to look up songs. He kept two microphones close to him and one on a stand for the singers. There were two giant speakers that sat on elevated stands on either side of the stage.

Kips smelled like booze and bad decisions. This could only be masked by the thick stench of cigarette smoke that loomed in the air. The walls were filled with bright neon beer signs and posters advertising different drink specials and the next concert dates. The pub wasn't overly crowded but the noise level did require that one spoke a little louder when you talked.

Ted quickly found us a table along a wall so that we could have some privacy. As we settled into our new place he asked, in a dramatic British accent, "Cinnamon and Fire shot anyone?"

"I think I will," said Sara.

Caroline and I looked at each other and agree to the selection. The shots came and Ted held up his glass. Still talking in a British accent, he said, "Everyone please raise your glasses to symbolize the start of tonight's most historic event."

We all complied and raised our glasses.

"Ted you know you don't need to talk in that accent right?" I asked with a tone that said *enough already.*

"Silence you simpleton! I am giving the toast," Ted responded quickly.

I rolled my eyes and allowed him to continue.

"Here's to honor. If you get honor, stay honor. If yo..."

"Woe, woe, woe Ted!" I interrupted. I'd heard this toast before and I didn't think that it would score points with the ladies. "I'll do it."

"Okay, that's fine Bro," Ted said now talking in his normal Indiana/Midwest accent. Then he said, "Do that one toast you like to do."

"Okay... May your neighbors respect you, trouble neglect you, angels protect you, and heaven accept you," I quoted, hoping that it would impress Caroline.

"Wow Sam that was nice," Sara commented.

Caroline chimed in, "Absolutely, I liked it too."

Ted walked over to the DJ and told him that we wanted to sing. He gave the DJ a slip of paper with the name of our song on it. The DJ nodded and within a few minutes, we were being called to the stage to sing.

Ted and I made fools of ourselves as we sang to the music of "Can't Get Next to You" by The Temptations. We were a combination of flat tones and high pitched squeals. At least the girls seemed to have fun with it all. Sara rolled her eyes and Caroline laughed so hard that she had tears streaming down her face.

We finished the song to a standing ovation of two women. Sara was cheering because it was over and Caroline because she hadn't laughed so hard in years. The last time she could remember laughing that hard was when her father took her skiing and he fell more than he actually skied.

Laughter can strengthen the power of love. It is a connector to our loved ones. Something as simple as an inside joke that only you and the people you love know, can make you think of the good times without that person being present. Instantly the laughter makes you feel that the ones you love are there. Through love, laughter can teleport a person to a moment in time spent with a loved one.

"Your turn," Ted said gesturing toward the two women.

"Wait a minute! You never said anything about us singing. There's no way I'm getting up there," Sara declared.

"Well then you lose the challenge and my Bro here wins," Ted said.

"I'll do it," rang the voice to my right. It was Caroline. "I'll sing for us, Sara."

More curious now than ever, I asked, "You really sing?"

"I've been known to hum a bar or two," Caroline said in a modest yet sassy sort of way. Even though she had denied saying these next few words, I'd swore she did in a court of law. She simply said, "Watch this."

Caroline walked up to the stage. The moment after the first note was enchanting. The noise from the bar, the laughing and loud talking, the glasses clinking, and all of the bar traffic stopped. Everyone was looking at Caroline and her eyes were on me. She sang, "I'd Give My All" by Mariah Carey. Her voice was as pure as a beam of light traveling from a faraway place that was designated for a single flower on Earth. I felt as if her voice was that of an angel ordained by the source of love to sing this tune to me.

As she sang nothing else in the world mattered. I felt what I would later come to understand to be Love. One of the many ways that love represents itself is in music. Music is one of the most powerful ways love can be wielded. The words and the melodies of the right person with the right song at the right moment are as strong as any magic that this world can conceive. Music created through love can disarm, silence, or encourage.

By the time Caroline finished her song I knew that I had to know more about this woman. The entire pub whistled, cheered, and applauded her singing. I knew that this was my chance and I would take my best shot. I felt a connection with her that continued to grow as we talked throughout the evening.

"Your voice... Wow!" Was all I could say at first. "Where did you come from?"

"I guess I sang quite a bit in church choir growing up," she said, trying to be modest.

"What else don't I know about you?" I asked still in awe of her.

"Well, there isn't much else to say... My father took care of me and loved me with all of his heart. He worked overtime and extra shifts so that I wouldn't have to take out a bunch of student loans for school. My mom died in childbirth so I never met her. My father tells me all kinds of stories about her, though. Oh, and I am an only child," she summarized.

"I'm sorry to hear about your mother," I said.

"No, it's ok. I never knew her so it feels weird to talk about her."

"Either way, I think it's sad that you didn't get a chance to meet your mother," I added.

"That's nice of you to say, Sam."

"So, how did you meet Ted?" I asked, trying to lighten the mood.

"Long story short, I thought he was cute but then we started talking. You know how someone starts talking and you immediately regret having a conversation with them. That was Ted. For some reason though, I knew he and Sara would hit it off."

"That is too funny. I know what you mean. Ted and I have been buds for a while. He's got a good heart and he's very honest."

"Great qualities to have in a friend," she said.

"Will you clarify something for me? I mean, Ted said something about you and I... Nah forget it," I said.

"What is it, Sam?"

"I don't want to go down the wrong path too quickly and scare you off."

"You scare me? I don't think you'd do that to me, would you? Go ahead and ask me," Caroline said.

"Well, Ted said that you... you were always talking about love when you guys dated. Is that true? Do you believe in love? What I mean is, do you think someone can truly be meant for one other person?" I asked, hoping I hadn't gone too far.

"You mean like love at first sight?" she asked.

"Well maybe more like love at first meeting," I said, anxious of her response.

She paused for a while and I started to get nervous. "Never mind," I said.

"No, I want to answer the question. I just didn't want you to think I was crazy or something," she replied. She paused a few more seconds and then asked, "Have you ever felt like you've known someone but you didn't know where from? I've always felt that I would know when I met the one," she said in a sure tone.

"Yes! I know what you mean." I said enthusiastically.

"When I was up there singing, I felt very nervous at first and then my eyes met yours. And a calm fell over me. It was as if your eyes were a guiding light helping me navigate through the song and hit the notes just right. It was like I was singing to you. While I don't know you very well, it all felt right."

I could agree that this was not a typical first date conversation but I felt something stronger than any force that I have ever felt. I made a decision quickly to see where this conversation could lead us. I wanted to see if she was feeling what I felt.

"Tell me all about you, Caroline. I want to know you. Has your hair always been Blonde? Tell me about this scar on your elbow. How did you get it?" I asked.

"Well if you must know, I have always been Blonde... except for the few weeks I tried cherry red."

We both laughed about that.

"Well blonde suits you quite nicely," I said to her with a smile.

"Why thanks, Sam. And as for my scar, I fell off my bike when I was a kid."

"Awe," I said with a fake empathetic tone.

"Are you making fun of me?" she asked playfully.

"Oh no, not me," I said starting to straighten my clothes. "I would never do that... now go on with the story about the scar."

"No, you don't want to hear me ramble on about my childhood," she said starting to blush a little.

"Really I do," I said.

"...So, when I was little, my father and I liked to go camping. We would camp all around different states but mostly here in Indiana. I was about eleven years old, we went camping at Eagle Creek."

"Do you mean Eagle Creek State Park in Indianapolis?" I asked.

She nodded and continued with her story, "My dad and I had been riding our bikes on trails and then on the gravel roads. There was a bend in the road which created a blind spot for me. Little did I know on the other side of my blind spot was one of those old school 'big boat' cars. I didn't see the car until it was right on me... This might sound funny but it is true... I'm not joking so don't laugh. Something pulled me off of my bike and onto the ground."

At this point Caroline's eyes were big and she glared at me for an extra beat before finishing the story. "There was a little boy that I had been playing with earlier. He rushed over to me first. I cut my elbow pretty good. My father came and saved the day. I had to get fourteen stitches."

I knew her story like a reoccurring dream. It was a memory from my childhood too. An event that stood out in my mind for some reason. The little girl that narrowly escaped my grandfather's vehicle.

Love has the power to keep a memory alive for as long as you need it. Love uses those memories to help souls navigate through their existence. One who can wield the powers of love to remember has the power to find love without even looking. In this way, love gives vision and clarity to all that need to see.

I didn't know how to ask her more details. What would her reaction be after she told me this story and how would I make her believe me?

She had been so receptive up to this point. I had to keep believing this was not just a chance meeting.

"Can I ask you questions about the near accident? …Would that be weird?" I asked, giving her an out if she felt uncomfortable.

"Well Sam, at this point I think that it's weirder that you are asking me if it's weird." I feel comfortable with answering your questions."

Her response was exactly what I was hoping for. After all, she had a point. The entire date was an appointment with destiny. I just didn't fully grasp it.

"Was the car baby blue with a white top?" I asked.

Caroline paused for a moment and looked at me with wonder. "How'd you know that?"

"I'm just asking."

"It was one of those really old cars. It was in great condition…"

"It had white leather seats, chrome wheels, and a White convertible top," I said interrupting.

"I don't…I don't understand," Caroline said, stuttering.

"I was there at Eagle Creek Park that day," I responded.

Caroline looked me in the eyes with some fear and some amazement.

"I was there. I was the little boy. I remember you with so much clarity. From time to time I dream about that moment and you. I could never understand why until now. You telling me that story. That car, your dad, and my dad always dragging us out there to that same State Park, year after year. That is one of the only things I remember as clear as I do." I explained.

"And now you do?" Caroline asked.

"Do what?"

"And now you understand why you remember this all?" She asked, with more clarification.

"Well, I don't understand, but I can tell you that you grew up and you are beautiful. Your voice has a sound angels stop to listen to. You… you are literally the girl of my dreams," I responded.

"Oh, my. Gosh Sam, this is getting a little odd. Well, I should be feeling weird. But, it doesn't feel as strange as it should. I mean as soon as you introduced yourself to me, I stopped feeling so nervous. You felt familiar. It's so amazingly odd that I don't feel more freaked out about this right now. You just described a part of a story about my life that almost no one could know."

"You want to know what's really weird though?" I asked.

"What?"

"I still remember how to slide." I said with a smile.

"Oh, that's right! I loved that game when I was younger," she replied.

The night went on and we talked for a long time. We swapped stories about our childhood. We talked about past relationships. The days went by and we kept seeing each other. While I fell in love with her that day, we didn't say it to one another for a few more weeks.

There it was, my entire life right in front of me. I knew that she would be my wife. I knew that there was no force on Earth that could ever stop me from loving her. I knew that my life was going to revolve around her. I knew that I would see death before I let her be hurt.

Chapter 2

Us Together

M Y MOM AND my brother welcomed Caroline in like she was one of us. My father had passed during my freshman year of college so he didn't get the chance to meet her. Caroline's father didn't worry about her as long as she was with me. I guess I won most of her family over after the time that she had broken her leg on a hiking trip. We were over near Brown County, in Indiana. I wouldn't leave there to get help. I had created a splint from the tree branches and a spare T-shirt. I carried her on my back for two miles down to the DNR station.

We got married a few months after college. It was an outdoor wedding at Cox Hall Garden in Carmel, Indiana. The venue was a place full of green grass and architecture. The inner sanctum consisted of an alter located beneath ground level, surrounded by tiered rows with stone benches. Above the alter arched a canopy supported by old Roman-styled columns. The officiant and I stood under the canopy waiting for my soon to be wife.

Caroline walked down the aisle to the Christina Perri song, "I

Have Died Everyday Waiting for You." I don't think I'd ever really heard the words to that song until that day. Each word of the song had a new meaning for me. I realized in those moments how she was my person. I know men aren't supposed to cry at these types of things but I did.

She was beautiful in her dress. She toiled for a long time over finding the perfect one. Should she get a strapless dress or keep the shoulder straps? Should she get plain or some type of pattern? For being a hippie chick, she seemed to care a great deal about the tiny details of our wedding. "Women dream of their dress from the time they are little girls. I want it to look perfect for you," she'd say.

I'd reply, "Caroline, you'd look great wearing a gunny sack for a dress. You will always be perfect to me."

I was telling her the truth. My Caroline looked absolutely stunning in her wedding gown. She went with a strapless dress with an embroidered flower design around the waist. The entire dress was off-white and flowed down to her feet. She chose white strapped sandals for shoes. She wore a veil over her face that was connected to her long flowing blonde hair, which she styled in bouncing spring shaped curls.

When I unveiled her, she had very little makeup on but it was slightly runny from the tears flowing from her face. We made our own vows and mixed them with the traditional ones. Her words were beyond satisfactory. I could not believe that the girl that was out of my league was now my wife.

Outside of work, we were always together. Even when things got busy, they weren't too busy for us to make time to be in love. I would find a reason to send her flowers while she was at work or have her bath ready with candles and relaxing music if I got home earlier than her. She would slip little notes in with my lunch bag. We had date nights every week. Usually, it consisted of me and her making popcorn and sitting out on the back patio deck looking at the stars and talking about life. It was enough for me. Just to be with her was all I wanted.

"Sam, Sam, wake up," Caroline said.

"I'm up. I'm up. Are you okay?" I asked, still a little groggy.

"I'm fine. I was just looking at you sleeping. But I couldn't sleep.

I wanted to do something special for you so I got up and made you breakfast in bed," Caroline said in a soft sultry voice.

"Where's the breakfast?"

Caroline merely smiled. At last, I got it. She was lying in bed wearing only black lace underwear and whipped cream covering her breasts.

"Oh, breakfast in bed," I said, quite stunned and very excited.

We made love for a little over an hour that morning. When we were finished we laid in bed staring at the ceiling, breathing and thinking. We didn't talk right away. We sometimes had comfortable silent moments where we could relax with each other and not have to say any words.

"How did I get so lucky? Millions of people in this world. You could have been with anyone else. Why me?" I asked.

"It was always you. You are the man of my prayers. I asked God for you long before you came to me. I only had to date a few jerks before you came along. I saw what's to see out there. But you Sam, you are different. You still do things like help old ladies across the street. You bring in the trash cans and do the dishes because you want to."

"I do the dishes because you always miss a spot," I said as we both chuckled.

"No really Sam. You are my nurse when I am sick. You send me flowers at work. That makes all of my co-workers jealous. You are my support system and you are my best friend. I could not go through this life without you."

"What about the next life?" I asked.

"What do you mean Sam?"

"I promise to love you forever. That means when we are old and gray and pass away. I'll be with you in this life and the next."

"In this life and the next, huh?" She asked, a little skeptical of my promise.

"Yeah, I'll be there waiting for you, if I go first. Heaven wouldn't be heaven if you weren't there."

"Well, Sam, that is a long ways away. I will love you till the end of time and then we will create time again to be together for longer. My soul would be lonely without you. If I passed away first, I would be here with you. My spirit would not leave your side. I would be next to you. The first face you see in the afterlife would be mine."

"How would I know you were there?" I asked.

"You would feel it in the air and in the silence. I would comfort you in a way that only my presence could. And if you didn't get it, I would knock something over or make some kind of soothing noise so that you'd know I was here for you."

"I feel like you've really thought about this... Tell you what, whoever goes first comes back for the other until it is time to be together again. No knocking glasses over to freak each other out. We make our presence felt by using a soft easy sound like a chime lightly tapping in the wind," I said offering up a feasible alternative to scaring each other.

"Deal... together in this life and the next," Caroline said.

"Deal... forever," I replied.

That phrase would become our mantra. Together in this life and the next forever. It was a strange conversation but we had those types of heart to hearts all of the time. Our commitment would be tested soon and we would hold on to those words to get us through a very challenging period.

We had been married for six wonderful years. Our love continued to grow stronger and stronger with time. We had learned each other's quirks and complimented each other well. Love has the ability to bend time. A day spent in loves bliss can make time stand still. True love can create a protective shield around your loved ones leaving them invulnerable to the pains that Earth can cause.

It was April 12, 2016. The date is something that love won't ever let me forget. It was a heavy Indiana rain. It felt like giant buckets of water were being poured right on top of us. Caroline and I were in the car driving home from work. Caroline was in the driver's seat while I was in the passenger seat. I didn't know at the time but this would be the first and only time that I would wield the powers of love on Earth. I had no clue that a driver texting would be the catalyst to me discovering my powers.

"Caroline, be careful honey."

"I know Sam. I have my flashers on and I'm ten and two on the steering wheel."

"I'm sorry, I don't mean to be like that. It's just that you and the baby..." I explained.

"Yes, the baby. I'll be careful."

Caroline took one hand off the wheel to gently caress her undeveloped belly. I placed my hands on hers. Caroline glanced back at me and cracked a half smile and was quickly back to driving.

Just ahead I noticed flashing lights... "Police? No... ambulance!" I thought. There was lots of chaos all around. I saw three bodies lying on the ground with covers over them. Three others being tended to. I had some first responder training from my time working for the forest preserves during college.

"Stop the car," I said. Caroline carefully brought the car to a stop and I jumped out to offer my services.

"Hello, I'm a trained first responder. Can I help?" I said to one of the ambulance drivers.

He was a black man with light brown skin. He had a thick raincoat and hat on that were both soaked by the rain. He seemed very overwhelmed and welcomed my assistance.

"Yes, that man sitting against the tree has a broken arm. Can you do a splint?"

"Splint, I know how to do that," I said.

"Take these. And thanks by the way," he said, handing me the necessary tools.

I quickly ran over to a young man. He looked to be in his early twenties. He was shocked by the gruesomeness of the scene and a little afraid. He was also cold and wet.

"Hi, I'm Sam. I'm here to help you. Do you mind if I take a look?"

He held out his arm and I began to splint what looked to be a broken forearm. After patching up several people, I learned that the accident occurred when a truck flipped over because of the slick road conditions. When the accident was tallied there were about a dozen cars involved, twenty-six people injured, and three fatalities.

The rain calmed. The wreckage was cleared away and traffic started to flow as usual again. As I walked back to the car, I noticed another car swerving between lanes. As it moved closer and closer, I saw that the driver had his head down. *Is he asleep?* I thought to myself.

"Hey!!! Hey!!!" I yelled while frantically waving my hands in the air. The driver never noticed me. His erratic pattern seemed to be closing in on our car. On Caroline...Now my attention was focused on her. I was at least a hundred feet away and my legs wouldn't move fast enough.

"Caroline!!!" I shouted as loud as one can yell. She heard me somehow. Caroline looked up at me. Then responded to my gestures. "Get out of the car!" I continued to shout. Read my body language. *Please, get out of the car my sweet beautiful Caroline,* I thought as I shouted. Caroline quickly jumped out of the car as the rogue vehicle plowed into it but was unable to clear herself from the impact. The car door swung backwards due to the impact and clipped just enough of her. Caroline was knocked to the hard, unforgiving asphalt and was now lying in the road. I heard screeching and saw that another car had jacked on its breaks and was on a collision course with Caroline.

"No!" I cried.

I liken how I felt to how you hear about a mother that sees her child stuck under a car. She is suddenly equipped with the strength to lift the car off the child and sweep him to safety. This was the initial rush that I felt flow through me the first time I used my powers. Everything slowed down. The laws of the universe became very clear to me. I had control of time and space and was aware of it. In that instant, a great light surged through my soul and around my body. It was as if the hand of God reached through me and helped me move faster than I had ever gone.

Caroline was on the ground and barely conscious. She did not see the car sliding out of control and headed directly toward her, but she instinctively sensed it, and curled into a ball to brace for the impact.

With my newfound understanding of space and time, I realized I could move very quickly. I was able to reach her just before the impact by lunging between Caroline and the vehicle. The car impacted us like a linebacker slamming into an offensive lineman on a blitz. I took on most of the impact but it was the car that took on damage. When it hit me, it stopped in its tracks and bent around my body.

As I began to regain my focus I looked at the car that had just crashed into me. It was a gray 2010 Impala. The bumper was completely crushed into the car. The windshield was shattered into pieces. The car had an imprint of my body bent into it.

The driver got out of the car. It was a white thirty-something-year-old man. He stood about five feet ten, wore a suit and had a neat haircut, like business types have. He was on his way back to work from his lunch break. The airbag had successfully deployed. Aside from a few bumps and bruises and a bloody nose he was fine.

"Sir, are you okay? How did you do that? You… you were glowing. Wow, that light. It was amazing," the driver said.

I couldn't stand but was able to get to one knee. Still not completely understanding him, I motioned with my hand as if to ask for a moment to assess.

"The woman… is she okay?" The driver asked, gesturing over to Caroline.

Caroline was injured. She had a broken leg from the impact of the door and a concussion from her fall to the asphalt, but she had survived.

It's amazing the things we are willing to do for love. Physically, I put myself in the way of a moving vehicle to save Caroline. Love's power of protection, as it relates to life and death, comes down to a simple math equation. A life for a life. This was a harsh rule about my powers that I had yet to learn. Love is a great power. It is created from Ekon himself. The power of life is rooted in love. The cost is a life for a life. I only had one life to give.

"Sam?" Caroline asked. She looked confused at first. But I soon realized it was not confusion on her face. It was fear.

"What's wrong Caroline?" I thought I said. In reality, it was all in my head. Caroline didn't hear or understand me.

"Sam?" she said with tears in her eyes, "Sam?"

I tried to respond but couldn't. It felt like a hot knife had pierced my ribs. It was then I realized I had been injured. I was able to protect Caroline from the crash but not myself. The impact of the car was too much for my mortal body to handle. I couldn't keep balanced on my knees and I fell to the ground.

"Sam!" Caroline cried. She pulled herself closer to me and held me in her arms. "I'm with you, honey. You're going to be okay." She said trying and failing to choke back tears. "Please Sam, don't leave me."

I laid there trying my best to fight for my life. I wanted to say something, anything…"I'm… n…not going an…y …where." I finally managed. "T…to…ge…ther forev…ever," I said just before coughing up blood.

"In this life and the next," she finished my sentence for me.

"I'll be there wi… th you."

She held me in her arms for a brief while before the paramedics made it to the crash site. I held on the entire time. She continued to try to comfort me and gave me her best smile. I was no longer able to speak. Every attempt was met with me choking on my own blood.

"Sam, please. Come back to me. I love you. You saved me. Now save yourself Sam. Please, stay with me! I can't do life without you!"

I took a deep breath through my nose and remember smelling Caroline's perfume. It was a brand that I bought for her last Christmas. In that moment I marveled at her beautiful face. I was so lucky to have her. Because I couldn't talk and continued to cough up blood when I did try, I decided to take in all of her features. I knew that these were our last moments together on Earth. I could slowly feel my life force changing. The strange part is that I felt my force getting stronger. The light I felt before the crash was back. It started to get brighter and brighter. Soon I could no longer see Caroline's face.

The paramedics pronounced me dead upon their arrival at the scene. Caroline was left alone, broken physically and mentally. There was nothing more I could do for her.

Chapter 3
The Awakening

Y EYES SLOWLY adjusted to the light. The pain in my ribs had disappeared and I could breathe normally again. I was not afraid even though I had no clue where I was. I started to look around. "Where am I?" I said under my breath.

I was lying in a field of deep green grass and bright yellow daisies. I felt the warm light of the sun on my body. It felt like a beautiful spring day. This was the kind of day where you call off of work and go for a walk. The fragrance of the air was fresh with a mixture of flowers and a salt-filled ocean. The temperature had to be in the mid to upper seventies. I'd guessed seventy-six or seventy-eight degrees. There was a very light cool breeze flowing through the air.

"Caroline would love this," I said, again to myself. My mind focused upon her and I found myself calling out, "Caroline, are you here?"

She was not.

In the distance, I noticed a dirt path. Further down the trail, it changed to a paved road. The pavement was made of a gilded gold color. I felt compelled to explore where it led. I began to walk down the path and took in all of the beauty around me. The field was butted up next to a forest. There were thick, enormous trees all around, more than in any forest I'd ever seen. The trees were so tall, one couldn't see over the tops unless they climbed them. I walked over to touch one of the trees and a feeling of pure understanding of the tree came upon me. I knew that the tree was a Sycamore. Sycamores didn't grow this tall on Earth.

"How did I do that?" I asked myself. To my right, I saw a squirrel eating a nut. It looked right at me and held it out as if to say, *Would you like one?* I smiled and gestured back by holding my hand out. The squirrel cracked the nut and handed it to me.

"Thank you," I said. It only seemed polite to say such a thing.

In front of me was a brook of water flowing from a small waterfall. Immediately I ran towards it. I loved to swim back on Earth. The fall let off a light mist which formed rainbow colors when the sun's rays hit it just right. The perfection in the flow of the water was remarkable. It was as if each drop of water had a formation and followed it to the letter. The water was crystal clear. I could almost see to the bottom.

I kneeled down and placed my right hand in the water. Its movement tickled my hand and I let out a slight chuckle. Having tested the temperature with my hand, I now placed my face into the brook. I started to hold my breath and realized that I didn't need to. I was fine keeping my head under as long as I wanted. Delighted by this revelation, I dove in for a quick swim. A large coy fish saw me and decided to swim with me. I could move just as fast as the fish did. The coy fish and I raced around the small body of water like two Indy Cars at the Indianapolis Motor Speedway. It was a joyful experience and I found myself laughing as I swam.

After several minutes underwater I waved goodbye to the coy fish and returned to the surface to continue to explore more of the path. There was a feeling of harmony in everything I saw. All of God's creatures and creations were one. The wind had a hint of fresh juniper aerating through the forest. I saw a bear together with a deer and a wolf walking with a rabbit. These things would seem strange on Earth but here in this place, they were not. I didn't talk to the animals but I could read feelings or emotions from them.

I walked for a long time and never really got tired or even warm. I felt no hunger for food or thirst for water. I was aware of the journey but the time did not pass the same way it does on Earth. I wasn't sure where I was going but the closer I got, the surer I felt that I was going in the right direction. Never straying too far from the golden path, I started to come out of the forest and into an open field again. This field had rows of grassy green hills of varying slopes and heights. Further in front of me, I saw what looked to be a city filled with beautiful houses. The architecture was not unlike Earth's buildings. The biggest difference was that they were grander and had cleaner lines and straighter edges. Each house had its own style and personality.

The city were guarded by a large gate featuring pillars made from the same gold of the path which emitted a blue and white light, much like one you would see in a LED light bulb. The gate was open and as I walked through I glanced at the doors, which had golden rods running vertically and support rods on the top, middle and bottom running horizontally. Unlike any gate on Earth, this one felt welcoming, as if it were made of pure energy.

As I approached the city I could make out moving shapes and figures. There were people! Some were walking into buildings while others were walking out or along the streets; they seemed to be free to go as they pleased. I was excited to see others since it had been some time since I had seen or spoken to anyone.

The golden path widened as I reached what must have been the main entrance, a tall, wide entryway paved in gold with silver light posts. It made for a very shiny beacon for someone who was lost. I'd hoped that the people of the city were welcoming. It felt right so I walked forward through the entrance.

The first person I noticed was an older black gentleman who looked to be in his early sixties. The man was standing next to a pond with a fishing pole resting horizontally across a wine barrel. He was turned away from me at an angle, focused on threading the pole. I couldn't see his face but he was about six foot-two. Even though he was older, he appeared to be in good shape. Age agreed with him like Laurence Fishburne or Denzel Washington. The man was wearing beige linen pants with a cotton button-up shirt. He had the top three buttons open and the sleeves were rolled to his elbows. He had pepper colored hair on his chest and a full beard that matched. He was wearing beach sandals and a straw hat. If I didn't know better, I would say that he was ready for a trip to the beach.

"Hello Sir," I said

The man looked at me and smiled. "Sam! Oh, you're here!" His voice was full and deep. His accent sounded Midwestern but with a hint of Georgian. It was slightly familiar but too hard to place. He offered his hand and I took it.

As we shook hands he said, "Welcome!" then reached past me with his other hand.

A little disordered, I went along with it and allowed him to pull me into an embrace.

"You don't recognize me." It was more of a statement than a question.

"I'm sorry, sir but I don't," I said a little nervous about the interaction.

"It's me, Gerald. Your father."

It still took me a moment to truly grasp what he said. It had been a long time since I had seen my father. I was only nineteen when he was killed in action at the age of forty-seven serving the US in Iraq. His role in the mission had been to lure the enemy away from his company's position in order to allow them to escape. Later, his comrades were able to double back by following a trail of dead enemy soldiers for eight miles before they found his body. His sacrifice saved eight soldiers and fifteen civilians. They told me the story in a private get together after his funeral.

"Dad? Is that really you? You look so different," I said with tears welling up in my eyes. I was very emotional about this meeting but the main feeling was joy. We hugged again.

"We are in The Land of the Promised. I believe on Earth the closest way to describe it is Heaven. Here we are able to take on any age or shape that we want. I could be myself at age ten." Without another word, he turned into a ten-year-old version of himself. He had on a white tank top and cutoff shorts. He was not wearing any shoes, just like his early years in Georgia. "Or I could be the age I was when you last saw me." He then looked like he did the last time I saw him at age forty-seven. He was in his army fatigues and his rank was on his collar. He gave a salute for old time sakes. "But I prefer to be the age I would have been on Earth, had I lived that long," he said with a smile. He was now back to his older version of himself.

"We are in heaven?" I asked in disbelief.

"Well, you can call it that. We call it The Land of the Promised. It is the place where all things begin and end and begin again. This place was promised to us by The Great Source, Ekon."

He saw that I was not sure what he meant.

"God, Ekon, or The Great Source; he has many names. However, it is more complicated than that. We are all a part of something greater than ourselves. That something is The Great Source. In some way, we are all God. Have you noticed how you can just touch something or concentrate on an object and know what you need to know about it?"

I thought for a minute, remembering the Sycamore tree. I nodded my head and said, "Yes."

"We are a part of The Great Source. We are in a harmonious state with all that surrounds us. Our emotions, personality, and thoughts originate from The Great Source. As we learn more and more about the universe, we can give that knowledge back to the source. The new knowledge is then distributed, if you will, back to each individual."

"So, we still have independent thoughts, right?" I ask.

"Yes, but you are also able to understand the thoughts of others, hence gaining new understanding about all things," my father explained. "Come now Sam, there is much for us to talk about. Let me show you around."

The gold paved streets continued throughout the city. There was not as much as a crack on a sidewalk or any building. There was a colorful market back near the entrance where one could find any type of cuisine. While there was no hunger, there was desire. If someone desired to eat something they could but it did not have the same effect as food on Earth.

Our bodies were not built to last on Earth but they were here. The market was a gathering place. If a person desired to be with people they could come here. If another person desired to be alone or at home, they could create food at the speed of thought.

The houses were as different as the people living in them. While it was unnecessary to have shelter. It felt comforting to have a space to call home. But home could always be changed or even moved with little effort in this land.

It had been so long since I had seen my dad and now he was right here in front of me. There were so many questions that I had for him. Some questions were about how he died, some were about how he lived, and some were about this place we were in. He knew all of my questions before I could ask them. He was able to communicate to me with just a touch of his hand.

As I continued to ask more questions he invited me to a celebration for me to see other loved ones. My grandmother, uncles and aunts, cousins, and friends that had long since been gone would be in attendance.

Slowly, I began to love the Land of the Promised. It started to feel like home. Earth was becoming a distant memory. I felt love in a very pure form. This feeling would be too much for any human body to contain. The feeling is indescribable but euphoric is as close as I can get to a description.

Chapter 4
The Funeral

Back on Earth, Caroline was preparing for my funeral. We had some money saved up for just in case purposes. Death was not the case that we were really planning for. I had some life insurance which was just enough to cover the casket and burial.

Caroline was sitting in the office of the Funeral Director, a man whom at his age of fifty-seven had presided over thousands of services. He wore a store-bought gray suit and black tie. Because of his line of work, he always kept a handkerchief in his jacket pocket.

"Caroline, we at The Final Resting Place Funeral Home know how difficult it is for you at this time. Unfortunately the cost of a funeral can be substantial, but I will do my best to work within your budget. It is a true tragedy that such a young man has passed. Let us know if there is anything we can do."

"Thank you," Caroline said with a sniffle.

Her longtime friend Sara sat beside her holding her hand. She was trying to be strong for Caroline but seeing her friend in her current state was devastating and she found herself tearing up as well. "It'll be okay. I'll be right here for you during the entire time." said Sara.

Caroline nodded her head and could not hold back her tears.

The memorial was held at the funeral home. The venue was modest but was big enough for members of our families and our closest friends. The room held about one hundred fifty people. Almost all of the seats were filled. Everyone in a seat was someone that I knew well and loved.

During the ceremony Ted got up to say a few words remembering me. He stood at the podium wearing a tailor-made suit that fit his physic perfectly. He was still at the weight he was back in college. The suit and tie were both black. His shirt was white. His entire outfit was designer made. Ted pulled out a folded sheet of paper from his inside jacket pocket. The room was silent as he slowly unfolded the paper from fourths to half and then from half to full page.

"Sam was a good man," Ted began, "He believed in true love. He loved and he loved hard. I remember in high school, Sam's girlfriend dumped him because he was too nice."

The crowd laughed a little and Ted managed a slight smile.

"...Which was true by the way, he was a very caring and giving person. He didn't care if you were rich or poor. If you needed it, Sam would give it to you. When I first met Sam we were 13 years old, I was being accused of shoplifting from a local gas station. The police had me sitting down on the curb in front of the store in handcuffs. Sam happened to be in the store at the same time as the shoplifter. Now, I had been in trouble before which made me a likely suspect but it wasn't me."

A tear rolled down Ted's face. He paused to gather himself.

"Sam saw the guy who had actually shoplifted, followed him out of the store, caught up to him, and made him come back and confess. I never did forget what he had done. When I asked him why...?" Ted cleared his throat and took a drink of water. He'd heard that you can't cry and swallow water at the same time.

"...Why would he do something so stupid and put himself in danger like that? He looked at me and said, 'it wasn't right what that boy did and it wasn't right that you were going to be blamed for it so it was the right thing to do.' We were friends ever since. It came as a shock to me when I was told about my best friend's death. I was not shocked that he had died saving the life of the woman he loved." Ted folded his paper in half then into fourths and placed it in his inside pocket. He walked away with his head hanging down trying to hide his pain.

Next up was Caroline. She wanted to speak despite Sara's advice not to. Caroline walked steady and firm up to the podium. She was aware of all of the people staring at her but she wanted them to know how much she loved me. "I am happy that you all came to honor Sam's memory. Thank you, Ted, for those beautiful words about Sam. He would have been proud of you."

And I was.

"Sam was wonderful. He was my best friend and the love of my life. Our love transcended space and time. We always talked about being together forever. I never saw this being the way life would go for us. I miss him terribly." She stayed strong while she was up there but she started to sniffle and reached for a tissue to wipe away tears before she continued…

"He'd want us to celebrate his life. Sam loved hard. He loved true. He helped others every chance that he could. But Sam would never want us to be here crying over him. Sam would want us to raise a glass in his honor," Caroline said while she cracked a smile through her now red and puffy face.

"I will leave you with his favorite toast and the one he gave on the first night we met. It was kind of a prayer… May your neighbors respect you, trouble neglect you, angels protect you, and heaven accept you." Caroline barely finished the toast before she finally broke down and cried. Sara quickly rushed to the stage and ushered Caroline off, comforting her all the way.

Caroline spoke true words. I never wanted anyone to cry over me. I wanted them to celebrate my life. I wanted lots of drinks and fellowship. I wanted laughs and cheers. While my life was short, I wanted to make some kind of impact on the ones around me. I wanted them to feel loved, honored, and cherished.

Chapter 5
Staying True

B ACK IN THE Land of the Promised, I was learning so much about the universe and the power of love. Here technology existed but it was so much more advanced. It seemed a lot like magic but it wasn't. Our abilities are so enhanced because we are not restricted by the laws of Earth. One only needs to have a strong evolved mind and one could make almost anything happen.

Gerald, my dad, taught me that it is possible to go back to Earth and check in on a loved one. "We are unable to disturb their lives," he explained to me, "But it is possible to emit energy such as a flickering light or a warm sensation to let them know we are there."

"So I could go see Caroline?" I asked eagerly.

"Yes, you can."

"Show me how."

"Give me your hand," he commanded. We joined hands and in a matter of minutes I understood how to make my way back to Earth.

"Thank you, dad."

"Before you go, son, can we talk a little more about your abilities?"

"My abilities?" I asked, pretending that I didn't know what he meant.

"Yes, you have a great power that you were able to wield on Earth. While you are not the first one to use these gifts, you are the first to defy the laws of Earth and use them there."

For a moment I tried to deny that I had used any abilities.

"Remember son, I was able to see you use these powers. All in the Land of the Promised know what you were able to do. Many have trained for years to perform the skills that you showed on Earth."

"To be honest, I can't tell you how I did it. I was able to save Caroline but I could not save myself." I was saddened by this reality.

My father sensing my feelings, placed his hand on my shoulder and I was comforted immediately. "A life for a life son."

I looked up at him with a question on my face.

"This means that when a life is destined to be taken, the only way to stop that life from dying is to trade. Caroline's only chance of survival was you, Sam. You made the ultimate sacrifice."

"What about our unborn son? He's ok right?" I asked

My father looked at me and repeated, "A life for a life. Your son would have never survived. He had not been in the womb long enough. You made the right choice."

He was right, I did make the right choice. Because my understanding of the universe had expanded, I was able to feel solace by my actions.

"My son is here with us?"

"It is more complicated than that but he is here. When unborn children die, they have the option to re-enter and try again. Your son's soul is in the waiting place. He is contemplating his decision. His soul cannot be disturbed during this process," Gerald explained.

I resigned myself to the realities of the situation and was pleased that he had another chance at life on Earth. "Dad, you said that others can do what I did and my powers can be controlled?"

The old man smiled and said, "Yes, my boy."

"Can I meet them?"

Still smiling, he said, "In due time."

Months had passed and things slowly got back to normal for everyone. That is to say that everyone but Caroline slowly moved on. She had just lost her husband, best friend and soul mate, as well as his unborn child in the same tragic accident. Having so much tragedy happen to one person can take its toll on anyone. Caroline was a sweet, caring, and loving soul that did not deserve her plight.

To visit Caroline I only needed to think about her current whereabouts. Like tuning an old radio, I needed to find her frequency. Once I could do that, I could transport my spirit to Earth. She wouldn't be able to see me but I could see her. I'd also learned that while I could visit, I could only stay for a few months. To stay longer, would mean assimilation. I didn't quite know what that was at the time but I didn't get the impression that it was a good thing.

I went to visit Caroline for the first time. She sat at her vanity holding a picture of an ultrasound in her left hand. With her right hand rested on the vanity, she propped her head up. On the vanity was a half-empty glass of red wine with the bottle sitting next to it. Caroline was drinking. She sobbed for the loss of her baby. Caroline did not reach for a tissue. She let the tears flow down on the floor. With each teardrop, another piece of her heart broke, never to be mended.

"My Caroline, my sweet, sweet Caroline, please don't be troubled. I am here." I said knowing that she couldn't hear me. I quickly remembered my father telling me that I could emit energy to her. I closed my eyes and concentrated. My hands started to glow a warm yellow light much like the gates of the Land of the Promised. I opened my eyes and reached out to touch her. Caroline stopped crying. I startled her. Her eyes moved from left to right frantically. Her breathing got heavier. Her heart beat rapidly.

"Sam?" she said with a sniffle.

"Caroline?" I said, almost surprised that it worked.

"Sam, is that you?" she questioned to the thin air. "Sam, sweetie, I need to know it's you."

"It's me! It's me!" I called. "Concentrate," I said to myself. I looked at the lights. I didn't want to scare her by making them flicker. Then I thought about the wine bottle; I could knock that over.

"No scaring each other," we'd said.

Finally, it hit me: the wind chime in the baby's room. We had already decorated the room once we found out that we were having a boy. The wind chime hung near the window. It had different sized metallic bells that knocked into each other to produce a gentle, tranquil series of tones. I moved to the baby's room and focused on moving the chime. After a moment of concentration, my hands glowed once again.

Ring, ding, bing, bong was the sound the chime made. It was a wonderful and beautiful sound.

"Sam, it's you!" she shouted. For a brief moment, she had traded her tears of pain and heartache for a joyous laugh and smile. Caroline walked over to the bed and sat down. I sat next to her and emitted a warm energy surge. She closed her eyes and was quiet for a time. "We lost him," she said suddenly, "We lost our baby boy." Tears returned to her eyes. "You are here but you are not. Sam, I miss you so much. I can't do this without you here with me. Everywhere I go and everything I do reminds me of you. I stopped going to Rick's Deli for lunch because we ate there all the time. I don't sleep. When I do sleep, it's usually on the couch for an hour or two. I usually wake up looking for you. The other day I got up and made this great breakfast. I cooked bacon and sausage, eggs, and pancakes. I set down two plates to eat, then it hit me, I was making breakfast for you and me to eat together. All of my routines included you, Sam." She wiped more tears from her face. "This house is full of memories for me. I need you so much. Why did you have to go? Why did you save me? You should be here," she said, crying in full force now.

My heart broke after hearing her words. I understood her pain. After some time, I was able to gently guide her to lay down on the bed. I emitted another energy surge with a kiss on her forehead. This comforted her and slowly she stopped crying. I spooned in close to her and gave her another kiss on the neck. She closed her eyes. For the first time in months, she slept through the night. I did not leave her side until the morning.

I stayed true to my promise and stuck by her side every day for three months. It was wonderful being in her presence again and I tried my best to comfort her. I stayed with her as long as I could but had reached the limit of my visit back on Earth. It was painful to leave her again but I would return to Caroline as soon as possible. That night as I lied by her side I whispered that I would be gone in the morning, that I loved her, and that I would return. I closed my eyes and thought of my destination.

When I opened my eyes I was back in The Land of the Promised. I was away from Caroline but hoped my visit had helped her. Being back meant that I had to focus. I wanted to learn more about my abilities. My father had agreed to introduce me to Griffin, who was the leader of an elite group of individuals called The Protectors. They were trained in the art of love. Protectors would be considered the Navy Seals of our world. They wield the power of love to save the souls that died and end up in Hinterland, which is loosely translated to mean the land of the unknown.

Hinterland is a middle ground where lost souls end up. It is between the oasis that is The Land of the Promised and the decaying ruins of Necropolis. There are a few ways to end up in Hinterland after death. People of questionable character arrive here. The Protectors use the powers of love to find the potentially worthy and rehabilitate them. There are other evil forces that take those that are found to be unworthy or the vulnerable because of their mental state while leaving Earth.

The most vulnerable are the mentally ill that commit iniquities against themselves or others. In most cases, the mentally ill have committed some type of evil and died. One is not automatically condemned to Necropolis. They may have even thought they were acting in the name of God.

If someone were to commit suicide or overdose on drugs, they would also find themselves in Hinterland. These people harmed themselves to the point of no works to be judged. They may have felt unloved on Earth and The Great Source gives them a chance to find harmony. If they do, they are able to enter The Land of the Promised.

Griffin was tall and had copper toned skin. His eyes were green and had a slight glow to them. He looked to be in his mid-fifties but his body had the appearance of a much younger man. He had a kind face that made it easy to talk to. His smile was familiar but he was no one that I had met to this point. He was wearing a navy blue button up shirt with what looked like a black Kevlar vest. His pants were also black along with his military boots. His hair had a military box cut look to it. His voice was firm with a hint of rasp.

My father greeted him first with a brotherly hug. "Griffin old friend. How long has it been?"

"Gerald brother, it's been too long."

The men smiled and talked like old army buddies.

Gesturing to me, Griffin said, "So this is the one that was able to wield powers that it took me years to perfect." He offered his hand and said, "It's a pleasure to meet you. What's your name?"

"Hello, I'm Sam." I said, shaking his hand and feeling at ease almost immediately. "Honestly I was hoping that you would be able to tell me what it was that I did. My father has shown me some of the basics of love wielding but nowhere near what I had done on Earth."

"You have power in you that is untapped. The Great Source has looked upon you with great favor. There are countless numbers of souls in the Land of the Promised and less than a percent of a percent are ever able to do what your father has been able to teach you. Even he does not wield the powers of love on the level that the Protectors can," Griffin explained. "I have been blessed as you have with the ability to understand my powers. There are almost no limits to them. This ability has made it possible for me to use the powers of love for protecting those who would be otherwise lost. I am here to teach you more about your abilities. I am here to ask you to join the Protectors."

I swallowed hard and shook my head. "I am flattered but…"

"It has been long since prophesized that the one with great powers of love would have the ability to walk through the gates of Necropolis and back to The Land of the Promised," Griffin declared.

"The Protectors? First off… you might not have the right guy here. I don't think I'm the 'one' you are talking about," I said, shocked that I was being told any of this.

"I think you may well be, but if you are not, you would still be a great addition to the team. The evil that exists beyond these lands is great. One protector is able to save countless lives each day. It is truly good work that we do," said Griffin.

"Evil, what evil? I am not a protector," I said looking at my dad for confirmation.

My father took a deep breath and said, "Son, you have the potential for greatness. You have been called by the highest power in the universe to serve. I understand that you cannot make this decision lightly. While it is completely your choice, it is a great honor to save souls for Ekon."

I put my head in my hands to think. My father walked over to me and placed his hand on my shoulder. Griffin put his hand on my other shoulder. The two men began to give me a greater understanding of my purpose. All of those people will be taken by evil forces if I was not there to save them. I was able to take away selfish emotions and concentrate. I felt less overwhelmed and resolved in what I had to do.

"But Caroline," I said.

"She will be here to join us soon enough. When it is her time, you will be united just like we were," my dad said.

"I promised her that I would be there for her always," I explain.

"She will always feel your love, Sam. You have not left her," Griffin said softly.

I took a few moments to think about what had been placed before me. I would need to go away and not see Caroline for at least two Earth years to train.

"What would Caroline want you to do if she were here?" asked Griffin.

Caroline would never forgive me if I did not help others. She would say, "Sam, we help those that can't help themselves."

"I will train with you to become a protector but I am not the one you spoke of. I am just Sam. No one calls me anything but Sam. And dad, I need you to check in on Caroline for me from time to time. If there are any problems, I need you to notify me."

"I will Sam. But there isn't much you or I can do on Earth from here. For you though, I will make your wife my first priority," he said looking into my eyes.

Griffin smiled. "Come... Sam. We have much to learn."

My Father embraced me warmly and wished me well.

Chapter 6

Longing for Love

CAROLINE WAS IN a diner having lunch with Sara. The diner was small and had a countertop for the regulars to sit and eat. It wasn't the cleanest joint but the food was full of flavor and the ownership boasted that the diner was the home of the greatest BLT sandwich. The two women sat in a booth in the back corner on the opposite end of the only other people in for lunch. Their plates of food were sitting in front of them. Sara's was half eaten. Caroline had only taken a bite of her BLT and moved some fries around her plate.

Caroline had lost fifteen pounds over the past two months. Her weight loss was noticeable in her face. She wore an oversized grey long-sleeved sweater. Her t-shirt looked to have been worn for several days without washing. Her hair was barely tamed and in a ponytail. She was not wearing any makeup and it was clear that she had been crying.

"It's so nice to see you, Caroline," Sara said in a concerned voice. "I heard that you have not been to work in two weeks and I'm worried about you."

Caroline looks down into her lap but said nothing.

"Sam has been gone for over a year and a half now. We need to figure out a way to help you move on," Sara said, still speaking softly.

Caroline looked directly into Sara's eyes. Her eyes were red with tears starting to roll down her face. She seemed almost defiant in her gaze.

Sara continued, "Honey, I know what he was to you. I was there when you first met. I stood up at your wedding, helped you move into your first house, and was there when we put him in the ground. I know..." Sara began tearing up but continued to speak, "When I say move on, it is as your best friend that sees her best friend hurting. There is no getting over this, Caroline, but you and I can get through this."

"Hurt," Caroline began speaking, "You think I feel hurt?" she said rhetorically. "I am so past hurt that you would need a seven forty-seven to fly me back to hurt."

Caroline's eyes moved back and forth as she searched for the appropriate feeling that she felt. "I am... I don't know, shattered into a million pieces, swept up and thrown into a frying pan, then scraped into the trash, and thrown into an ice freezing cold dark space! So hurt is not the word I would use."

"Caroline, I know..."

"There is no way you could know. Sam was the love of my existence. He was the air that I breathed. I cannot breathe right now. I need Sam to help me breathe."

Sara reached out her hand to grab Caroline's.

Caroline pulled back and said, "Sam knew me. He knew my soul. He loved me through it all. He would always seem to show up on a hard day of work and take me to lunch or buy me a single rose just because. I won't make it without him."

"Caroline, please don't talk like that. No one wants to replace Sam. I just... want to see you in a better place than you are right now. Have you tried to talk to anyone?"

"They don't get it. They don't get what Sam was to me. I cry myself to sleep at night. Sam is in my dreams. He is in my thoughts. I can't get him out of my head. I miss him so much it aches. I just want to end the pain and see him again."

"Care, please don't talk like that. You're not serious. You have so much to live for sweetie."

Caroline heard these words and knew Sara didn't understand her. She took a deep breath and started to clean her face. She did her best to suppress her need to cry. Caroline mustered up a half smile and wiped her eyes again. "You're right Sara. I have so much to live for. I can call my boss tomorrow and smooth things over with him. We can start spending more time together too." Caroline reached out her hand to grab Sara's.

"Absolutely," said Sara, convinced that Caroline was ready to turn the corner.

Caroline realized that she couldn't share her true feelings. Sara didn't want to believe how deeply hurt she was. Caroline let out another half-smile. It was much easier this time. Maybe because she knew that her friend needed to see her smile. She didn't want to burden Sara with her issues anymore. Caroline kept the conversation about Sara as the women caught up. Caroline always had a way of deflecting her issues and keeping the focus on others in order to hide her feelings.

After two hours of conversation the pair decided they had touched on all subjects and agreed to stay in touch. They planned to meet up the following week at the same time. The place would be at a "to be determined location." Sara walked away thinking she had been helpful to her longtime friend. Caroline walked away feeling even more isolated than she had ever been.

Later that night, Caroline sat in the bedroom at her vanity. The song "A Thousand Years" by Christina Perri played loudly in the background. It had been the song that played at their wedding. "I have died every day waiting for you. Darling don't be afraid, I have loved you for a thousand years." *These words are the soundtrack to our life together* Caroline thought to herself.

She wrote a letter as tears flowed from her eyes.

To Whoever Finds Me:

It has been too long since I have felt Sam's touch. I cannot live in a world without my one true love. He is waiting for me on the other side. Growing old together was our plan. We promised to spend forever together. Because God saw fit to take him, I must now see fit to find him on the other side. I am sure that he and our son are together in heaven waiting for me.

To my father, I love you and I hope that you understand why I am doing this. You are remarried and Cathy is a wonderful partner for you. Sam is my one true love. I cannot find anyone that will make me feel the way that he did. Forgive me for what I have done.

Please tell Sara that she did all that she could. My heart was in too many pieces to get back to a normal life. I will always love her for being with me through the good and the bad. I cannot be a burden on her any longer.

The world will never miss me. My family is waiting.

Caroline

Caroline finished her letter and reached for a nearby bottle of cheap vodka. She was known to enjoy a glass of wine but she hated vodka after the time in college she got really sick drinking it at homecoming. Next to the bottle is a prescription pill container one of the shrinks had prescribed for her but she had never taken. The label warns that no more than two should be taken at night. It also says that high levels of alcohol should not be consumed with the medicine. The pills were intended to help her sleep.

Caroline dumped about six pills in her hand. She breathed out, then a deep breath in. She put all six pills in her mouth and washed them down with a big gulp of the cheapest vilest tasting liquid. She let out an "Ugh!" Then exhaled before attempting another swallow.

She looked at the bottle of pills and decided that six was not enough. She reached for another handful of pills and consumed those as well.

With about half the bottle gone Caroline started to feel drowsy. Her eye lids began to feel heavy and she could feel the effects of the pills and vodka. Her body started to numb and she found it difficult to control herself. She stumbled over to the bed that we shared, slipped under the sheets, and slowly fell into a deep sleep. As she faded away she mumbled, "I'll see you soon Sam."

Chapter 7

Love, Hate, and Castro Thorn

"**W**HERE ARE WE?"

Griffin and I were standing in a huge room full of books on large, tall shelves. There must have been several thousands of books all around me. The room had no windows and one door, and was rectangular in shape, being about one hundred feet long by fifty feet wide. The floors were hardwood and partially covered with oriental styled rugs. The walls were not visible because of the books on the shelves. The ceiling was painted the same as the Sistine Chapel and I found myself gazing upon its beauty.

"That is the original. Michelangelo was remembering this painting when he conceived it on earth. Lots of the art on Earth is created based on the art here in The Land of the Promised," Griffin explained.

"So we have all been here before?" I asked.

"We originate from the Great Source. Everyone and everything starts here and ends here if there is even such a thing as starting and ending."

"Why would we ever leave here?"

"To leave is to learn. We need to learn about our own selves within our existences. Earth is like a training ground for learning. Some souls want to experience love and wonder. Some souls want to experience fame and fortune. There are even those that want to know about pain and suffering. You must beware of the souls that have chosen to learn about pain and suffering. They are the reason that the city of Necropolis was created," Griffin summarized.

"Necropolis? What is that?" I asked.

"You would call it Hell back on Earth. Necropolis is the city for the damned and the unfixable souls that have been consumed by hate and self-loathing. On Earth, these souls had become the heroes of slavery, greed, and mass murder. They no longer feel the powers of love. If one finds himself in Necropolis, it is too late for them to be rescued."

"Why doesn't the Source just destroy them?" I asked, frustrated to hear that such a place existed in the midst of all of this wonder and joy.

"Like a mother is to a child, Ekon is love. He uses the power of love to battle hate. Destruction is not in the nature of the Great Source. He creates and constructs, nurtures and cares for. Hate must exist for love to exist. It is two sides to the same coin. The Great source created souls such as you and me to be the physical manifestation of the powers of love. Beware of the powers of hate and self-loathing. In some ways, they can prove to be equally powerful. The demons who wield the powers of hate choose to deceive, destroy, and conquer the minds of the weak and unknowing. Our work is to protect and convert the minds of the souls trapped in Hinterland. These books that you see around you hold the secrets of love. Think of them as training manuals. The books will train you on the tricks of the enemy. Once you have gone through these books, we will move on to mental and physical combat," Griffin explained.

"We?" I asked.

"Yes, the other Protectors. I will introduce your training partners to you soon. For now, you need to focus on all of this..." Griffin said as he raised his hand, palm open, and motioned towards the massive amounts of books before me. "Remember, this task is not as insurmountable as it looks. You are in the Land of the Promised. You have the ability to understand quickly." Griffin smiled at me and left the room, closing the door behind him.

I stared up at the top shelf and eyed a book with a faded burgundy cover and said, "That looks like a good book to start with."

Immediately, the book slid off the shelf and floated down to me. It looked old and dusty. The cover had no title. I opened it and begin reading. My eyes started to glow a bright blue and white color. My hands were now glowing the same as they did when I would visit Caroline. In an instant, I knew that I could heal a wound by focusing on how the healthy tissue should be. The knowledge of the greatest power in the universe was starting to become more and more a part of me as I absorbed the information from the books. After about a dozen volumes I learned that I could absorb several books at a time just by stacking them and focusing on the top and the bottom books simultaneously.

As my understanding grew, the glow from my hands and eyes shined brighter. Soon I no longer needed to touch a book. My entire body was surrounded by an awesome light. My soul was consumed with the teachings of love and how hate could be conquered. I learned that in fact hate and love were very close to each other and the slightest of manipulations could change one to the other. I learned that hate, while a worthy opponent, was actually no match for love. But hate did have the power to consume the mind and create the illusion of a greater power. Hate uses fear and hopelessness to source it's potential. Once someone feels these emotions they are unable to see love for what it truly is.

Lots of the same instruments are used in the fight for both love and hate. You see, the lines between love and hate are very close. Love is like a magnet. You have two sides attracted to each other. Hate works in the opposite manner and attempts to push away or separate. Love is the stronger of the two because there is strength in unity. The powers of hate have a strategy of dividing in order to conquer. With love, the sum is always greater than the one.

I knew that I'd have to be very careful if I'd ever come into contact with beings that were able to wield this power. The people that can use the powers of hate are also very deceptive. They have the power to tap into your insecurities that you had on Earth and use them to convert you into one of hate's disciples. While they almost never lie, the truth is distorted enough to persuade unsuspecting souls into their world.

I also learned that the leader of Necropolis was Castro Thorn. He lived on Earth over a thousand years ago. He was once a member of the Land of the Promised but descended to Earth because of his curiosity for emotions that did not revolve around love.

Castro Thorn was the weakest of all things created from love. For many years he did not understand why he lacked the strength of others within the Land of the Promised. While he gained knowledge and understanding he could not feel love. This bothered him.

He requested to see the Great Source and query about his inability to harness the powers of love. Even in this time, it was thought to be impossible to be in Ekon's presence and live. Somehow he was equipped with the ability to resist assimilation. He was granted permission to descend to Earth and learn about all types of feelings. He'd hoped that this would allow him to understand and be as powerful as the others.

Castro Thorn lived a hard life. He was born on a vineyard in what is now Greece in the year 1023. His mother was unknown to him. She was killed by his father when he was a baby. This was after she admitted she loved another. Back in those times, a man was the judge of his household and would not be punished for exacting vengeance for such a crime. His father was full of hate and self-loathing. His name was Devan Thorn.

On nights when Castro's father was sober, he would be beaten with a leather strap for the slightest misstep. On the frequent occasions that his father was drunk with a belly full of ale or wine, he was beaten for sport. Castro grew to resent his father for the relentless pain and suffering inflicted upon him.

When Castro was fifteen years old, he decided that he had had enough of his father's abuse. He was a gangly kid but stood tall at six feet. His muscles were just starting to develop and his body always had some type of bruise on it from Devan or work in the vineyard. The motivation was years in the making, but at last, Castro felt he was ready to enact his revenge.

He devised a plan to kill his father at the next chance he found. Thorn kept a sharp blade on him at all times in case a wild animal or the occasional wine thief would show up unexpectedly. After his father passed out from drunkenness he would slit his father's throat in the night.

Castro would not have to wait long for his opportunity. Devan had been drinking wine from their testing batch and began to provoke Thorn, as he so often did, "Come here you little disgrace! If you don't... come now... you will regr... regret it." His speech was slow and slurred from the night of drinking.

Castro approached his father.

"What took you so long? I've been calling you and you took too long. Do you know what I do to boys that don't come when they are called?" Devan asked.

He looked down and away for fear he would say the wrong thing. The only problem was that it didn't matter what he said or didn't say, his father was out for blood.

"Oh, so you don't thi... think you nee... need to answer mm... me?" Devan reared back and struck Castro to the ground with his closed fist. Feeling the sting from the blow, Castro stayed on the ground a moment to perform a quick self-check. He slid his tongue across his lips and tasted the blood streaming from the corner of his mouth. He slowly removed himself from the floor and stood up. His body surged with anger and contempt. As he looked at his father, he knew there was only one action to take but he needed to make it count.

"Don't loo... look at me bo... boy. You think you... you're a man? Trrry i... it boy!"

There was something about the way that his father said "boy" that struck a nerve with Castro Thorn. He had taken his father's blade minutes before. He now tapped the heel of the knife to make sure that it was still on his hip hidden under his shirt. His heart began to beat quickly. With his hands shaking, he drew the weapon from the back of his belt.

"You better kill me, boy!"

He sounded almost sober in that moment. Castro charged with the knife above his head and thrust downward. Instincts kicked in for Devan and he caught the knife hand at the wrist. The boy and the man grunted and groaned as they tussled for life. Devan, even when drunk, was much stronger than Castro. He managed to pry the weapon from Castro and threw him to the ground.

Devan only showed one mercy. He did not kill Castro. But there are things far worse than death. Devan tortured him through the night with his leather strap. He tied his son up to his own bed. He used his knife and sliced Castro's back slowly in multiple places. Devan found pleasure in watching the blood stream down from each wound. He poured wine in the wounds as an added insult. The wine made his back burn like fire. Castro Thorn cried for help but none came.

After Devan finished, he left Castro on the bed bleeding. He pulled and yanked as hard as he could to get free of the ropes before his father awakened from his drunken slumber but the knots were too tight and he was too weak to get loose. Thorn eventually gave up and passed out due to his blood loss and the fatigue that had set in.

The morning came and soon the light of the sun shined directly over top the vineyard. Thorn's father slept off his drink for the entire day until close to dinner time. He walked into the room where Castro lied in his own blood, still moist from the night before.

"If I untie you, will you try to kill me again boy?" he asked.

Castro did not answer right away because he knew the truth. His dad should have killed him when he had the chance. His attempt had failed but another opportunity would present itself. For now, he knew what he needed to say.

"No, Sir," Castro said with a whimper.

His father pulled the knife from his belt and cut the rope. Castro's wrists were red, black, and blue from struggling to get out. Instead of getting him help for his cuts, his father made him put on an old worn shirt and make dinner.

"I think I'd like some potatoes with beef. You know how to make that right?" Devan asked.

"Yes, Sir."

Castro kept his hatred for Devan bottled up for years in fear of what his father might do if he failed again. His wounds healed. The scars remained as a reminder of what his father was capable of doing to him. As Thorn grew older and stronger Devan grew older and weaker. The beatings happened less and less because Castro could fight his father off and make him tired. He didn't win any of the fights with Devan but he wouldn't say that he lost all of them either. He waited for the right time to wreak his vengeance.

During this time he also directed his hatred outward against his peers. He would find any reason to fight someone. Sometimes it would be because he suspected someone of stealing from him or something as trivial as looking at him the wrong way. Young men around his age came from all over to fight the undefeated Castro Thorn. They all failed. Thorn used his hatred for his father as motivation to win.

One of Thorn's best fights was against a younger boy named Alex Raven. He was two years younger than him but he fought with a fury that he had only seen in himself.

"You fought well Raven," Castro said as he helped the younger boy off the ground.

"Not good enough to win," Raven replied.

"You were close for a moment. You are the toughest that I have ever fought. Where are you from?"

"I'm from all over. My parents were killed when I was young. I was sold as a slave when I was five years old. I ran away when I was nine. I've lived on the streets and have worked odd jobs to get coins for food. For now, I'm working for a nearby sheepherder." Raven answered.

Even though they had fought against each other, they felt a certain kinship. Thorn decided to accept his first and only friend. The two were inseparable. When Raven came into the picture, they would both fight Thorn's dad together and won a few times. Devan did not like

Raven but respected that he was willing to fight for his place in life. In some twisted way, he felt as though he was nurturing Castro and Raven into manhood by beating and bruising them.

By the time Thorn was twenty years old, his muscles were developed and he had the body of a man. The work on the vineyard required a physical tax that Castro paid every day. His upper torso formed a perfect V shape and his abs rippled like a washboard. His skin was tanned and dark, kissed by the sun while working in the fields. He was as tall as his father now standing at six feet four inches. His hair was jet black and reached just past his shoulders. He braided it in the back to keep it out of his face while working. His physicality was noted by most in the community, as few men boasted his combination of size, strength, and athleticism.

Thorn's father was one of the few men that was not intimidated by his size. Devan had grown older and gained some weight. He knew he moved a step slower but was still a large, strong man who could hold his own whenever he needed to.

One day Castro walked into the house after a long day's work. Devan was ready to sit down for his first drink of wine. "Castro, come join your dad for a drink."

"Ok father, but first, I'd like to take a bath and wash some of the stink off of me."

"Now boy! Come drink with your father. There comes a time when a father and son should drink together." There was that tone again. Five years later but somehow being called "boy" from his father enraged him.

"I hate it when you call me that! I have not been a boy for a long time," Castro growled.

"What did you say to me? I will kill you for taking that tone with me. Now sit down and have a drink."

Castro gritted his teeth. He knew he was too exhausted at that moment to fight his father and decided it would be best to have a drink. Devan poured him a glass and drunk from the bottle.

"A good vintage," Devan said as he tasted his wine.

Castro simply nodded and pretended to drink from his glass.

"I was timid like you but look at me now. I can handle my drink from a bottle. Don't be afraid. Drink up son." Castro continued to sip slowly, feeling his pent up anger ready to explode. He didn't like spending time with the man that beat him on a constant basis. With every swig of wine, Castro plotted on Devan's life. He was going to take it and this time his father would not stop him.

The evening air was cool with a slight breeze that came in through the open window carrying the smell of the grape leaves and wood oak barrels. It would have been a peaceful evening to most but on this night peace was not on Castro Thorn's mind. The window was his father's bedroom window. While Devan lied in his bed, sleeping off his wine, Castro and Raven had snuck into his room. Castro drew the knife from five years earlier. This blade that had carved lifelong scars into his back would finally find its intended victim. "Father," Castro said, just loud enough to startle him out of his sleep.

"Wha... Wha... What is going on?" Devan asked. He quickly noticed that something was afoot, as his arms and legs were pinned down by rope. He writhed for a moment until he noticed the gaze of his son. It was dark with only the light of the moon to illuminate the room. "You coward! You couldn't face me like a man! You tie me up like this and give me no fighter's chance?" Devan implored.

"This is for all of those years that you have beaten a weak little boy and all of those years that I came close but could not find it in me to win. I've decided not to take any chances." His voice had changed and had a sinister tone to it. He felt no fear of his father. Five years of hate engorged his confidence.

"Ah ha ha! You think that I am afraid of death? You little cock boy. I will not shed a single tear. I will not give you a faint whiff of fear. Get on with it boy! Ha ha ha ha!"

Castro was not swayed by Devan's laugh. He could see the fear in his eyes. For the first time, his father was afraid of something. It made Castro smile. He looked at Raven to signal that it was time. Raven drew a knife from his belt. It was blunt on purpose.

"I hate you," Castro whispered in his father's ear just before taking the first blow. Flesh makes an interesting sound when dull instruments pierce it. And so did Thorn's father as the two young men continuously jammed their knives in and out of his body. He pleaded and begged for it to stop. It did but only after he was dead. Castro Thorn felt great satisfaction from killing his father. He also developed a great hunger for murder and torturing. The hate inside of him began to grow. It made him stronger somehow.

Raven, who had to fend for himself for most of his life, was not moved by acts of violence. It was a way of life for him. It was how he survived. Killing Thorn's father was him surviving by keeping the only person he trusted alive.

Years passed and many bodies fell at the hands of the two men. They began to amass wealth by taking it. At first, he was a hero to the poor. He took from the rich. He freed slaves under the condition that they would fight for him and free other slaves. He enslaved the rich and killed the ones that refused captivity.

Thorn became obsessed with the abilities hate gave him. He was power hungry and needed to see people suffering. He believed that he was as boundless as a god and his strength continued to grow. Thorn only found peace when he was hurting someone or something. Hate was his new ally and he felt nothing else. Somehow, hate made him stronger, faster, smarter, and more deceptive. He started to feel a spark, almost like literal fire, in his veins.

He began to realize why he was weak in the Land of the Promised. He was the physical form of loves opposite. Thorn's powers couldn't be harnessed because he couldn't love. His abilities came from love's polar opposite. He could feel hate and hate consumed him.

As his number of followers grew, it became more difficult to feed them all. Many of them defected or rebelled against him. Thorn resented their resentment towards him. He called his people together in a field that reached forty acres. This was land that he had seized from a slave owner and was now using as a base of operations. There were over three thousand men, five hundred women, and one hundred children. He stood on an improvised stage made up of lumber from nearby trees to give a speech to his followers:

"I freed you and you repay me by rebelling and running away from your obligations. You may go and find new lives. I only want the most loyal. I only want the men that would lie, cheat, steal, and kill for me!" Thorn declared.

The crowd began to rumble and most took their things and walked away. There were about five hundred men and fifty boys that decided to stay. Once the people had scattered away, Thorn gathered the men for another discussion.

"All who left are no longer your brothers. I am your brother. Raven is your brother. The men standing next to you are your brothers. If the man standing next to you has let you down for failure to keep his promise as a brother, he is no longer your brother. He must be put down like the farmer does his sick cattle. The weak men and women who have fled us must not see freedom. They have not earned it. We have put forth the effort and they have benefitted and remained steadfast until it was inconvenient to do so. They moaned and whimpered and wet themselves like babies when they did not get fed. We are the warriors that found them food, clothing, and a better life. They will be forever slaves, either it is in the mind or the physical. My charge to you is to hunt them all down. Take the children as slaves. Then kill the men that refuse slavery and take their wives to be your whores. They are no longer your brothers. They must fall!"

The men cheered at his speech and did Thorn's bidding. In total, he took back only two hundred men as slaves, four hundred women, and forty children. The others were slaughtered even if they hesitated for a moment. As word spread of Castro Thorn's escapades, many feared that their cities would be next. They called his men the Marauders and Thorn embraced the name. The cities banded together and formed a large army tasked with killing Thorn and all of his followers.

Thorn, Raven, and a small group of his most trustworthy soldiers had been lured into a trap. Castro and his men were surrounded on the battlefield by two thousand soldiers. The Marauders had no fear. While they were a small posse of 15, they had seen similar odds before. They knew that to beat so many, they only needed to make an example of a few. This had been their strategy in conquering all that had opposed them.

"What fools these men are to oppose me," Thorn said to Raven.

"Fools indeed," Raven responded, "Why do they think they will win this time?"

"They have been fed lies by their leaders," Thorn answered, "We will give them the option of perishing here or surrendering. I am feeling generous today."

"Right away." Raven walked out to the front of the multitude of soldiers. With a booming voice, he declared, "What foolishness is this to oppose Castro Thorn and his Marauders? Our great leader has offered you a chance to leave with your lives and serve him. Any of you that decide to stay and fight will die today. Your children will be slaughtered and your women will be forced to watch. After they have seen their children murdered, they will be our servants and winches to do with as we see fit!"

He paused as some in the crowd start to murmur. Over 500 men were persuaded by Raven's words and fled the battlefield. They had either seen or heard this offer before and feared what could happen to them.

"We are not afraid!" said a voice from the crowd of remaining men.

"You will die today!" shouted another man.

A great roar of cheers raised from the crowd.

"We are too many, we will win!" said another voice.

Their superior numbers provided them confidence. They believe that there was no way that Thorn and his Marauders could defeat such a large group of men.

The army attacked. Hundreds of men started running at the Marauders. Thorn felt the spark of fire in his veins again. His mind went clear and he felt pure hatred. A flash shot out of his hands and pierced through three men confronting him. He was able to manifest hate into its physical form. His Marauders were able to take on two and three men at a time. Thorn was able to make quick work of ten to fifteen men by using his powers of hate. Every man that dared to swing a sword or sling an arrow in Thorn's direction was met with a powerful wave of electricity.

Thorn's hate continued to gain strength as the men attacked. Now he was able to take on twenty then fifty men. As the crowd bared down on him and his men from all sides, Thorn felt a rush of energy greater than any he felt before, even during his time in the Land of the Promised.

"Marauders, come close to me," Thorn ordered.

His men repositioned themselves closer to him so that Thorn and his Marauders now formed a circle. Thorn began to glow a magnificent purple then red light. His men looked at him in disbelief. They had never seen anything like it.

"Join hands with me," Thorn said in an ominous voice.

His men quickly complied. They started to glow as well.

The army of men, once attacking, stopped. Some were afraid while others were in awe. For a moment, all was silent.

Someone shouted, "Retreat!"

The militia of men commenced retreating they were too late. The aura energy expanded out like a tidal wave in all directions. True to his word… Thorn slew everyone not bound hand to hand with him. The Marauders all felt the hate that flowed through Thorn and into them. They were all amazed by the fact that none of them were killed.

Thorn was no longer glowing. He started breathing hard and fell to one knee.   Raven rushed to his side. "Thorn! Are you ok? What was that?"

The Marauders looked around them. In all directions bodies covered the battlefield; laid to waist by their energy surge.

"I'm not quite sure but I believe that it was hate. I hated those men, I hate almost everyone except my brothers and sometimes I hate you all as well." Thorn said, with a little chuckle.

"You are more powerful than anyone on Earth. What will you do?" One of the men asked.

"…I will take over the world," Thorn said as he stood back up to his feet.

That, he almost accomplished. He and his men conquered and burned villages and cities with ease because of Thorn's abilities. He made kings bow to him and become his slaves. The people of Earth prayed for mercy. Thorn told them that he was their god and the only way for them to have salvation is to follow him.

Ekon saw that his children were suffering at the hand of Castro Thorn. He gave a select few his power of love. They became known as the Protectors. They built a place specified for Thorn and his men. It was expanded because his seed of hate was planted deep and others would follow in his footsteps. Ekon cracked open the sky and linked the realm of Earth to The Land of the Promised. The Protectors ascended to Earth on golden chariots. They were in their heavenly forms which made them too strong for any mortals. Led by the Protector called Liam, the Protectors easily captured the Marauders. The earthly bodies of the Marauders perished as soon as they crossed realms. The sky was sealed again. Thorn and his followers were the first to be cast into the unholy place.

It was called Necropolis. The Great Source had given Thorn free will. He'd hoped that one day he would choose to be with him again. Now Thorn would have almost no chance of that.

Chapter 8

The Protectors

S TILL IN THE hall of books, I was distracted by the creaking of the door. It slowly opened. It was Griffin. He was not alone. He had three other people with him. There were two more men and a woman. All of them were dressed in black, wearing what appeared to be some type of protective gear similar to what SWAT units use.

"How are your studies coming along Sam?" asked Griffin.

I must have had a concerned look on my face.

"I see..." Griffin said in an all-knowing tone of voice. "You have learned about Castro Thorn."

I nodded in confirmation.

"He is a very powerful and disturbed soul. The Great Source has created several precautions because of him."

"What do you mean?" I queried.

"Well, we don't remember life in the Land of the Promised while we are on Earth for a start. One of the reasons that Thorn was able to use the powers of hate on Earth with such ease is because he could remember how the powers of love worked. The knowledge gained in the Land of the Promised is so great and vast that one could conceivably be a god on Earth. Think about what would happen if they are able to harness powers like they can here. Even remembering that the powers exist is dangerous for a human. You were unknowingly able to use the powers of love. Imagine if you knew that these powers could be manifested in the physical form all along. The power you have comes with a great deal of accountability. You must be careful when using it."

I nodded again, understanding the scope of my abilities a little better.

Griffin explained further, "It is now forbidden to leave the Land of the Promised without permission. There was a time that Hinterland was the only other place that souls would go after leaving Earth. Thorn's hate spread throughout the Earth and continued to plague humanity long after he was gone. There are souls that go directly to the evil city because they are lost and consumed by the forces of hate."

"I am beginning to understand now," I said.

"The Great Source also created the chosen ones to protect our Hinterland. This was one of the biggest changes in this world."

"You mean the Protectors?" I asked.

"Yes, and that leads me to the reason these fine people are here." Griffin looked behind him toward the people that had entered the hall with him. "These are Protectors. There are 10 of us in total. You will make 11. These are my strongest and bravest team members. They have proven themselves in the battle for Ekon's people time and time again. You will learn all they know. Be sure to listen closely."

The Protectors were all standing side by side facing Griffin and I. He began to introduce them. Starting from left to right:

"This is Chandra, Tate, and Liam."

"Nice to meet you," I said. I paused after noting the last name he mentioned.

"Liam from the book?"

"Yes, I am the same one," Liam responded with a partial smile. Then he said, "You should have a great deal of knowledge about love by now. The knowledge you've gained will help you wield and control these powers."

Tate was responsible for teaching me hand to hand combat. Chandra would instruct me on how to use my glow to create weapons and tools. Liam was responsible for helping me reach my power's full potential and controlling it.

Liam

Liam and I stood in a green field of grass that was enclosed on both sides by trees. It almost looked like the fairway to a freshly cut golf course. We needed the open space so that we didn't blow anything up. He was first to start teaching me about my capabilities.

Liam was a man of average height and weight. He had the look of an older man in his late fifties. He still had most of his hair but it was partially white. The other part was brown. He had dark tanned skin and his hands had bruises on them from years of fighting against the Marauders. He could easily heal himself but he liked the reminder of what he was fighting for.

His eyes were grey and had deep crow's feet wrinkles on each side. His face had stubbles of grey and brown hair forming a five o'clock shadow. He'd been with the Protectors for much longer than the others but was still just as capable. He had a hidden strength and was often underestimated because of his older looks. Liam liked the element of surprise that his appearance afforded him.

"Out of all of us, you have shown the highest energy levels with your power," Liam said to me. "Most of the Protectors have never surged their powers to the levels you did on Earth. My job is to get you to do that again but this time on purpose and without destroying yourself."

"That can happen? Can we die here?" I asked.

"Death has no power over us here. But souls can lose their energy force. Only The Great Source can absorb them back into the light," Liam said, attempting to explain.

"Is that a bad thing?"

"If you are absorbed or assimilated into the light, you are no longer an individual. To become one with The Great Source is a prestigious thing. That is to say, to choose to be part of the Great Source is an honor. If your energy force has been lost or taken, you are lost. The Great Source takes what is left of you and you can only exist in the force. It is the closest thing to death that we have. Now let's get to work." His eyes started to glow a dull sky blue and soon the color morphed to a bright light blue. "Love is a feeling Sam. You can harness the powers of love from a memory or a smell. You can close your eyes and feel the Great Source flowing through you. It is important that you are in control, my student. If you lose control, you are risking letting hate in." The glow from his eyes dissipated. "Now, you try," he instructed.

I closed my eyes and thought about that day back in college when I first fell in love with Caroline. I thought of the feel of her hand as she shook mine. I remembered her kissing me with her soft full lips. My eyes started glowing bright white. I thought about Caroline some more. She was standing in the baby's room next to a brand new crib. To her back was an opened window. The sunlight hit her blonde hair just right and there was a cool breeze flowing through the room. She held a pregnancy test in her hand and had a big smile on her face. I walked behind her and wrapped my arms around her waist. She turned to face me. We held each other and cried tears of joy. By this time my hands were a bright blue color. I could feel the power surging through my body.

"Easy Sam," Liam cautioned. "You want to control it. There is no need to go too far too fast."

The surge started to feel like needles prickling all over my body. I grunted a little.

"Try to pull it back, Sam," Liam urged.

"Ah...I'm losing it!" My entire body was now glowing a bright white color. The needle sensation changed to electricity.

"Ah, help!" I cried. One memory started to merge into another. This one was about the time we got into a fight about wanting to purchase a gun for our home. She was worried about guns in the house with the baby. I felt that we needed to protect ourselves in case of a home invasion, especially because the baby was coming. My aura turned purple. I was feeling angry and upset. My body began to burn. At that moment I felt a hand on my shoulder. It was Liam. The negative memory faded away and my glow dissipated. The electricity stopped. The burning sensation eased as well. I fell to my knees and panted heavily. I looked up at Liam.

"What was that?" I asked.

"You lost control. You'll need to regulate your thoughts in order to control your powers. There are other ways to summon your powers without a memory but it is easiest this way. The other way is to tap into the power of The Great Source."

"I can do that?"

"Yes, you can and more. The Great Source is love. Few people can harness loves powers in this way. It is as pure as power gets. If you are not careful doing it that way, you can lose your energy force," he warned. "I will show you that after you have proven that you can control your thoughts. Now let's try again. Remember to keep your thoughts positive."

We continued to train for what I could only describe as weeks to help you understand the time that lapsed. But the knowledge gained would have been equivalent to ten or fifteen years on Earth. I was able to master many skills during this time. I was becoming a warrior for the citizens of Hinterland. Little did I know, I would also be training to help and save Caroline.

Chandra

Chandra and I were sitting on two logs over a campfire in a forest thick with trees. The thick trunks of the trees allowed for stealth and organized ambushes. The night sky was full of stars. I felt as though I could reach up and grab one in my hands. The constellations that we know on Earth were among those in the stars but there were others that Chandra showed me. I wasn't much for stargazing back on Earth but what I saw in the sky was majestic. Along with the stars was a blue and white cloud formation that looked like dust. The dust cloud twisted and twined around like candy cane stripes. The two colors were bound together and moved in unison across the night sky, almost like a dance.

Chandra appeared to be a very fit woman. She had the model female warrior look. Her physique would be compared to Grace Jones in the eighties. Her arms and legs were toned from many years of training and combat against the Marauders. Her face and skin were flawless and she had high cheekbones which helped extenuate her beauty. She had the classic lines of a ballerina and moved with grace and seamless effort on the battlefield.

She had a tattoo of a dragon on her wrist. When she lived on Earth, she was Japanese. She kept this as her form in the Land of the Promised as well. She spoke perfect American English, except for certain words. Her accent peeked out sometimes. On words like "the or that" she would say, "da or dat." Generally, she seemed to have trouble with all "th" words. But the reality was that she just liked to accent them.

Chandra was very quick witted and very serious. She used lots of sarcasm to help her keep calm in frustrating situations. Chandra was slow to warm up to new people and would rather keep her distance if she had her way. She was also very protective of the people that she loved and would be the wrong person to make your enemy.

"Why do you have that?" I asked as I gestured towards the dragon tattoo.

"It is a remembrance. I need to stay sharp at all times. The dragon reminds me of the evil that awaits us in Hinterland. It also reminds me of the souls I loved and why I must fight to protect them. You will need to find motivation and a reason to fight, Sam. Now, enough talking..." Chandra's eyes began to glow the same smart white glow as mine had done when I wielded the powers of love. She put her hands together and stood straight as if she were beginning a yoga session or was saying a prayer. In between her hands, I saw a small light. She slowly pulled her hands away from each other and the light expanded filling the space in between her palms.

"Think of the light as clay. You can mold it into anything you want it to be. The more connected you are with your powers, the more powerful your weapon will become." The light flashed bright and dissipated. What was left was a Samurai sword. The sword appeared to be made of steel. It had a black leather woven handle. The blade was sharp enough to cut through...

"See that tree," Chandra said.

I looked over to a tall oak tree. A moment later she was charging towards it with a swift and powerful stride. She raised the sword which combusted into a blue flame. "Hee-Yah!" she yelled as she unleashed a mighty swing. The blade of the sword sliced through the tree. *Crack, snap, woosh* was the sound of the tree as it tilted and fell to the ground with a thunderous thud.

"Remind me never to get on your bad side," I said, shocked at what I'd just seen.

"If what they say is true about you Sam, you will be able to do that and far more. I feel the love of the Great Source within you. Your inner chi is strong. Now, you do it... Like I just showed you. Focus on the weapon you desire to hold."

I thought for a minute. "Let me see. How about a gun?" I asked.

"Whatever you'd like," Chandra said.

She was standing off to my left but was close enough to whisper in my ear, "Focus on the gun. Be specific. What type of gun is it? What size is it? Does it have a smell once the bullet leaves the chamber? The more detailed you get the better."

My hands began glowing and I could feel something within my grasp. When the light disappeared, I was holding a six-shooter. It was a Colt single action. A gun belt, much like the kind that you'd find in an old western movie, was on my waist. Another gun was holstered on the other side.

"Okay cowboy, let's try it out," Chandra said. She waved her hand in the air and in a whirl we were in a room full of bullseye targets. It is a shooting range. We stood in one of the cubicles. It had bulletproof windows on either side of me. Straight ahead was a countertop and further in front of me were bullseye targets.

"Like I said before, your weapons are only as strong as you are. Let's see you shoot."

I found a target about thirty feet away and pulled the trigger...*Pow, pow, pow, pow, pow, pow!* I shot out all six bullets.

Chandra walked over, looked at the target, and said, "You're a pretty good shot cowboy... Try again but stop limiting yourself." The room started to stretch. The target is now the equivalent of two football fields away.

Chandra, standing behind me said, "Now hit the target."

I look back at her wondering if she was joking. She nodded her head as if to say, *go ahead.*

"So, I'm supposed to hit that target way down there... from here... with a six-shooter?" I questioned, doubtful that the bullets would even reach.

"Just do it," she said in an impatient voice. "Remember you are not confined here. Love is limitless. Now, harness your powers and shoot!"

Not being eager to trifle with Chandra I replied, "Okay," and began to focus; *Caroline, sweet, sweet Caroline* I thought to myself. My eyes started to glow blue, then white. I inhaled deeply and slowly pulled the trigger on my exhale. *Bang, bang, bang!* The shots rang out as each energy burst left the chamber. I stopped shooting. My Colt smoked from the heat of the energy bursts. I slowly lowered my arms as I wondered if I had made any of the shots. I turned back to look at Chandra but she was staring through me.

I holstered my gun as I inquire, "What is it, Chandra?"

"Do you realize what you just did?"

"What do you mean?"

"You just hit those targets. No one has ever done that from this distance unless they had a rifle. Even I can't do that!" Chandra exclaimed.

"But you made it sound as if anyone could do it," I said a little annoyed.

"Well, in theory, anyone can. But you are the first that has," she said, smiling.

She placed her hand on my shoulder and I was instantly calm. "All I did was try to make you think that it is possible. I knew that the chosen one would possess the abilities to make that shot. I'm not saying you are the one but I am saying that you and the chosen one are the only two that I am sure could make that shot."

"So that wasn't just a lucky shot, huh?"

"No, but you will still need to practice this same skill more in order for you to be ready. You need to be able to call upon your weapons quickly and make that shot in a short amount of time. The Marauders have been at this for much longer than you. They are very skilled and do not hesitate."

As was the case with Liam, we practiced to the point of mastery. Chandra started warming up to me. I think it was because I let her continue calling me Cowboy. I managed to call upon many weapons such as a Viking battle ax and medieval long sword and learned to use a M-16 assault rifle as well as a bow and arrow. However, my favorite weapon remained the two six shooters. They were reasonably light and easy to carry around. I also learned how to continue shooting with them without needing to reload. It turned out the power was actually in me the entire time. The weapons were only limited by what I'd allow them to do.

Tate

On Earth, Tate was a gladiator forced to fight in the Roman Coliseum. He traded his life for his village. The Marauders agreed not to touch his people if he'd fight. Thorn loved his size and agility. Tate was his slave and Thorn had made a great deal of his wealth from betting on his gladiator.

Tate was a large black man. He stood much taller than any of the other protectors. He was barrel-chested and his uniform was form fitting. You could easily see his muscles bulging through his shirt. His build is less like a bodybuilder and more like a strong man, the kind that you would see throwing kegs over his shoulders on ESPN. One would think that because of his size he would be much slower but this was not the case. Tate was very flexible and could move like a fleet-footed running back.

Tate was a funny person or at least he thought so. He always had a song in his heart and was quick with a joke. He was as strong as an ox but as gentle as a teddy bear. Tate's own hands had been the weapons of death for so many men, which is why I think he could appreciate the important things about life. He attributed his abilities to the years in the arena fighting diverse opponents. "Every man was different," Tate would say. "One day I was fighting a strongman such as myself. The next time my opponent would be a long, tall yoga man from India. Each man had a strength and a weakness. I was fortunate enough to find theirs before they found mine."

Tate and I were standing in an old boxing gym. The walls had lots of dents and looked old and dingy. Some of them had chipped paint around the edges. It had the typical equipment in it. There was a heavy bag in the far left corner and a speed bag along the middle of the same wall.

"The first rule is to know your opposition," said Tate. "If he is best as a puncher, then you make the fight a kicking match. If he's good on his feet, you take the fight to the ground."

"Ok, that sounds easy enough," I said.

"Sure easy enough but I have no weakness. I can do all of those things," Tate said, with a laugh.

I chuckled with him a little.

"Study his movements." Tate said, bouncing like a fighter would in his stance. He had a rhythm in his motion. "Follow me Sam. Like this," Tate instructed. He started to show me how to move like him. My motion was not as fluid as his. "Try not to think about it. Just feel yourself being ready to strike and block at the same time. Keep a rhythm but don't be predictable." Tate said as he faked at me.

I jumped back to block his advance.

"Not bad! Now as you are moving, let's try a few punch-kick combos."

Tate began showing me how to punch and kick. Next, he taught me the differences between wrestling and jujitsu. He taught me mu ti kickboxing. I was becoming an all-around fighter.

"You picked those up very quickly. None of this will work against the Marauders or any other fighters in Necropolis City."

"Huh?" I said, a little confused by why I had taken the time to learn these moves.

"They won't work unless you use your powers. All of these styles originated from the Protectors. The Marauders learned from fighting us and eventually adapted some of our techniques."

"Oh, I see."

"Your powers will make you faster and stronger. Things will slow down for you." In that moment, Tate began to glow. His aura was different, it was orange like the sun. "Get into your fighting stance. We are going to roll around a bit." Tate said with a gigantic smile.

I knew right away that I was in trouble. But I knew that I had to train. We put on MMA styled cloves which allowed us to punch and grab each other as we practiced.

"Why is your aura a different color?" I asked.

"You'll see."

I made my aura glow too. My aura was bright blue. Tate had taught me how to identify the type of fighter by how they stood. I also knew that he was a very versatile fighter so he would likely be able to deceive me. My plan was to move quickly and try a few combinations of kicks and punches. Tate was much larger than me. I figured that trying to wrestle with him would not benefit me much.

Liam was now standing up on the outer edge of the boxing ring. He was holding on to one of the tern buckles near Tate and whispered in his ear. Tate grinned and looked at me.

"Don't hold back Sam. Tate can handle anything you have," Liam declared.

"Ready?" Tate asked.

I nodded my head and we started to dance around. *Stick and move,* I said to myself. I threw out a test jab to find my range and see his reaction. Tate quickly blocked my hand down. There was a good amount of force in his block but I could tell that it was effortless for him. Next I attempted a combo. Tate blocked my two punches and checked my kick. He then countered with a punch to the gut. He knocked the wind out of me.

"Ugh!" I said, as I back away from him, still in guard.

Tate continued to press forward like a lion that had wounded his prey. He hit me with a thrust kick to the midsection and followed up with a tackle to the ground. I gathered myself enough to block his first set of ground and pound punches. Somehow, I managed to buck him off me. We both scrambled to our feet and back to defensive positions.

"Oh, nice one!" Tate said, brushing off his gloves.

"Thanks," I said, breathing hard.

"Let's see if you can handle this…" His orange glow started to burn brighter. I ran toward him and I landed a punch combo but I felt slow and couldn't keep my chi powered up. Tate took advantage of this. I remembered a large flash that looked like a fist come directly at my face…

I woke up to the sound of slapping. Tate was smacking my face. Liam is also standing near me. I was okay but confused.

"What… How did… huh?" I asked, unsure as to what happened.

"You lost your glow and I was able to knock you out with just one blow," Tate said, with that smile on his face. "My orange glow allows me to block your chi for a short period. You slow down and I get faster. I did have to focus more to lower your glow. That is unusual for me."

Tate could use the powers of love to create joy and laughter. He was able to channel his sense of humor to calm his opponent and weaken him. "Why don't you try Sam? When you are powering up, think of a joyous or funny moment to channel the orange aura," said Liam.

I began to think about the time that I was washing my car and Caroline was there. I had my wireless headphones on and I was listening to John Legend's song PDA. I had the sponge in my hand and a bucket of soapy water on the cement of the driveway right beside me. The day was hot for October. The sun was shining and a slight breeze blew the smell of autumn leaves through the neighborhood. I was wearing a tank top and a pair of old basketball shorts. I also had on a pair of flip-flop sandals. I was really into the song so I didn't notice her behind me.

"Psh!" cold water was all over the back of my shirt.

"Hey!" I said as I yanked off my headphones.

There was Caroline standing there wearing one of my raggedy old college t-shirts which was wide on top, exposing her shoulders. She also had on cutoff jean shorts and no shoes. One of her eyebrows was raised and her smile gave her away. That and the fact that she was holding the water hose and she was the only person around. She shot it off again. It was another direct hit. I looked at her, amazed and shocked. She was in the mood and wanted to play. I let out a sigh. She started laughing hysterically. I picked up the bucket of soapy water as I laughed and I started running towards her.

"Oh no!" Caroline screeched, as I gained on her.

"Sam please no!" she yelled, with a high pitched scream of dread.

"Oh, it's too late for that now!" I pulled back my bucket in launch position.

Woosh! I'd hit my target. The water splashed her hard enough for her to fall.

"Ah!" she screamed as she hit the soft green lawn.

I jumped on top of her so that she couldn't get away. I gave her just enough room to turn and face me.

"I got you," I said. We both laughed side-splittingly. I rolled over to lay on the grass next to her. Soon our laughs were traded in for a romantic gaze.

Still smiling, I said, "You are crazy."

"I know, *crazy for you*," she said in a soft whisper.

With her smile permanently stuck on her face, I took charge of the moment and gave her a kiss.

"Ready for another go?" Tate asked.

"This time focus on what makes you laugh or brings you joy," said Liam.

I got up to my feet and took a Bruce Lee like stance. With a fresh thought of Caroline on my mind, I felt more confident about my chances.

Tate was glowing bright orange again. He stalked forward towards me.

I produced an orange glow as well. Tate grinned.

"Our auras will neutralize us. But I'm the more skilled fighter. What will you do?"

"What will I do? Come get some," I said as I wiped my thumb across my chin.

Tate leg kicked me to get me off balance.

I stumbled but countered with a kick of my own which only grazed him.

Tate faked a low kick then connected with two gut punches before I blocked his uppercut.

His skills were stifling. I found it hard to get room to try anything.

"Focus!" I heard Liam grunt in the corner.

"That's it!" I thought. I was going about fighting Tate all wrong. I was playing to his strengths. He was great at all of these fighting styles but his strength was in his ability to dictate what he wanted to do next. I needed to take control of the fight and put him on defense.

Just then, Tate landed a hook shot to the ribs. The blow dropped me to one knee. This was my chance. I dropped my defenses and stopped glowing.

Tate gave a half smile and pounced. He attempted a superman punch. I moved out of the way just in time. Back on my feet, I began to glow again. This time it was the bright white light that Liam showed me.

"Yes!" Liam grunted with enthusiasm.

Tate, a little surprised, forced his glow brighter orange. He sprinted for me and attempted a double leg takedown. My light stayed strong. I sprawled down to stop his attack. Still holding him in my sprawl, I put him in a front neck choke and gave him two hard knees to the chest. He couldn't absorb my bright light like he could my blue one. It had too much power.

The giant man collapsed to the mat on all fours. I let him go and

I took a few steps back. He shook off the effects of my counter. Tate balled up his fists in determination. Next, he attempted a flying kick.

Now it was him slowing down for me. I was able to duck his kick. All in one motion, I maneuvered behind him and wrapped both arms around his waist. I locked my hands together and I launched him in the air behind me like a German Suplex.

This time Tate was the one that needed help off the mat. Liam grabbed a stool from the corner where he had been standing. We sat Tate in the seat.

"Tate. Tate. You're gonna be okay my good friend," said Liam.

Tate finally came to.

"Are you ok?" I asked.

"Yeah, I'm good. Wow! You must be the chosen one."

"Aren't we all?" I responded.

"Yes, we have been chosen by Ekon," Tate said.

"The Great Source has truly honored you with this gift," Liam added.

"It's just one fight. How does that make me the chosen one?"

"Up to this point, Tate has been the strongest of all the Protectors. You are the first to defeat him. He and Thorn almost fought once. The two traded a few hits before Raven and Arawn "The Hunter" wanted to join in to make the fight less than equal. Chandra and I rallied behind Tate and they retreated before anything of consequence happened," Liam explained.

"I didn't know about that... Have you ever assimilated anyone before? I mean it seems as though Thorn is as mean and nasty as they come but he is still around."

"There are extreme cases where we do have to assimilate a soul. Ekon does not wish for any of us to be assimilated before we are ready. There are times when the opposition poses an immediate threat and we need to neutralize them," Liam explained.

"There are those that have committed atrocities everywhere they go. If we ever get our hands on one of them, it is imperative that we neutralize them right away... But remember, our real job is to Protect and assist those that are ready for The Land of the Promised in the conversion process," Tate added.

This training was extremely beneficial to me. Tate was very skilled in combat. I learned from a true master. He and I continued to train together. As I realized my now blooming powers, he too got stronger. We slowly became best friends, much like Ted and I on Earth.

Chapter 9

Caroline in Hinterland

⚬◆⚬

HINTERLAND WAS A miserable place. While it only rained on occasion, it always felt like rain was on the horizon. Days and nights felt the same. Gloomy gray clouds covered the landscape like the shadow of a tree covers the ground in mid-day. The dry, cracked dirt ground was hard and brittle. The city was not full of bright blues and vibrant yellows. Instead, one would see melancholy beige and disconsolate browns.

While it is possible for one to believe that this was hell, it was not. This was a place for the sad and the lonely. The buildings and shelters were not built to last. Mostly made of sticks, mud, and clay, they would be easily destroyed once its inhabitants had made their choice. Hinterland was created to be a choosing ground. It was designed for a soul to desire something different.

The Great Source did not want to send evildoers or the self-haters to Necropolis City to become Thorn's slaves until the soul could no longer desire to be free and happy. Choice was the key to where one would spend eternity. Hinterland was for the ones that harmed others in life or didn't find the beauty in purpose on Earth. Not every sin is equal and the lesser evils were given a chance for redemption here.

The Protectors were needed to save the people in Hinterland. Before Thorn found a way into Hinterland, all souls had the chance to go to the Land of the Promised. Some needed more time than others but they all saw the light eventually.

Thorn and his men were well practiced in the art of seduction. He was able to deceive because he is one of them. He knows the sorrow that they feel from his time on Earth. He paints a picture of a better place and a better world in Necropolis.

Now my sweet Caroline was there. When she made her transition I was in training and had no idea she was no longer on Earth. Caroline was very strong-willed and would never submit to the charms of Castro Thorn. Unlike my experience, however, she was greeted with odors and smells that were hard to describe when she reached Hinterland. There was smoke in the air along with the sounds of hustle and bustle in the distance.

Her setting was quite primitive. She sat upright in a dirt-filled alley way. There was a hut made of dirt and clay behind her. In front of her, about 20 yards away, the alley ended and opened to a thick dark forest that didn't seem to be very welcoming. She wasn't aware of it but she was only a few hundred feet from the cliff that separated her land from mine. *Where am I?* Caroline thought to herself.

"Sam! I'm here, Sam. I'm here for you!" she cried, but I was nowhere in sight. "You said you'd be with me, Sam." For a while, Caroline was saddened at the thought of not seeing me. Ending her life apparently did not provide the reunion she so desperately sought. Soon though, she would gather herself and decide to walk towards the sounds of this busy yet lonesome place. As the ambience grew louder, she saw a faint light through a space in the wall of a building built with sticks and straw. There were people sitting around the fire. There was little talking except for an occasional grunt for someone to put on another log. Caroline slowly walked over to them.

The people were wearing modern styled clothes but they were torn and worn, likely from sleeping and moving about the rough terrain.

"Hello," she said to the group. She was able to make out that there were six people sitting around the fire. There were three women, one man, a boy, and a girl.

One of the women looked up at her. "Are you lost?" she asked in a Northern British accent. Her voice was cold and had a hint of melancholy to it.

"Um... yes. I'm not sure where I am." Caroline said.

"Oh, I see. It's your first day here? Well, welcome to Hinterland. I'm Joann and that's my son Abe."

"Hinterland?" Caroline asked.

The woman nodded and looked back down towards the fire.

"Do you mind if I sit?"

"I don't see why not." Caroline found an empty space near Joann and slowly got into a comfortable position. She leaned over in Joann's direction and asked with a somber tone, "Would you mind telling me what Hinterland is? You see, I'm not exactly sure how I got here or..."

"This is Hinterland. I've heard others call it that and it seems to me that people around here don't stay very long. They stay as long as they need to." Joann didn't have an expression on her face. She didn't seem sad to Caroline. She was more... lonely.

"Have you seen a man named Sam?" Caroline asked. "...Sam Connelly. He's my husband. About 6 feet tall. He's black, about two hundred pounds?"

"Sorry, I can't help you there," Joann said.

"But it's important that I find him," Caroline said in a desperate tone.

"Look, lady, I'll have to ask you to leave now! I've got my own problems." Joann said. She was talking with her teeth clenched together almost as if she was growling.

"I see," Caroline said as she slowly stood up and walked away. She was very frustrated that Joann had nothing more for her. All she wanted to know was what this place was and how to find me.

As Caroline walked down the dank and dimly lit streets of

Hinterland, she happened upon a man. He was not dressed the same as the other people of Hinterland. He wore a black suit and white shirt that seemed to be tailor-made for him. His tie was a solid dark blue shade. This tie mainly stood out to Caroline because it was the first time that she had seen color since her arrival. She couldn't see his hair cut because the top of his head was covered by his authentic Dorfman Pacific Straw Western Cowboy Hat.

He was called Jester. Jester was five feet ten inches tall. He was thin in the way that younger men in their early twenties are thin but his face appeared older, as though he was in his late forties. His face had a scar about an inch long just under his ear. His eyes were hazel gray. He was a white man but had a very dark tan as if he spent lots of time in the sun. He wasn't a large guy but his body language said that he could handle his own if it came down to it.

His appearance being so different from everyone else, Caroline believed he knew a little more than the average resident. He was standing near a mud hut that was much larger than most of the others and seemed to have a feel of class.

Yes, this must be someone that could help me find answers, Caroline thought.

"Excuse me, sir," Caroline called over to Jester.

He smiled and pointed to himself as if to make sure that she wanted him.

"Yes, you sir. I was wondering if you could help me."

"Why, for a beautiful woman like you I'll do my best to try," Jester responded in his best Texas car salesman voice.

"Well, you see... um... it's my husband," Caroline stuttered through her first few words. "I am looking for him." She then gave a brief description of me.

Jester listened to Caroline attentively. He had a hand on his chin and looked upward as though he was thinking. "I'm not sure...but he sounds familiar," he surmised. "Well if you are here and he's not, I bet you that he's in Necropolis city," Jester said sounding like he just solved a tough crossword puzzle.

Caroline was excited to finally get some answers. "Where is Necropolis city?"

"Well, it's just over on the other side of that river. Over there where the water stops running."

The gates of Necropolis could not be seen from where she was standing but she did notice that the water just seemed to stop flowing right at the point that Jester told her about. There were dry rocks and dead trees just on the south side of the river stream.

"What is Necropolis city?" Caroline inquired.

"Oh, wow!" Jester said. "It's where I live. It's a city that was created for a special group. It isn't so easy to get into the city if you have not made the choice to be there. This place here is a waiting place. Hinterland. You stay here until you have made a choice between two lands. One is filled with fools that believe that they should rule over everyone. The other, a city where you have the ability to choose what rules you. Necropolis is a great city where great men and women strive and fight for the right to choose what rules us. It is an unbelievable place where our leader Castro Thorn keeps our feet planted firmly on the ground."

"Why would you need to have your feet planted?"

"Because a war is coming! Our leader wants us to prepare and get ready to fight those that would stop our way of existing. Castro Thorn is a strong leader. He has taken many of us into Necropolis City. You could say that he is a hero. Necropolis does not have much. I'll give you that. But it's ours. Our City is not made of gold and doesn't have flashy bright lights like the Land of the Promised. But... there is beauty to be found in all of creation. The so-called 'Protectors' hunt us down and fight us all the time. Heck, I could get in a lot of trouble from just talking to you. It's not really very safe here for someone like me who has chosen to live in Necropolis. I'll have to go soon before they come back. So, I can take you to Necropolis now. But you need to choose."

"I don't know. I'd want to be sure that Sam was there."

Jester paused for a few beats and looked down at his black lizard-skinned boots. His gaze then returned to her eyes before asking,

"Caroline, do you think that Sam would support a cause like ours? If he knew that there were people being oppressed or hunted down for being different, would he do something to stop them? Would he risk his own life to save others?"

Caroline started to answer Jester's questions in her mind. She knew me to be a good person. She knew that I would help even a stranger in need. She soon found herself thinking back to the time that I had chased off these two teenagers that were ganging up on an old man. Next, she thought about the time that I almost got tasered and slammed to the ground by the cops for trying to help a young teenager not get arrested.

Caroline and I had been driving home and we were near the east side of Indianapolis and saw the situation unfolding.

"Stop the car babe," I said as I started unbuckling my seat belt.

"What?" she responded. "Oh no honey, it looks like the cops have the situation handled."

"But honey that's a kid over there. Do they really need guns?" I asked.

Caroline stopped the car. I jumped out and walked closer to the scene. There were four police officers standing in a line with guns drawn. The young teenager was standing scared with his hands in the air. I could tell that he was looking for a way out. I also knew that it wasn't smart for him to run.

"Get on your knees and keep your hands where I can see them!" one officer shouted.

"Excuse me, officers!" I said with an authoritative yet respectful tone. Almost immediately I'd begun to feel a little bit of fear for my own life. But he was just a kid.

"Is it necessary for you to have your guns out? I mean... he's just a kid. A Taser could work just the same." I said, trying to appeal to their humanity. There had been several police shootings in this area of town in recent months and I didn't want to see another one happen when I could do something to prevent it.

"Sir, sir, you need to calm down sir," Officer Romanowski replied in my direction. I knew his name because I read it on his shirt.

"With all due respect officer, I am calm," I said, starting to feel less afraid.

"You need to back away, this is a delicate situation."

"I didn't do anything!" the kid shouted as tears streamed down his face.

"It's going to be ok young man," I said.

"Sir, I said to move back," Officer Romanowski was starting to get agitated.

"I have the right to observe you and the other police sir!" I declared. "What did this boy do officer?" I turned to the boy and said, "Young man just do what they say and everything will be ok."

"I didn't do anything," said the boy.

"He started running as soon as we pulled into the apartment complex," said one of the officers. "That means he's got something to hide."

"Not necessarily," I said. "Why were you running young man?"

"My mother had called me and told me to come home right away!" the boy cried. "And I can't get in trouble for coming home late again or I can't play on my Xbox for a month."

"Come on officer," I said. "He's just a kid. He's guilty of being a kid. You know how it is when mom says it's time to come home, right?"

Romanowski looked at me and gave a half smile. "Ok, fellas stand down. Olsen, take the kid home and let his mom know that it was a misunderstanding and he shouldn't be punished."

"And you," Romanowski was pointing at me, "What you did was stupid and you could have been arrested or shot yourself. Doing this job means we see a lot of bad people in all shapes and sizes. I guess sometimes that gets the best of you. Thanks for your help."

"No, thank you for showing patience."

We shook hands.

Caroline had recorded the entire moment on her phone. While no one was arrested. That story made the news. It was a great PR moment for the police.

⌒⋅⋅⌒

"Caroline, I can't force you to come but if you choose to come, it must be because you want to be there. I'm not saying that Sam is there. But he might have chosen to be."

Caroline believed that I would choose to fight for the rights of others, which I would. She knew that I would stand up to bullies and put myself in harm's way to save a life, which I had. These were some of the main qualities that she loved about me. My love for others was great. She had felt my love each and every day. It started to make sense to her that I would have chosen Necropolis City and that I would be fighting for its citizens. The problem was that I had been preparing to fight and save the souls in Hinterland. She was being deceived into thinking that Necropolis was on the right side.

"Sam must be there. Will you help me look for him, Jester?"

"Of course, but you will need to join our cause and be a fellow warrior. I will train you myself. There are great powers that you can manipulate with your love for Sam along with your sadness and loneliness that you feel without him."

Caroline was very strong-willed. On Earth, she had played several sports including soccer and swimming. She was even on the gymnastics team for a short while. By training with Jester, she thought that she could prove to me that she was strong. We would be strong together once she found me. Then she made a decision that would change my path forever.

"I choose Necropolis City. I will fight for and defend the city as Sam would do. I will make him proud of me. He will love me again."

Jester smiled and held out his hand. Caroline joined hands with him and they began their journey.

Chapter 10

Something's Not Right

"**D**ID YOU FEEL that?" I asked Tate.

"What?"

"That!" there it was again. "I felt the ground shaking underneath me."

"Are you okay? I don't feel anything," said Tate.

"Something's not right."

We were walking in the forest after a training session with Liam and Chandra. The winding dirt path started to blur. I lost my balance for a moment and stumbled before Tate grabbed my arm to help steady me.

"Let's head back to my home. I may have something that will help," Liam said.

I sensed a pain in my stomach. It was a sharp sting followed by butterflies.

"Ugh!" I groaned out loud and fell to my knees.

"Sam!" Chandra shouted.

I put my hand to my head and closed my eyes. Images started to race through my head. At first, they made no sense. The first was of Caroline. She is sitting in our bedroom on Earth. I see the pill container and the vodka bottle. She looked hurt. The next vision is of her wandering around a dusty dirty place. She looked lost and lonely. She was calling my name over and over but I was nowhere to be found. The final image was of Caroline and another man. He reached out his hand and she grabbed it. They walked through a cast iron gate. My vision stopped.

All at once the pain is gone and I am feeling better. The visions were just fragments but they felt very real. "It's Caroline! Something has happened. She is in trouble," I explained to the group.

"What did you see?" Chandra asked.

"She was looking for me and couldn't find me. She was walking with a man wearing a black suit. My vision stopped once they reached an iron gate."

Tate, Liam, and Chandra were all listening intently. The look on their faces was grim. It was as if they knew something that I did not know. They were all wondering who was going to do the honors of telling me what they knew.

"Sam," Tate said while he rested his hand on my shoulder. "Caroline... it... it sounds like she was in Hinterland."

"That can't be! Caroline is one of the best people I know. She would come straight to The Land of the Promised. She is caring and she volunteers her free time at a homeless shelter. How can she be in Hinterland?"

"Sam!" Liam said authoritatively, "...there has to be a reason she ended up in Hinterland. The Great Source would not make a mistake on this."

"Liam, she's a good person. She should not be there. There has to be some kind of mistake or something. Why was she in Hinterland? Where was she going?"

Liam had to choose his next words very carefully. He knew that I was upset and he knew that in order for me to clearly understand, I needed to be composed.

"Let me show you." He reached out his hand to me. His eyes were glowing a bright blue. Liam grabbed my shoulder and I felt a rush of energy flow through my body. I focused my eyes to find myself in new surroundings. Liam was standing to my left.

We were in my old bedroom from Earth. Caroline was there. She was listening to the song that we played at our wedding. I saw the bottle of pills and the vodka.

"What is going on?" I asked. "Caroline, don't do this."

She couldn't hear me.

"Liam, we have to stop her. Not like this Caroline!" I ran to her side and I fell to all fours. A tear streamed down my face and I looked at her laying in the bed, her body lifeless. It was like she was peacefully sleeping.

If I could just wake her up somehow, I thought. "Caroline... please no. Why Caroline, why?" I cried.

Liam placed his hand on my shoulder again and I was pulled back into the forest. This was the first time that I felt true sadness in the Land of the Promised. I sat down against a tree. Slumped over, my head felt too heavy to lift up. Chandra and Tate looked at me as if they understood my pain, but they also knew it was too late for Caroline.

"We have to go get her! Let's go to Hinterland and bring her to the Land of the Promised. Will you help me, Tate?"

Impulsively, Tate responded, "I've got your back brother."

"Tate you know we can't do that!" Chandra snapped at him.

Tate grunted. "We have to try. It may not be too late."

"Too late for what?" I asked.

Chandra explained, "Look, Sam, if Caroline is in Hinterland that means that she can be deceived into entering Necropolis City. You said that she passed through an iron gate with a man in a black suit. The only gate that you could be describing is the entryway to Necropolis."

"She has to make a choice. The Land of the Promised or Necropolis. As you have learned, Thorn and his men are very persuasive. If one of the Protectors was able to stop them then she would be okay and there would still be a chance," said Chandra.

"Okay, so what's the problem?" I asked.

"One of the Marauders wears a black suit and goes by the name of Jester. He is one of Thorn's most loyal and deceptive recruiters. He is very skilled in the art of trickery. If you say that they were standing at a gate… it is likely that she has already made her choice," Chandra said, with her heavy words lingering in the air.

"That just doesn't make sense Chandra. Why would she ever choose Necropolis over all of this?" I asked.

"Like I said Sam, they are very persuasive. Sometimes they threaten to take the life force from someone in order for another to choose. Sometimes they use lust or greed or even self-pity. My guess is that he appealed to her heart. I believe that Caroline came here looking for you. They must have made her believe that you were somehow in Necropolis City." Chandra surmised.

"So she is here because of me. This can't be the end." I said in disbelief. "There's only one option I can see and that is to go to Hinterland and pray that it's not too late. Will you please help me?" I asked, looking at Chandra then Liam. They both looked at each other and back at me. Both gestured in agreement and the four of us began in the direction of Hinterland.

We arrived at a cliff that overlooked Hinterland. It is a one hundred foot natural barrier that separated the two cities. My companions and I scanned the city for a time and began devising a plan for finding Caroline.

"This will be a double mission," Liam explained. "If we find any Hinterlanders that want to come back with us to the Land of the Promised, we will accept them as well."

The three of us nodded in approval of the task. I had never attempted a crossover before but I had read about it in the hall of books. Crossovers were one of the major functions of the Protectors. It was considered an honor to perform this duty. With our plan set we walked along the ridge until we found a slope to descend. Once we were on the lower elevation of Hinterland we strode forward. It wasn't long before we entered the city and found ourselves walking amongst the many mud huts. We split off into two groups with Tate staying with me. We wasted no time and began questioning people about Caroline.

"Excuse me, have you seen my wife? She goes by the name, Caroline." I asked a stranger.

He seemed too involved with his own problems to care. The man grunted and went on his way, never actually responding to me with coherent words. This type of reaction was very common as we searched. Then it happened: the pain was back. Not as strong but it was back.

"Ugh." I grunted as I slowed down and hunched forward.

"Is it Caroline?" Tate asked.

"Uhgg! Yes." I said, with a growl. "She was here. That fire over there," I managed.

We walked over to them. Instantly, I knew her name.

"Joann?"

"Yes, I am. And you are Sam," she responded

"Are you and Abe ready to go home?"

"Yes, we are," she answered.

"Leave your troubles behind." The words came to me with ease. I felt as if this was my true calling. "Now be restored," I commanded. A colorful bright light overtook their bodies. With a flash, the woman and the boy were transformed. They were now wearing fresh new clothes. Their faces were no longer beat up by the worries of life on Earth. She had spent her time in this dusty city and was ready for her life in eternal paradise. "Joanne? Before you go, would you please share with me what you know about Caroline?"

"Sam, I am very thankful for you helping me with my transformation. But... I am afraid to say, Caroline has chosen Necropolis City." Her voice was somber and full of regret. "The one called Jester told her that you might be there. He made her choose. I was not in a state to help her and he is one of their strongest fighters."

"Thank you, Joanne. Now go in peace. The light will guide you home."

"Thank you, Sam. You are truly a gift from God. Do look me up for tea when you are back in the city."

"I will."

Joanne and Abe floated in a ball of light upwards toward the cliff and disappeared once they made it to the top.

I let out a deep sigh.

"That was a beautiful crossover, Sam. It took me several trips to Hinterland before I was able to cross anyone over properly," said Tate.

I heard his words and they gave me comfort for a moment. I found great relief in knowing that I was saving souls. The souls that were ready to crossover were easiest. It only took me being near them to feel that they were ready to transition. My abilities allowed me to sense them. The more difficult souls to save were the ones that had been talking with Marauders. Most people found themselves in Hinterland because of their mental state before leaving Earth. They needed time to get their minds clear. The Marauders wanted to keep their minds clouded in order to make it easier to trick the Hinterlanders. Sometimes a mind would be so twisted that the soul believed we were the enemy. In these situations, we would need to help them find happy memories and moments of joy. Sometimes a parent only needed to hear their child's laugh. Other times they needed to feel a kiss from a loved one. Our powers allowed us to see deep into the minds of people and show them the love that they had forgotten about. The hardest cases were the souls that died with hate, vengeance, and malice deep in their hearts. These were also the ones that Thorn and his people would recruit first.

There was one man that had killed his neighbors. They were a family of seven. He ended their lives by burning them alive while they slept through the night. My powers were greater than the others so I took him on. He was looking for a fight. His mind was twisted into thinking that the family that he had murdered was part of a crime syndicate. They all needed to die in order for the neighborhood to be safe.

"Ford! It is time to crossover," I said, knowing that this would likely agitate him.

Ford was a thickly-built white man. He took the form of a middle-aged man and was very athletic. He kept his orange prison jumpsuit on. His arm muscles bulged from his shirt. His voice was gruff and deep. He'd lived in prison for over thirty years. He was beaten and taken advantage of by his roommate and other prisoners. He was labeled a baby killer. Even the world's most hardened criminals have a problem with baby killers.

"I'm not crossing anything you devil!" Ford shouted over to me.

"You are the one that is coming with me. I spent years in prison after protecting my neighborhood. They all turned on me. Those ungrateful SOB's and now you think that you can take advantage of me too."

"Ford, I'm here to help you. You have paid for your crimes and the Great Source wants to ease your pain. He forgives all."

"Forgives all! I don't need to be forgiven. I killed them to keep my mom and family safe. The 'Great Source' should be thanking me!" Ford said.

"They were not a threat to your neighborhood. You have to see that what you did was wrong."

"I did nothing wrong!"

"Some of them you killed were kids. What threat were they?"

"Enough!" he shouted as he charged towards me. He swung his giant fist toward my head. I moved just in time. I followed up with a tackle from behind, using his momentum against him. Moving quickly, I grabbed him by the neck and my body glowed white. Ford's mind cleared. The feelings of hate and betrayal faded from his mind. He saw the reality of what he had done. He knew that his act was gruesome. The weight of his decision to take the life of a father, mother, and young children mounted on top of him. I felt his body stop fighting. I let him out of my chokehold. Ford proceeded to cough violently. Eventually he caught his breath before beginning to weep. "I killed those people. How could I have been so blind? But it felt... so... real," Ford said, heavy hearted. He then looked at me and asked, "Will he ever forgive me?"

"Even you can be forgiven. But first, you need to forgive yourself. It is the will of the Great Source that all of his children come back to exist with him in the Land of the Promised," I explained. "Your time of hurt is over now. Be restored."

Ford, on his knees, reached up to the sky. The great light overtook him. With an explosion and a flash, his jumpsuit converted to a tailor-made suit of white. He was not wearing a tie and his shoes were also white. "Thank you, Sam! Thank you for helping me see the light." Ford's eyes filled with tears of joy.

"Sam...I saw your thoughts when you merged with my mine. Your powers are truly great. The love in your heart for Caroline is pure. She needs you."

"But it's too late," I said, resigned to the fact that I would likely never see Caroline again.

"Yes, there was a time when it would have been too late. You Sam, have Ekon's pure love flowing through you. You are the one that can go from heaven to hell and back. It is not impossible. It has just never been done," Ford said.

"What makes you so sure that I can do that?" I asked

"I am one with the universe now. My mind is clear. The love that you have for Caroline gives you boundless powers. You are the chosen one. If you want to bring her back, you must start to believe this simple truth. If it wasn't too late for me, it isn't too late for her even if she is in the Necropolis."

He reached his hand out to me. We shake hands.

"I must go now," Ford said. He turned and walked away into a beam of light.

That evening back at my father's place, Chandra, Tate, Liam, my father, Griffin, and I discussed the merits of going to find Caroline.

"It has never been done!" Griffin shouted. We are all gathered around a large circular table. The table was made of thick oak and could fit all of the Protectors around it comfortably if needed. There were several empty chairs because the others in the group were on duty in Hinterland.

"I know, and there is no way I can do it alone," I said.

"You expect us to go to the Necropolis just to save your wife?" Chandra interjected. "If I am going to go along with this crackpot plan, then we need to free all who want to come back with us. Just like in Hinterland."

Griffin said, "I cannot go. The Protectors are here to help the people of Hinterland crossover to the Land of the Promised. I implore you all to let this go. There is danger and certain loss of your life force if you enter Necropolis. Sam, your powers are great but you are not ready."

"I'm almost done with my training. I don't have a choice, Griffin. My wife is there and all of the love in my heart is with her. If she is not here to enjoy this paradise, then this is not paradise. It is a hell that I would not imagine on any of you. Somehow Caroline was tricked into thinking that I am there in that city which means she is there because of me. The longer she is there, the less hope we have of getting her back."

"He's right you know," Tate said. He took his time to glance around the table to make sure everyone was looking at him. "Sam is one of us now. We need to help make him whole. Caroline must come back here."

Liam said, "None have ever walked in the gates of Necropolis with the intention of leaving. The Great Source allows for Thorn to enter into Hinterland and Thorn only allows his most loyal followers to join him in enlistment. To enter into the Necropolis is to wage war on hate. It is a suicide mission…but I am in. Sam, you are the chosen one of the chosen few. We will prevail."

I was surprised at first by Liam's comment. Then I was grateful that he was willing to sacrifice his life force for me. "Thank you, brother," I said.

Griffin was not as excited about Liam's speech but he understood the nature of the journey.

"Griffin, we will make it back. We will rescue the other souls. The Great Source will guide us through this voyage," I proclaimed.

"I'm afraid that I cannot send any other Protectors to aid you. They are needed here."

"Yes, sir!" I looked at the Protectors that would be accompanying me. "Thank you so much. We will make it back and we will save many souls."

"Be careful son. I know you can do it. Now, go get your wife back," my father ordered.

Chapter 11
Necropolis

CAROLINE ENTERED NECROPOLIS. Jester was an excellent manipulator. He explained the beauty in all that they saw. The weeds and poison ivy lining the black iron gates of the city were merely Ekon's way of protecting the occupants on the inside. He pointed out the beautiful green and red colors that are present on the leaves of the itch filled pest of a plant.

Necropolis is a city of torture and hate. Where there is grass and fertile soil in The Land of the Promised, there are weeds and baron dirt in Necropolis. Its citizens include some of the most deceptive and hateful people to ever walk on Earth. While there is pain and suffering there, most of them find an almost masochistic pleasure in watching the others suffer alongside them. There are very little comforts in the world of Necropolis but somehow, the Marauders thrive inside its walls.

Necropolis gets hot and humid during the day. At night the temperatures drop to cold and frigid levels. The shelters in the city were like those found in a third world country. They were made of tin and dead rotted wood. Even though one is protected from the elements in these shelters, it's hard to say that the living quarters were comfortable. Someone like Castro Thorn could survive quite easily in a place like this. He was used to living a hard life.

They walked along an old dusty trail as they made their way towards the main hub of the city. There was beauty to be found there. Caroline spotted a flower that had green leaves around the base and two layers of petals. The outer layer of the flower was a pink fuchsia and was shaped like a heart. The inner layer was white and looked like it was dripping from the pointed end of the heart. She was delighted to see the beautiful plant and reached to touch it.

"Oh no, don't touch that!" Jester warned. "Those are Bleeding Hearts. They are native to Siberia and some parts of Asia on Earth. They could harm you on Earth. Here, they have the power to paralyze and weaken your life force."

"Oh, but they are so beautiful. Can you believe such an innocent looking creature could be so dangerous?" she asked.

"You'd be surprised at what isn't as it seems," he mumbled.

"What was that?" Caroline said not hearing his tone.

"Nothing, it's just that some things are not what they seem. Most of the vegetation here is very dangerous. Take that tree over there, we call it the Little Apple Tree. The fruit looks like a small green apple and the leaves appear harmless. If you break the leaf open, you'd find a toxic liquid that will severely burn your skin. The apple looking fruit, if eaten, will cause you great pain in your stomach for months."

"Oh wow," Caroline responded. It was her steadfast belief that I was there somewhere that prevented these discoveries from triggering some type of alarm in her.

"Don't worry Caroline. We do have edible food. It may not be the best but it will keep you going. We have been banished here for a long time. The group called the Protectors see to it that we can only hope for what little we have here. They keep us trapped in this place. Soon there will be a war. We will be ready for them. Those saps living in the Land of the Promised want us to stay here and rot here. We are constantly weak and malnourished while they reap the rewards of a full belly and glutinous comfort. But our hunger for justice will help us prevail against them."

Caroline nodded in agreement.

"Come on now, we are almost at the main hub of the city. I think you'll find it to be unique." Jester smiled at Caroline and she smiled back. They continued forward for a while longer. Caroline saw a bright yellow and red neon styled light in the near distance.

"What's that?" she quarried.

"It's the main hub," Jester said with a grin. "Come on Caroline, I'm so excited to show you around."

Chapter 12
The Plan

"CAROLINE... CAROLINE ... Caroline!" she heard me calling her. "Sam! I'm right here Sam!"

I was walking through thick weeds and past dangerous plants. She saw me looking for her but for some reason, she was unable to get any closer to me. It seemed to her that the harder she ran the slower she got.

"Sam! Slow down! Sam, Please!"

"Caroline, wake up. It's Jester. Caroline..."

She was jolted awake by her newfound traveling companion.

"Caroline, it's me, Jester."

For a moment she was disoriented and was not sure where she was. She shook her hair away from her face and rubbed her eyes. As things became clearer to her, she took a deep breath and pulled her hair into a ponytail. They were in a hot tin roofed hut. The floor was made of dirt. Besides the four walls, there wasn't much else in the shelter. *It's better than sleeping outside,* she thought to herself.

"Necropolis Main Hub, we made it. We stopped here for a rest. You must have dozed off."

"Hmm... I can sleep in this world?" she asked.

"Sure you can. You don't need as much sleep or food like you did on Earth but it still is a necessary thing to get every once in a while. We have a night and a day but time moves differently."

They left the shelter and headed on their way.

"Well, sleepy head, there is someone I want you to meet," Jester said.

"Who would that be?"

"Our leader and a good friend of mine, Castro Thorn. If we want to find Sam, we will need his help."

"Do you think he'd help us?" Caroline asked.

"Well, he's a very complicated man. But he also owes me a few favors and he rewards his most loyal followers."

"That's great, Jester. Thank you so much for your help."

"No problem Caroline. You know, he's going to like you right away. I can tell."

"What makes you say that?"

"There's something about your energy. When you were sleeping, I felt it radiating strongly. You are special indeed."

Caroline gave him a smile as they approached Thorn's home. The home looked different from the rest of the shelters. It was made of tin and wood like the others but it seemed to be rustier. The home of such a great leader was very modest from the outside. It was, however, the largest of all the homes near the main hub. There were two guards standing in front of the house stationed at a doorway. Both wore tattered war-torn armor. It could have been the kind worn in Rome one hundred years BC or something.

"Let me do all the talking, Caroline."

"Jester, what brings you here? Thorn told you to stay in Hinterland," one of the guards said.

"I was in Hinterland, son, now I'm back, and I have someone that he will want to meet."

"Who's the woman?" the other guard asked.

"She is the 'someone' that he will want to meet," Jester said as his smile turned into gritted teeth. "Now get out of my way."

The men did not appreciate those words and sized him up. They knew that he was known for his fighting skills but they wouldn't be Thorn's personal guards if they weren't formidable themselves. The guards looked at each other and simultaneously decided that they could take him.

Necropolis is a rough place. To survive in a habitat like this, one needs to be ready to face any and all challenges. To back down from even one fight meant that you were weak and made you a target for stronger fighters looking to build their status.

Jester was no easy prey. He knew he needed to gain Caroline's trust even more in order for the next step in his plan to work. He noticed that she had a great power in her, just as the Protectors noticed in me. Because our love was so strong for each other, our powers were potentially equal. Jester was in Hinterland looking for Caroline. She was the fallen one and somehow Jester knew she would be there. Hinterland would be their best chance to find her. She sacrificed herself for love. It was misguided and selfish, but love was still in her heart.

"I don't like your tone Jester. It's like I said, you're not supposed to be here. Neither is she. Thorn is busy. Now you get out of my face before we give you what for," one guard said.

Jester was left with no choice but to fight. It was what he wanted all along. This would not likely be an even fight with it being two on one. The guard on the left swung at Jester and missed. Jester countered with a left jab and a right cross. The guard to his right jumped on his back and was quickly tossed over head first into the ground. Jester gave him a swift kick to the ribs and turned back to the guard on the left. This time, Jester made the first move. His body started to glow neon red. He grabbed the guard and they clinched like rams jousting on a mountain. Jester gave the guard a head-butt to the nose then two body shots. Jester let out a roar as he finished his opponent with a powerful uppercut.

Both guards were on the ground holding their bruised parts.

Jester looked down at them and snidely asked, "May we pass now?"

His smile returned as he waved Caroline over to walk with him. They strode up to Thorn's thick, beaten up front door. Jester knocked and with only a brief wait, a servant opened the door.

"Hello, Smith." He was always friendly with the staff. He found that even in a place like Necropolis, people appreciated a friendly face. He was good at not letting his feeling show on the outside. But he was full of rage on the inside.

"Do come in Mr. Jester. I shell alert Mr. Thorn to your presence." Smith responded in a British accent.

The inside of Thorn's home looked much different from the outside. There were servants to wait on him hand and foot. He had a cold pool for the swelteringly hot days and a hot tub for the artic like cold nights. The furniture was made of quality crafted wood taken from Hinterland. The ceilings were vaulted and made of tin. The inner walls were paneled with wood. One could say that it was as comfortable as possible in a place like Necropolis.

"Mr. Thorn, you have a visitor," Smith said.

"Who is it?" Thorn asked.

"It is Mr. Jester, Sir."

"Is he by himself?"

"No Sir, he is with a woman."

Thorn was curious as to why he would be back and why he had a woman with him. *That sly fox,* he thought to himself. *He always comes through for me.* "Send him in."

Castro Thorn sat on a hand grafted wooden couch that had woven wicker seats. The other furniture matched. He was in his study where there were shelves with rarely found books. The room had no windows but good lighting from the lamps and the overhead lights.

"Jester, I see you're back. This better be something very important, because you were to stay in Hinterland as ordered."

"I'll let you be the judge of that, Castro," Jester replied. He was smiling his patented smile. "Meet Caroline."

"Caroline." Thorn repeated. "What is so important that you had to come all this way?"

"I'll let her tell you."

"Well… you see, it's my husband." Caroline said in a soft voice. "I believe he is here fighting to help the people of Necropolis. I need to find him. I came all this way to be with him."

Thorn glanced over at Jester, still curious as to why this woman was standing in front of him. Jester had always come through for him so he decided to let it all play out. "Smith!" Thorn called out.

In a short moment, Smith appeared. "Yes, sir."

"Caroline here needs some help with finding her husband. I want you to find him for us."

Thorn looked at Caroline and asked, "What is his name?"

"Sam Connelly," she replied.

Thorn only needed to gesture with an eyebrow raise and Smith understood.

"Right away sir."

"Thank you so much, Mr. Thorn," Caroline said, grateful for his assistance.

"Please, call me Castro or simply Thorn."

Caroline acknowledged his request with a head nod.

"Now would you excuse us for a moment? Jester and I have some business to take care of. If you need anything, just ask Smith for it."

"Yes, sir… I mean… Thanks again, Castro."

The two men walked out of the room to an adjacent one with a sliding glass door between them. Caroline could see them where she was standing but she could not hear what they were saying.

"I feel that I have been very patient with you Jester," Thorn said with an annoyed yet intrigued edge to his voice.

"You're right and you have been patient Chief. You'll be happy because she is the one," Jester remarked.

"The one what?"

"The one that is going to help us defeat the Protectors." Jester had a big grin on his face. Jester was really excited now that he could finally sell his idea to Thorn.

"I saw her with my own eyes. I felt her energy force when she slept last night. I'm not even sure she knows how powerful she can be. Our problem with defeating more of the Protectors has been that our energy comes from the darkness of hate. We both know that love is stronger than hate. And she is off the charts, Castro. She may be stronger than Tate from what I can tell. You've been in the Land of the Promised. You know more about love's power than anyone on this side of Hinterland."

"Why would she fight for me? This place is fueled by hate."

"Have you ever heard of the saying, 'it's a thin line between love and hate', Castro? We understand what it takes to harness our powers. I believe that she could do the same with a few tweaks. We will make her love this place and the people here. She will think the Protectors are the foul ones and our oppressors. Which they are."

Castro Thorn gave the idea some thought. Jester had made some very valid points. While he was able to crush the souls of the weak, the Protectors were very powerful and stopped him at every turn. Having someone with their abilities fighting for him could only benefit his campaign for greed and power over everything. "...I think you are on to something," Thorn finally said. "...Now to get her on board. What do we tell her about her husband? I have a feeling he is not in Necropolis."

"Leave that to me. For now, we need to figure out the limits of her powers and how to persuade her to train with us," said Jester.

They invited Caroline to join them in the room.

Jester started, "Caroline, you have been very patient with me and I have some news for you."

"Is it about Sam?" she asked.

Jester put both hands out in front of him before replying, "Well yes, that is part of it. We are still trying to get the details on where he is but there is a chance that he is with the Protectors. We have not confirmed it but Smith will let us know when he knows something for sure."

"Okay, I have to keep the faith that he hasn't been taken by the Protectors. Sam is strong. He would have given them a fight, I know."

Jester quickly glanced at Thorn before continuing, "That also brings us to the second part of what I wanted to talk to you about... You have a gift. This gift may be more powerful than any that we have ever seen. Your gift may make it possible for us to defeat the Protectors and find your Sam."

"You mean… gift as in powers like what you did to those guards?"

"Very perceptive Caroline. Your gift is not quite like mine. It's more… unique in these parts. Have you not felt it? That feeling in your belly. Those are not butterflies sweetie," said Jester.

Caroline grabbed her stomach and started to think a while. "Well, yes. I guess I have felt it."

Thorn said, "It has been your compass. It has guided you to Jester and to this place. If you wanted, I could teach you everything I know about your powers."

"I don't have time," Caroline said. "Sam is out there somewhere."

"Yes, you're right. He is out there somewhere. My trackers are the best in the realm. They will find him if he is here. And when they do, you'd want to do everything in your capacity to help him get back to you. Let me show you what you are capable of."

"But I thought Jester was going to train me."

"Castro is a much better teacher than I am. He actually taught me about my powers."

Caroline was curious as to where I could be. She was very unfamiliar with the land but had felt safest with Jester so far.

"Well Caroline, it has to be your call," Jester said, "I brought you here for a somewhat selfish reason but it does benefit you if we can find Sam. Once you have learned half of what you can do, you will be able to stop most any Protector and help your husband. I think you should do it for Sam and more importantly yourself."

"If I train with Castro, you will let me know as soon as you hear something about Sam?" she asked.

"I will, Caroline."

"Well, we have no time to waste," Thorn announced. "Let's get you in something more suitable for training."

Chapter 13

The Gates of Necropolis

W E STOOD AT the towering black cast iron gate, which was chained shut with a formidable pad lock. The foreboding entryway was creepy and ominous; reminiscent of the type that would be seen in an old cemetery back on Earth. This gate, however, was protected by a force field of some kind, making it impossible to touch.

I was in full black modern warfare gear. I kept my six-shooters holstered on my hips. I was with Tate, Liam, and Chandra who were also in full Protector clothing.

"Ok, team, let's follow the plan," Tate commanded. He would be the point man for this mission. The team started to move into position.

"Will this work?" I asked.

Chandra shrugged her shoulders and Tate said, "Let's find out!"

Liam announced, "This has never been attempted, Sam. The last time that a Protector had to touch these gates was to cast Thorn and his followers into it. We can only pray that the Great Source shows favor with us."

"Don't worry about it Sam, we will get your wife back as well as some of the others," Chandra said.

The team formed a semi-circle around the massive gate. With arms stretched out wide, we all began to glow a vibrant white and blue light. The lights expanded in height and in width like bread rising in an oven. The ground trembled. Loose rocks and nearby tree branches moved and shook. The wind swelled up and howled like a wolf to a full moon. The gray sky turned black and lightning struck all around us.

"Hold steady!" Tate yelled over the noise. "I think it's working!"

The gates rattled and shook. With a loud *Ping, pang, boom* the gates of Necropolis flew open.

"Yes! It worked!" Tate exclaimed.

I gave a fist pump in the air, relieved that I was that much closer to Caroline. "Thank God," I said.

"Let's get going. I'm sure most of Necropolis heard us banging down the door," said Tate. "Chandra you and Liam head northeast. Sam and I will loop around and meet you in the main hub of the city."

"Be careful of the vegetation around here. They can be very lethal if you are not alert," Liam warned.

"We will. See you on the other side," I said.

We headed off on our mission to bring back as many souls as we could. This was more complicated because most of the souls here made a conscious decision to be in the city. My powers merely gave a person clarity but the individual still had to make the choice to go back to Hinterland and then to the Land of the Promised. With the blurred lines of deception out of the way, the citizens would be given another chance to choose. Perhaps after spending enough time in such a forsaken place, the choice would be simpler. Tate and I moved through the outskirts of town relatively unnoticed. But things were just too quiet. We had to keep our eyes peeled.

"We are about five miles away from the main hub Sam," Tate said. "We expect a try..." He did not get a chance to finish his statement before we heard a snap sound from behind us.

"Freeze!" a voice from the distance said. The voice had a Middle

Eastern accent. It was higher pitched so I couldn't tell if it was a man or woman right away.

"Put your hands up where I can see 'em. You are not supposed to be here. Protectors don't come around here. There's no one to protect. Why are you here?"

"We are here for his wife and to save anyone that wants to come back to the Land of the Promised," Tate said, never turning around to face the voice.

"That's a lie. Once you are here you have to stay here. There's no way back to the Great Source without losing your life force," the voice said.

"That used to be true," I said, "but that's not the case as long as we are here. Would you like to go?"

"Horse crap. There is no way that you have the power to do that and there's no way that Thorn would allow it."

"Thorn has no power over us," said Tate. "Ekon has given us abilities beyond your imagination."

"If you would like, I can demonstrate for you. I understand that in a place like this deception is commonplace. But have you ever known a Protector or anyone in the Land of the Promised to lie?" I asked.

The voice stayed silent for a few beats.

"You have my word," I said. "Would you like to go to the Land of the Promised?"

The voice sounded like it was trembling as it spoke this time.

"I want it to be real. But there's no way this is real."

"It is real. Come closer and allow me to see you. I will show you," I said.

As the voice moved closer, I saw a man. His clothes were ragged and worn from the difficult days and nights in the city. He had tears flowing from one of his eyes.

I asked him again, "Would you like to leave this place for a far better one? A place where you do not suffer and there is no pain. Would you like a new life in the Land of the Promised?"

"Yes," he said, holding back tears of joy.

"Give me your hand and tell me your name," I said.

He reached out and took my hand. "I am Amir Abdul. I have committed many transgressions in my days on Earth."

"Like a father teaches his son, Ekon wants you to learn from your mistakes and he has forgiven you. It is time for you to forgive yourself. Find your self-worth and feel the love flowing through you."

Amir closed his eyes and felt true and pure love for the first time since his death. He let out a sigh. His mind was no longer consumed by his past. A luminous light appeared in front of him and engulfed him. He began to laugh.

"Wahoo!" Amir shouted. "I'm free! I'm forgiven!"

"Now go in peace, my friend. You have many family members that will rejoice when they see you," I said, feeling the warmth of Ekon's love radiating off Amir.

Amir walked with the light. It was much different saving a soul in Necropolis. It is an unholy place but a holy act had just occurred. The light served as a shield until the soul reached Hinterland. It was properly transferred into the Land of the Promised after that.

We were able to take in hundreds of lost souls. While it felt great to help Amir and others, the bright lights drew attention to us. The Marauders would not be pleased to lose so many of their foot soldiers.

"Hey you!" a man called out to us. He had a thick southern twang and a tenor voice, perhaps being from Arkansas on Earth. "Are you the ones converting people over to the Land of the Promised?"

"We are willing to take all who want to go," Tate responded.

"Well, you need to stop it this instant," the man said. "These folks have done unspeakable things. They deserve to be here. You need to mind your own business."

"Our business is to protect all of the souls that were created by the Great Source," Tate stated.

"Well, there ain't no one else here wanting your protection anymore. You have until the count of five to start walking the other way."

"Or what?" Tate asked.

"Or you will be meeting the Great Source personally. We're going to take your life force, sir."

"Who's we?" I whispered, leaning into Tate's ear.

My question was answered soon enough. From the shadows of the tin buildings around us emerged several men and women with weapons. I would estimate around nine or ten fighters were there, ready for a brawl. We were outnumbered but only three of them were Marauders.

"Don't try any of that hocus pocus crap either," the man said. "We like it just fine right here."

"We can only bring back those that want to come back with us," I responded. "If you don't want help from us, feel free to stay here and live your life. We are here on a special mission. So please move out of our way."

"Your mission has been canceled," the man replied.

The others chuckled, as they felt this comment passed for wit around here.

"Surround them, fellas."

The group complied and soon Tate and I were walled in.

"Easy folks," Tate said. "We don't need to fight at all. Please kindly allow us to pass and we will not have to hurt you."

"Let's get them!" A voice shouted from behind me.

"Whoa, whoa, wait! You told us you would count to five first." I said trying to buy some time with one last plea.

"Five!" The man shouted and they closed in on us at once.

Tate let out a sigh and shrugged his shoulders as if to say, *they were warned.*

I pulled my six-shooter and commenced to taking down the first two attackers. It took two wave blasts each. I was sure to only disable them.

Tate was a purest. He only used weapons when the opponent was a worthy challenger. He easily took out the first aggressor with one hook shot to the jaw. The next two also proved to be a minimal challenge.

Tate quickly attacked one of the Marauders before he could power up and cause any trouble. "Beat them before they get strong enough to make you worry," he'd say when we trained. The strategy was effective.

Now there was the man and two Marauders standing in front of us in a fighting stance. Tate and I stood side by side only slightly breathing hard. I could feel my heart race as I saw the man leading the charge. His aura turned a deep, dark red.

It was Arawn. He was known for his skills as a trapper and a hunter. During his time on Earth, he pillaged, plundered, and murdered hundreds of men and women. His favorite assignments involved torture and extracting information by inflicting pain. He was not one that could be swayed to show mercy. Arawn was the same height as Tate but slimmer. He wore a cutoff blue jean jacket and no shirt. His arms were naturally muscular and had tattoos of lions, snakes, and bears running down them. His legs were long and wiry. He loved to wear combat boots so he could, in his words, "stomp the life force out of a man's head."

"You!" he pointed at Tate. "Your time has passed. Like an old mare with a broken hoof, it's my job to put you out of your misery."

I grabbed Tate on the shoulder and said, "Let me take him."

"That's not the way things are done around here, friend. If you are challenged, it is your duty to answer the call or be branded as a coward. The Great Source's powers flow through me as they do you. There's no need to worry. We have a mission and we are not going to let these unworthy souls stop us," Tate assured me.

Arawn chose to wield a machete. The blade glowed fire red. He held the handle with two hands for better grip. Just as his legend was known by us Protectors, Tate's was known to the Marauders.

Tate chose what looked to be a metal club but they pulled out into nun-chucks. The nun-chucks burned a blue flame all around them. Tate's body aura had the same colored flame around him.

"Let's tango!" said Tate.

Arawn swung his large machete in a downward slashing motion. Tate managed to move out of the way but not before being nicked.

Tate grinned at Arawn and said, "Nice one."

"There's more where that came from," Arawn growled. He slashed and slung a few more combinations but Tate blocked these attacks.

"Get him Arawn!" The other Marauder shouted. Arawn jabbed and sliced his machete and nicked Tate a few more times but never a clean shot. Arawn was a hunter and he was used to being patient and waiting for his prey. But he grew impatient and frustrated as his attempts failed.

Tate hadn't attempted an advance of any kind. He was waiting for Arawn to show his weakness. He knew that Arawn was one of the few souls that had the potential to beat him in a fight and that would mean his demise. One of them would have to lose their life force before either would stop trying to defeat the other.

"Ah!" Arawn bellowed out as he tried a different tactic. He launched his weapon at Tate and charged behind it. Tate was able to maneuver away from the machete but not from Arawn. Arawn attempted a tackle and was stopped when Tate jabbed his weapon into his gut.

"Uff!" was the only sound Arawn could make. He was bent over as one does when one has the wind knocked out of him.

It was Tate's turn. He was currently holding Arawn in a front headlock choke with one arm. Next, he began to pound on Arawn's back with his free hand which was also holding the nun-chucks. After a few more hits to the back, Arawn's legs gave out on him. This was a new sensation for the hunter. He had never been broken before.

Tate could feel the fight leaving the hunter and stopped working on Arwan's back and started spearing his side with the butt of the nun-chucks. "Like all of the souls that you have murdered and tortured you will be relieved of your life force. But first, you will answer a few questions," Tate said.

"Never," Arawn grunted, struggling to get enough air to breathe.

"I was hoping you would say that." Tate pounded on Arawn's ribs some more. He was very careful to hit him in the exact same spot each time.

Arawn attempted to reverse the hold but he was weak from the blows to his rib cage. To further weaken him, Tate changed his aura to the orange glow that he used on me when we first trained and tripped him to the ground. He let go of the chokehold and took full mount position on top of Arawn. "It's time for a little ground and pound," Tate said, with a slight smile on his face. He seemed to get some pleasure out of making the hunter suffer. Tate reared back his fist. It glowed and turned into a large bolder.

"Wait!" the Hunter called out. "What would you like to know?"

"Oh, now that's more like it," Tate said. He gestured over at me. "That man over there? He is looking for his wife. We have reason to believe that she is here. Her name is Caroline Connelly."

Arawn looked up at me and laughed. "Ha! Ha! Ha! You? Well, you sir are in luck." He said coughing and wheezing between words. "She is with Castro Thorn himself. He... huh huh... he's training her to fight for us."

"What are you talking about? There is no way she would do something like what you are saying. Caroline does not have enough hate to be a Marauder," I contested.

"You must be mistaken," Arawn said. "She is training and I am hearing that she is more powerful than any of us. Even... Thorn thinks she could be as... powerful as him. Ha ha ha! So do your worse Tate. I am comforted by the fact that you all will be destroyed soon by the hands of someone that you people love. Bah ha ha ha!"

"You won't be around to see it," Tate said just before he smashed Arawn's head with his boulder hand. Within moments, Arawn's light aura flickered like a broken neon sign then stopped. He turned into ash as his spirit left his body.

The man with the Arkansas accent and the other Marauder saw what Tate did to their leader and made the decision to retreat.

As they fled, Tate shouted, "Let Thorn know that the Protectors are here! Those that want to be freed will be freed! This is the will of the Great Source!"

Once they were gone Tate and I agreed that we should try to regroup with Chandra and Liam. The new revelation that Caroline had abilities was one thing, but the fact that she was working with them meant that we needed to devise a new plan.

Chapter 14
Qurina

WHILE CASTRO THORN was accustomed to training his men from a familiar place of hate and destruction, he found it quite easy to slip into the role of teacher for Caroline's undiscovered powers. "Focus, Caroline. Your powers are great and we want to respect them."

"Okay," Caroline responded. She was the best of his pupils. She did not fight back much and listened carefully to all of Thorn's instructions. Her abilities blossomed very quickly. She was standing in a desert under the hot suns of Necropolis. For miles, there was nothing around her but Castro Thorn and her thoughts. The ground was dry and cracked. It seemed to be a place where water may have existed at some point but had not for thousands of years. Thorn had decided to train her in this tough environment because her powers were greater than anyone he had seen. If she could wield her powers in a place of hopelessness then she would truly be the warrior Jester thought she was.

"That is a glow rarely seen in this part of the realm," Thorn said.

"What do you mean?" she asked.

"My abilities were created out of oppression, despair and even hate. Which means that I am strong because I have seen and felt those things for a long time, but I had to learn to use my abilities. You were created and born to love. Therefore, it is more natural for you. It is a feeling not to be learned, just tapped into. It is a pure light. Now don't focus on anything but the love in your heart. I want you to harness your powers. Let them build up and hold them until I tell you to release them. Think about the beauty of Earth. The green grass, the rainbow in the sky after a storm, and majestic beasts that roam near the pastures and river streams."

Her light started to dim.

"What's wrong Caroline?"

"Well…nothing," she said.

"Caroline, it is clearly something."

"…Well, I love green grass and rivers and all but they make me sad. As I think about them, I think about Sam. He and I did so much together. He was the love of my life. He was love for me. Sam could be anywhere in the world and he'd always find a way to communicate with me. And I him. There was one time we were in Paris and his phone had died. We were split up because I was out shopping and he wanted to go check out a local jazz club. Sam had gotten lost and didn't have a way to contact me. He had one of those converter plugs but it was back at the hotel. His French was barely understandable but somehow he convinced some random stranger to send me a text message." She started to chuckle at the thought of me trying to speak French.

Her glow brightened again. Even in a land where there was no hope for a single blade of crabgrass to grow, my Caroline shined like a beacon of light casting from a lighthouse on a troubled sea.

"Yes, there it is Caroline," Thorn said. He was truly winging it at this point but it seemed to be working. Thorn was just familiar enough with the powers of love to pass as an expert to an untrained novice. Caroline had so much love in her. She only needed to be given the idea.

Her powers would ignite as a flame does when sparked by two flint stones rubbing together.

"I'm doing it!" she cried. Something else happened as Caroline's aura cast over this dry land. It began to turn green, then became multi-colored. In a small circumference of ten feet around her, grass and flowers started to sprout up. The ground became blessed by the love of the Great Source.

"Castro, look. Was that me? Did I do that?"

The look of bewilderment upon his face suggested Thorn may have been just as stunned. "...Yes... I believe you did," he said softly. "It's your own little haven in the middle of the barren desert. The Great Source has smiled on you. Your love must run very deep for Sam."

Caroline smiled. "He means a great deal to me."

"Well, I'm sure we will find him. One way or another," Thorn said. At that moment, Castro looked up at a cloud of dust heading towards them.

"What is that?" Caroline asked.

It wasn't uncommon for sand storms to plague this land but the dust cloud looked different.

"Be steady Caroline and try to use your powers to identify what that is."

She took a deep breath and focused in on the cloud. Her eyes converted to pure white light. She could see through the dust. It was Jester heading towards them. He was riding on the wave of dust. His face looked rattled. It was an unfamiliar look for Caroline to see on him. He was normally a cool, calm, and calculating man.

When Jester reached them, almost like magic, he willed the dust cloud away.

"Jester, what brings you out here?" Thorn inquired. "You know these trainings are off limits to everyone."

"There is much for us to talk about, Castro. I think we need to do that in private," Jester explained.

The two men looked at Caroline at the same time with the same expression.

"I can take a hint," Caroline said a little annoyed that she was the one that had to leave.

"Continue to focus on building your chi." Thorn instructed. "We may need your powers sooner than you think."

Once she was out of ear shot, Thorn asked, "What is so important that you needed to interrupt our training session?"

"It's the Protectors. They are here."

"What do you mean here?" Thorn asked, with a hint of disbelief of what he heard.

"Here as in here in Necropolis City!"

"That is not possible! They wouldn't dare come here. The Great Source wouldn't allow it."

"He must have because they are here and have been causing quite a ruckus, Jester explained.

"What kind of ruckus?"

"Well, they have reclaimed some of our foot soldiers and Tate defeated Arawn quite easily. Arawn is gone. Tate assimilated his life force."

"This is a hard pill to swallow, Jester."

"There's more. Sam, he is not only with them, he is one of them. Some are saying that he is their best fighter. They are saying his power levels exceed Tate's."

"Well then, this throws a monkey wrench in our plans now doesn't it? As soon as she sees Sam fighting with the Protectors, she will know that we deceived her and the two of them together will be an unstoppable force."

Jester asked, "What if we help her believe that her husband has been deceived by the Protectors? She already believes that they are our oppressors. Is it too far out to believe that the Protectors were strong enough to brainwash Sam?"

Thorn was once again impressed by his faithful follower. *Jester is always thinking,* he said to himself. "Okay, that just might work."

Castro summoned Caroline over to where the two men were standing. "Caroline, we have some news for you. Jester has multiple confirmed and reliable sources that have stated that they've seen Sam."

Caroline began to fight back tears. "My Sam is here? Where is he? When do I get to see him?"

"Well, that is the problem, my dear. We don't have him. He is here in Necropolis but so are the Protectors. The reports that we have indicate he is either with them or in their custody."

"He's not with them. He must be there against his will. Sam is a very smart man. He will snap out of it once he sees me. We need to figure out a plan."

"Right you are, Caroline. Fortunately, I specialize in such matters. Jester, go get Raven for a strategy session. You know where to meet."

"I'm on it." Jester called for his clouds of dust to reassemble with a wave of his hand. He jumped on it and rode away with haste.

"I've waited so long to see him face to face. I can't wait!"

"We must be careful of the Protectors," Castro warned, "they are fierce fighters and have already neutralized some of my most important combatants. In fact, one of my best men had his life force taken from him by Tate. He was a great hunter. But my pupil, you will be the one that saves us from them. They will fear your abilities and will be no match for you. If Sam is with them, he will need for you to be in full force in order to rescue him. I think we should train a while longer until we can efficiently plan our counterattack."

Thorn's logic made sense to Caroline so she decided to continue training with him. He encouraged her to remember so many loving, touching, and intimate moments. Each time Caroline shared her feelings with him, a bond of trust was made stronger. Caroline was in her final stages of training. Thorn had been with her every step of the way. She learned several styles of combat. Once she mastered a skill, Thorn would send her challengers. She defeated them all quite easily.

Thorn was wary of challenging her himself. He didn't want her to learn his movements and style of fighting, mainly because he was unsure whether their plan to use Caroline as a weapon would work. He knew that he likely would not be able to defeat her himself so he needed to use any potential advantage that was at his disposal.

"Caroline, this is your final challenge," Thorn announced. "You will face my right-hand man Raven. I will instruct him to show no mercy and to fight you with all that he has. Do you think that you are up to the challenge?"

"Yes," she answered with a little hesitation. Caroline was excited that she had almost completed training. She was impatient to see me and wanted to test her new skills.

"Then come with me... but first, put this on." It was a thin white full-length robe very similar to what a boxer would wear before a fight.

"Wow, this is nice," Caroline said.

"It is time to finish what we have started," Thorn said.

Thorn and Caroline walked through a dense forest. The area was full of dangerous trees with poisonous sap and spikes along the trunks and branches. Caroline could see a crowd of people gathered in a large circle near a clearing on the other side of the forest. They were Marauders.

"Wow! What are they all doing here?" Caroline asked.

"Word must have gotten out," Thorn said with a mischievous grin. "It has been quite some time since we allowed a new member into the inner circle. These are my chosen warriors. They are the ones that I allow to roam in and out of Necropolis. After today, you will be one of us as well."

Caroline nodded, accepting Thorn's words. She had a strange sense of belonging in a way that was unfamiliar to her. Slowly she realized she wanted this. She wanted to be part of the elite forces of Necropolis.

As she approached someone in the crowd yelled out, "She's here! She's here!" The others in the crowd went crazy with excitement. The noise from the cheers was almost deafening. The crowd parted like the Red Sea as Caroline approached the center of the circle. It was getting dark. There was a bond fire lit with giant logs and tree stumps just outside the circle of people.

Raven sat on a stool prepping for the fight. Caroline had time to study her opponent. His shirt was off and he had a large tattoo of a raven that spanned his entire torso. The tattooed bird was in flight and its wings stretched out to his biceps. Raven stood six foot-two and was built like a division one college linebacker. His hair was as dark as the night sky. He kept it long enough to stretch down below his ears. His hands were massive. They had blisters that told the story of a man that had to fight for his existence. She could hear the crack of his knuckles over the crowd.

Caroline made a mental note to stay away from his grasp because she could be in major trouble if she didn't.

Caroline had picked up a few noticeable features during her training. Her abs were nearing six pack while her arms and legs had definition. She took off her robe revealing a dark gray sweatshirt that was cut short around the waist so that her abs were in view. Her arms and hood were also cut for better circulation. Her sweatpants matched her shirt and were cut short so that she had a better range of motion. She began shadow boxing as she continued eying her opponent.

Thorn put both hands in the air and the crowd grew quiet. "This is a test to see if she is worthy to be called 'One of Us!'" The crowd erupted at the sound of Thorn's booming voice. He indulged the crowd for a few moments but then held one hand up and the crowd grew quiet once again. "The challenger has defeated some of the best that Necropolis has to offer. But she has never seen a fighter with as much skill and instinct as the Marauder known as Raven! Challenger and champion, toe the line!"

Raven and Caroline dragged their feet across the dirt to form two lines. The lines ran parallel about ten feet apart. Caroline took two deep breaths and put her foot down on her line. Raven had a look of pure malice in his heart; angry, and all business.

His aura glow surged and turned dynamite red. Someone from the crowd tapped him to get his attention. They handed him an old brown leather satchel. Raven reached inside of it and pulled out a pair of oversized black gloves. The gloves were cut off at the knuckles and spiked with metal on the backhand side. He pounded his fist into his palms and formed a heavy steel chain. Raven let out a grunt and then toed his line.

Caroline had seen Raven around but they never had words with each other. She always considered him bad news and chose to steer clear of him but there was no avoiding him now. Just before the fight started, Caroline felt a calmness in her spirit. Everything began to move in slow motion.

Thorn signaled the start of the fight. Raven quickly closed the gap between them and whipped his chain at her leg. It wrapped around and he pulled her down to the ground. He moved to pounce on top of her hoping to make quick work of the match. Caroline was stunned but gathered her wits quickly and pulled her legs up and Raven landed unprotected onto her knees. She rolled him off of her and got back to her feet. Raven had the wind knocked out of him but he returned to his feet quickly.

Raven whipped his chain forward again and this time hooked Caroline's right arm. He pulled her in quickly and landed a punch to her gut. The spikes added to the damage and she collapsed to her knees. She tried to take in a deep breath but was stopped mid inhale as Raven maneuvered behind her. He wrapped the chain around her neck. He squeezed tighter and tighter. Caroline reached for the chain to create slack but he was too strong.

Raven leaned down close to her ear. "You were never going to be one of us. You are too weak," he said, taunting her.

Caroline took advantage of his proximity to her and whipped the back of her head into his nose. The impact caused Raven to release his grip just enough for her to get loose. Caroline rolled forward, sprung to her feet, and turned around to face her opponent. She had a new found determination and felt that it was time to summon her powers of love. She began to think about what Castro Thorn had taught her. "Sam," she whispered to herself. She thought about a simple love letter that I wrote her years ago.

Caroline,

I've loved you since the day I met you. We've been through a lot together. There have been some struggles along the way but we faced them together. I wouldn't want to go through those struggles with any other person. Know this, every day, I am thinking about you. I am rooting for you to be successful. I am praying for peace in your heart. I am hoping for blessings around you. Every day, I love you. Even if we are miles apart and it seems that I am long gone, this will always be true. Trust in me. Trust your gut and your heart. Let them guide you to me. I will be there with an unwavering love that has been blessed by God himself. While you may fear a future that is without me by your side, put the truth in that deep place in your heart. Know always that I love you and I will be there with you soon enough, in this life and the next.

"In this life and the next," she whispered to herself. Caroline began to glow a color never seen before. I believe it is because of her training with the powers of love in a place that love does not dwell. She had to first conquer hate, despair, and loneliness. Caroline had to fight through her own hell and create her own heaven inside of it.

Her glow was not as bright as mine but I could not mistake the power of love that flowed through her veins. She emitted a luminance that radiated more like a black light than a bright one. Her aura was blood purple. Her determination to find me wherever I was drove her to power up to levels much higher than Raven could dream of.

Raven was not detoured by her power surge. He lashed his chain at her once again. Caroline caught it and snapped it in half. Raven appeared to move in slow motion to her. He was slower than he had seemed earlier in the fight. Every punch that he attempted was blocked and countered with a jab. Next, she decided to see how fast she could hit. She punched in hyper speed. Raven could only accept the punishing blows. By the time Caroline stopped, Raven was ready to drop to the ground.

She held him up long enough to whisper in his ear, "Don't ever underestimate the power of love." She pushed him down and he landed flat on his back.

The crowd that was once rowdy and ready for a show was now silent and stunned with amazement. They had seen more than they had bargained for. Even Thorn didn't think that Raven would be defeated in the manner that he was. Caroline had reached her potential.

Thorn was also stunned, but it only took him a moment to snap back. He strode to the middle of the circle, held Caroline's hand skyward, and shouted, "And the Victor!" The crowd cheered the successful challenger while Raven lied nearly motionless on the ground. "From this day forth Caroline will be known as Qurina, which means, 'The Great Female Warrior!'"

The people begin to chant, "Qur-i-na, one-of-us! Qur-i-na, one-of-us!"

Caroline was filled with joy. She was accepted by the people of Necropolis as one of their own. She was feared by many but perhaps for the first time there were those that respected her power. Thorn was delighted at her victory for other reasons. After seeing how powerful she was, he believed that he could beat the Protectors at their own game; Love.

I could only hope the Great Source had truly made Caroline's love for me as strong as my love was for her. If this was true, Thorn would underestimate the power of pure love.

Chapter 15
Dampener Cuffs

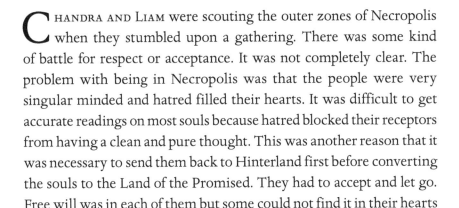

C HANDRA AND LIAM were scouting the outer zones of Necropolis when they stumbled upon a gathering. There was some kind of battle for respect or acceptance. It was not completely clear. The problem with being in Necropolis was that the people were very singular minded and hatred filled their hearts. It was difficult to get accurate readings on most souls because hatred blocked their receptors from having a clean and pure thought. This was another reason that it was necessary to send them back to Hinterland first before converting the souls to the Land of the Promised. They had to accept and let go. Free will was in each of them but some could not find it in their hearts to liberate themselves.

Liam was able to make out that there was a woman named Qurina involved in whatever had taken place. She had to be a force because she had defeated Raven. Raven was rarely beaten and almost never lost to anyone that was not a Protector.

He was responsible for taking the life force from many that

opposed him. There were always spats in Necropolis and it was rarely an event worth watching unless there was a well-known fighter like Raven involved.

"Liam, did you see that strange light that she emitted? It was as if she was not wielding the powers of hate. She seemed as strong as us."

"You're right, Chandra. She wielded a great power. I would have almost said that she was using the powers of love. But how could that be possible?" Liam would ponder over this for quite some time before he would learn the truth.

"We need to meet back up with the others and figure out a plan."

"I agree. Let's get out of here," Liam said. "Be careful. If they see us we could find ourselves in serious trouble."

They left the area and began to make their way to meet up with Tate and I. Unfortunately, as soon as they cleared the forest they were identified by Jester. Protectors stick out like a sore thumb in a place like Necropolis. It is something about the way we move. We have hope and purpose to our movement, careful not to waste a step for they are all precious and should be appreciated. Citizens of Necropolis are very weak minded and are fighting to survive every day. They learn to blend into their surroundings and make themselves noticeable when it is necessary to be noticed.

Jester signaled over to the crowd of people who were now celebrating Caroline's victory. A group of ten or so made their way to assist him. Caroline slipped away to join the group as well. Jester was in a crouched position where it was hard to see him. She had her robe back on and kneeled close to him.

"There are two of them right there," he said as he pointed in their direction. "I'll bet they know where Sam is. Let's follow them. Maybe they will lead us to the others."

"No, Jester, think about it. You and Castro are always telling me how powerful they are. Wouldn't we have better odds if we fight them here, with just two of them?"

"You have truly become Qurina. I'm following your lead ma'am," Jester said with a smile.

She moved very swiftly and caught up to Chandra and Liam. When she was close behind them she called out, "Stop right there you two!"

She had the hood of her robe over her head and her face was barely visible. They did not recognize that Qurina was Caroline but they knew they were being challenged and got ready for a brawl.

"What are you doing here?" she asked

"We are the Protectors from the Land of the Promised. We are here to bring back any who want to come with us," Liam said.

"You mean take anyone that you want to come with you," Qurina responded, quick-wittedly.

"No, we are not here for trouble," Liam said.

"It is not too late for you to come with us. I sense a great power in you. It is not hate. It is something else," said Liam.

"You have it all wrong," Chandra said. "Ekon created a place for the pure of heart. One needs to first recognize and forgive themselves before entering the gates."

"If it were that easy, why are these people still here? They are noble and brave. These people have helped me. Where were you when I was stuck in Hinterland?"

"We are so sorry… what did you say your name was?" Liam asked.

"I am Qurina, not that it is any of your business. The Great Source has given me an awesome power and I am here to free my people and avenge Castro Thorn."

"Thorn is evil," Liam said.

Qurina began to glow. Her aura was blood purple again.

Liam couldn't help but be in awe of her light. He was also starting to understand that this woman was very powerful and somehow she learned to harness the powers of love in a place that Ekon does not visit.

"You better be very careful with your next words old man. I am this close to making you pay now. What is keeping you alive is the fact that you may have some information that I need."

Just then Jester and the other ten Marauders reach them.

"Qurina, are you ok?" Jester asked.

"I'm fine. We need to get these people to a place where we can interrogate them."

"Jester how could you trick this woman into…" Liam started to say before Jester knocked him out by hitting him in the back of his neck with a karate chop.

"You're making a mist…" Chandra managed to say before Jester knocked her out with a similar blow.

"They are really good. I almost believed them," Qurina said.

Jester simply motioned in agreement and ordered half the men to take the Protectors to be interrogated. "The rest of you, go ahead and celebrate. We can deal with those pretenders in the morning."

"I feel like Sam is here somewhere," Qurina said. "They have him hostage. I have all of these powers and I'm unable to help my husband. We need answers soon."

"Let's chase our tails in the morning. You are one of us now."

"I guess you're right. I'm just…anxious to see Sam."

After Jester and Qurina made their way back to the celebration, Jester slipped away. He found Thorn and Raven, who was still licking his wounds from being beaten by Qurina.

"Qurina stopped two of the Protectors. They are in the holding cells waiting to be interrogated. They tried to convince her that she is being tricked by us. We need to find out all they know so we aren't surprised in the morning," Jester said.

"Raven, what are your thoughts?" Thorn asked.

"I think it was a mistake to even let her in. Aren't you worried that she will find out and destroy us all? You saw what she did to me. That's what I normally do to other people. If I couldn't beat her, I'm not sure who can."

"I think you have your angles crossed, Raven. She has the best of both worlds. Her powers are greater than any one of us because of love and she trusts us. That's something that you've never had."

Raven let out a grunt. He could see Jester's point.

Jester continued, "She thinks that the Marauders are here because the Protectors took the Land of the Promised for themselves. This is all based on her trusting us and the fact that she only knows what we tell her. We can see this through."

Thorn liked what he heard. Raven was reluctant but he also had trouble finding a reason not to go along with the plan.

"Raven, you and Jester will go and find out where Sam is and any additional information that could be useful. After we know that, we can figure out how to involve Qurina. I'll stay here and make sure that she enjoys the festivities," Thorn said.

Chandra was alone in her cell, sitting with her knees in her chest and her head down in her knees. She was chained to one of the tin walls. Once the Marauders had left her alone she had tested the chains, but after several attempts, she was unable to break free. The room was cold and dank from the night air. The lighting was dim which made it hard to see every corner of the room but she could see two chairs on the opposite end of the room, well out of her reach.

The chains were created to dampen the ability to harness powers of both love and hate. The creaky wooden floor was stained with the sweat and tears of previously interrogated tenants. Her protective gear had been taken from her and she was now only in a white tank top and black pants. Her shoes were also taken for fear that she would find a way to craft a weapon with the laces. Chandra was not used to these conditions but she was very strong-willed.

Her cell door clicked and squeaked. She heard keys jingle and the door opened. The artificial lights from the outside shined into the cell with two shadowy features blocking most of it. Chandra looked up and instantly recognized the two men.

"Jester, Raven, do come in." she said, sarcastically. "Who can I thank for sending you two?"

"Cut the crap, Chandra!" Raven said. "We're looking for Sam."

"Sam... hmm... I don't think he lives here."

"You're right, he doesn't, so where is he?" Raven asked again.

"Well I can't say for sure but if you let me go, I could show you."

Jester gave a fake chuckle. He grabbed a chair and dragged it across the room and placed it near Chandra. "Please do sit. Is that more comfortable?"

She got herself onto the chair and glanced up at Jester standing over her.

"Chandra, just make this easy on us all and tell us where Sam is," Jester said.

"Why do you care about Sam?" Chandra said, trying to turn the tables.

Whump! was the dull thud sound that Chandra's stomach made after Raven punched her in it. "You don't get to ask the questions, get it?" He pointed his finger at her face and gritted his teeth as he warned her.

"Hey, hey, Raven take it easy buddy," Jester said. Jester stood between the two with his hand on Raven's shoulder. His voice was calming enough and Raven backed off. He now turned his attention back to Chandra. "I'm sorry for that. Please forgive my friend. You see, we are kind of on a time crunch. So, I'll make you a deal. You answer all of my questions and I'll keep this guy off of you."

"How about I make you a deal Jester, I won't take your life force from you after I kick your ass. I can handle myself," Chandra said defiantly.

He gave his smile and looked around as if there was an audience in there with them. Jester walked back to the opposite side of the cell and grabbed the other chair. He pulled it across the room and sat it down backward next to Chandra. He sat in the chair and faced her ear.

"Bring him in," Jester said as he waved at the cell door. Raven gave three bangs on the door.

Liam walked in escorted by a guard. Both his wrists and legs were shackled and he was also wearing dampener cuffs which prevented him from using his powers. He had fresh bruises on his face and was limping. Raven dismissed the guard who closed the creaking door behind him. Raven then grabbed Liam by the collar of his shirt and slung him to the ground.

Chandra gnashed her teeth and started to pull at her chains.

"Hey, stop struggling. You know that isn't going to help anything," Jester said, trying to appeal to her rational side.

"Now, we have a new deal on the table. You tell me where Sam is and Raven won't take his life force." Jester was pointing at Liam.

Raven kicked Liam in the side and Liam gave a yelp.

"Don't worry about... me Chandra. They... can't hurt me," Liam said panting.

"Now start talking!" Raven yelled at Chandra as he offered another kick to Liam's ribs.

"Where... is... Sam?" Jester asked slowly.

"He's here," she said, with a whisper.

"What was that? I couldn't hear you."

"He's here, about five miles east from the main hub."

"Now, see that wasn't so bad was it? Let's try another question. Why are you hear in Necropolis?"

Chandra stayed silent.

"Come on Chandra, must we go over this again?" Jester said, almost sounding impatient.

Raven formed a sword with his light. He held the sword to Liam's back and pressed down. He used just enough pressure to make Liam moan with agony. He then slowly slid the sword down his back.

Liam tried not to scream. It was more of a growl and heavy labored breathing.

Raven was very skilled in this form of torture. He took his time marking Liam's back with stripe after stripe. He was like a painter creating his masterpiece on a blank canvas. Liam was helpless without his powers.

"Okay! I'll talk," Chandra said.

Raven stopped his work of art.

"Okay, but you need to know that if you delay any further, Raven will finish him."

"Yes, I know."

"So please, for Liam, answer my questions without hesitation."

"Okay," Chandra whimpered.

"Why are The Protectors here?" Jester asked.

"We are here to rescue the deceived souls that want to come back with us."

"So you're telling me that after all of this time The Great Source wants the people of Necropolis back?" Jester asked. "That doesn't make sense. There has to be another reason. You are not here for all of these people. You are here for one person."

Chandra stared back at him. While her face was expressionless her eyes gave her away.

"Yes, Sam is here looking for his wife. Am I right?" Jester said with a half-smile. "I am right, aren't I? Why would the Protectors be here with Sam? What is so important about his wife?"

"Sam's love for his wife transcends anything you could even imagine. Your hatred won't allow you to understand why we are able to do the things we do. Sam knows the power of love is so great that a place like this hellhole could not stop him from finding the love of his life. You go find Sam and you will know why he is here. You better bring an army because he's with Tate," Chandra said as she put on her best defiant smirk.

Jester glanced at Raven to see if he had caught on. If he did, he wasn't showing.

"Is Sam one of you?" Jester asked.

"You mean, is Sam a Protector? Oh, you don't know that part... Yes, he is. If you have done anything to his wife, I don't know what he would do to you. He's more than a Protector. He is the chosen one."

Raven and Jester locked eyes when they heard Chandra's words.

"Guard!" Raven called. A moment later the door swung open revealing the same guard. "Take him back to his interrogation room." The guard roughly helped Liam to his feet and they made their way out of the room. Raven and Jester followed close behind. The door slammed shut leaving Chandra alone once again in her darkened cell.

"We need to tell Thorn about this," Raven said.

"What is there to tell?" Jester responded.

"Well for one, Sam is part of the most elite force in the universe. For two, Tate is here and we need to start preparing."

"Raven, that is all true but what do we really know? Sam may be a Protector but Chandra said we will know why he is here. She called him the chosen one. That means he would have to be stronger than Tate. We can't properly prepare without knowing more. I say we find Sam first. Feel his aura and assess from there. If he is the chosen one then that means that Qurina is not and we were wrong."

"How do you propose that we get close enough to feel his aura?" Raven asked.

"Let's give them something they want back," Jester said with a smile and a wink.

Chapter 16

Laying Low

Tate and I were camped out in a thick brush. We chose this area due to the coverage the brush provided as well as its secluded nature. We were surrounded by poisonous plants and nocturnal creatures that hunt through the night. We needed to be very careful and undetectable so as not to be eaten. Snakes and spiders, black panthers and wild dogs also were all around us looking for late night dinner. We had planned to meet up with Liam and Chandra near this area to form a plan for rescuing Caroline. Tate and I stayed low upon the rocky, uneven ground. It was dark and miserably cold for most of the night. The cold by itself would have been bearable. The problem was the wind. It cut through the body like a sharp knife being sold on one of those infomercials.

We had to direct our breathing so that a stalking creature did not see the steam floating in the air. We were concerned about the creatures because they were creations made from the Great Source. We didn't want to hurt them unless we had to protect ourselves. Soon, dusk would be upon us but there was still no word from Liam and Chandra.

"They should be back by now. Maybe we should go out and try to find them," Tate said. There was a slight hint of concern in his voice. We were very reluctant to do something like that and miss them because we were gone.

"Okay, but let's wait a few more minutes. It will be daylight soon and we could try to blend in better," I said.

Just then, I heard a crackle in the distance. It sounded like a stick being broken from someone stepping on it.

"Did you hear that?" I whispered.

"Shh!" Tate said. Like a shepherd that had just spotted a wolf, he was already sharply surveying the direction of the sound.

I began to study the scene as well. Was it Chandra? No, Liam. He wasn't alone. My spirit felt cold for a flash.

"Tate!" a voice called out. It was not Liam. "We have something you want. You'd better show yourself."

"I'd know that voice from anywhere, Raven. What do you want?" Tate responded, still not revealing where he was.

"Like I said, I have something that you want," Raven taunted.

"Well, what is it?"

"You'll want to show me where you are first. I don't want to be ambushed. But trust me, it is some… one you will want to have back."

Tate glanced at me and I confirmed with a look that it had to be Liam or Chandra. He signaled to me to stay down in case something were to happen.

"Ok, I'm coming out." Tate slowly revealed himself from behind the brush.

The dawn light made the scene brighter and visibility was less of a problem. There was a slight fog from the rapid changes in the temperature of Necropolis. The mixture of the hot suns heating the area and the cold night made this brief moment the most comfortable time of day.

"Now, which of my people do you have?" asked Tate.

Raven whistled. From behind a thick oak tree that had been torn in half by a lightning strike, appeared Jester. He was holding up Liam, who was visibly beaten, still shackled, and stripped of any dignity. His bruises were unable to heal because he was unable to use his gifts.

"What did you do to him?" Tate growled. His aura started to burn bright blue.

"Now calm down Tate. We are here to give him back to you." Raven said.

"In exchange for what?"

"In exchange for Sam," Raven said with a mischievous smile.

Tate was careful not to react right away. "What do you want with Sam?" he asked.

"That… old foe is our business," Raven said.

Tate drew his weapon and scowled. His face looked like an angry Rottweiler ready to attack at his owner's command. He breathed hard. There was a grumble in his voice as he spoke.

"Don't forget who you are talking too, 'old foe'. Why should I not just hunt you both down and take your life forces right now for what you have done to my friend here?"

"Well Tate, your weakness is that your powers come from love. You won't harm either of us because we have someone else that you love," said Jester. "…We also have Chandra."

"You fellas are really pushing your luck," Tate snarled.

"Tate, while that may be true, you are also pushing your luck with us," Jester said. We have your friends and you know that we wouldn't hesitate to make good on our promise to end them. If something were to happen to us, we have given specific instructions to assimilate her. We will make you a deal. Let us meet with Sam and we will let you have Chandra back along with Liam."

"Why would you do that? You just told me that you wanted to take him. This is some kind of trap," Tate said.

"No, it's not. I just want to meet him and give him a message," Jester said.

"Yeah right." Tate scoffed. "From who?"

"It is about his wife."

"No one said anything about him having a wife, Jester. Now you're reaching."

"I don't think that Caroline would feel the same way. She talks about him all the time," said Jester.

"You know Caroline?" I asked, blowing my cover.

The two men were startled by my sudden appearance into the conversation. Jester smiled. He knew it was me. The man that he'd heard so much about.

"Ha ha ha. Sam! Boy, you look exactly how I pictured you. You're even built like a super hero."

"You know Caroline?"

"Why, sure I do."

"Where is she? Is she okay? Take us to her," I demanded.

"It won't be that easy. You see, my new friend, Tate and Liam aren't exactly fans of ours. For the most part, they have valid reasons for this to be the case. As you can see by the shape of Liam, we also have our own issues with the Protectors and their allies. But to answer your questions, Caroline is in our stronghold near the main hub. She is okay. I'm sure that she would love to see you. There's no way for us to allow anyone but you to come back with us," Jester said.

I had been searching for her for as long as she had been here in the afterlife. I wanted to see her badly. Chandra was also there and in captivity because of me. There are few greater burdens to bear than to put everything that is in your grasp on hold in order to accomplish a more deserving cause.

"I need to talk with my travel companion," I said, trying to buy some time and think of a plan.

"That's all well and good but we need to get back soon if you don't want anything to happen to Chandra."

"Got it," I said as I hurried over to talk with Tate.

Tate and I met just far away enough for them not to hear us. "What do you think?" I asked.

"I don't know that it's a smart idea, my friend. If you go there, we will have a hard time keeping you safe," Tate responded.

"But they have Caroline. Anything could happen to her here. This isn't a place for someone like her," I argued.

"He could be bluffing Sam. If you go, you could be running into a trap."

"I'm almost positive that it is a trap, Tate, but this is our best shot at finding out about Caroline without having to fight. Trust me, I will be able to handle myself."

Tate took a deep breath and sighed as if to say that he still doesn't think it's a good idea. But knew that I wouldn't stop trying to convince him. "I know you can Sam but the plan was for me to be there with you. We are hard to beat together, aye?"

"That's right Comrade. I'll be back once I know more about Chandra and Caroline. Then we can finally end this," I promised. We walked back to the area where Raven and Jester were standing with Liam.

"I'll go back with you Jester, but you must leave Liam here so that he can get proper attention to his wounds. I also expect to leave with Caroline and Chandra."

"Well chief, there is no way that you can take Caroline with you right now. We may be able to work something out with Castro Thorn for Chandra," Jester said, being careful not to commit too much. While he'd done most of the talking, he knew his place with regards to Thorn.

I looked back at Tate. He looked down and away and gestured with his hands stretched out to me. "It's your call. You know how I feel about it."

"You'll need to put these on," Raven demanded. He held a pair of hand cuffs.

"Hold on, no one said anything about needing to wear those," I said lobbying to have my hands free.

"Sam, we need to get going. Caroline is going to be so happy to see you. But Chandra may not be if you don't get a move on," said Jester.

I was between a rock and a hard place. We needed to figure out where Chandra was to free her and Caroline. So, I agreed to put on the handcuffs. They were cold and unforgiving. I learned that certain movements in these menacing toys would mean a tighter grip on my wrist. The handcuffs seemed to have some sort of dampening properties to my abilities. I didn't feel as fast or as nimble as I did without them. This would make it very difficult to thwart any attacks or traps.

"Tate, if we so much as think about your aura being close to us or that you have followed us, we will end all of your friends," Raven threatened.

"I got it. I got it," Tate responded.

Jester removed Liam's cuffs and shoved him toward Tate. He was very weak and fell to the ground. Tate rushed to him and kneeled down by his side.

"I got you old friend," he said as he lifted Liam off the ground. Tate rushed Liam back to the Land of the Promised.

Jester, Raven, and I headed to Necropolis. They stayed behind me the entire time that we traveled. They were discussing my abilities. At the time, they were able to communicate without my knowledge. This was mostly due to my lack of heightened senses from the cuffs. It was a funny thing about the cuffs that I had to wear. While they did not look like much, they were able to keep me from feeling the emotion that I needed to feel in order to use my powers. I could still process that I loved Caroline but I could not get the butterflies and the warm feelings all over my body. They made me weak.

"Did you feel that?" Jester asked Raven. "His power levels were amazingly high. He is gifted, I'll give him that."

"Yeah, I felt it. Is that something that we need to worry about? I'm not too sure just yet," Raven responded, asking and answering his own question.

"Do you think he has more power than Qurina?" Jester asked.

"Hard to tell. Their abilities seemed equal in power but different from each other. It's almost as if they complement one another instead of conflicting," Raven said.

"I see. But now that we have Sam, how do we get him on our team too?" Jester pondered aloud.

"I don't know. This is your show. It's on you if this doesn't work."

"Not to worry old compadre, Jester always thinks of something," he said, speaking in the third person.

Raven shook his head. In some ways, he admired Jester for his gutsiness and ability to plan. In the back of his mind though, he knew that if Jester got too careless, he would soon fail and have to deal with the inevitability of losing his life force.

Chapter 17

Seeing is Believing

WE MADE IT to the enormous gates of the main hub. They were heavily guarded with men standing and patrolling every inch of the massive structure. Every ten yards along the top of the fence stood a guard stand flanked by two men. They were all qualified marksmen. The wall itself was made of several layers of the same tin that the homes were made of. The gate was rusted in most areas but was painted over by the blood of would-be intruders. It was clear that very few prisoners were taken by the Marauders.

By this time the frigid winter air had evaporated leaving only the Sahara-like daytime temperature, which began to cook the metal on the cuffs. My wrists burned as if they were in an oven preheating before a Sunday roast. My only source of comfort was the fact that my clothes were drenched from my sweat.

Somehow Raven and Jester managed to stay cool. I assumed that it was because they were able to use their abilities. As we made our way closer to the entrance, I could hear the hustle and bustle of the city.

The main hub was where business got done. If there was any hope for comfort in the city, it would be here.

At the gate the men quickly recognized Raven. "Hello, Sir." Saluted one of the guards.

"As you were," Raven said. "We have a prisoner here that is very high priority. I need you and two of your best men to take him to the interview room."

"Right away, sir." the guard said.

"And don't let anyone in unless you have orders from me or Thorn," Raven commanded.

"Yes Sir."

"One last thing, you need to do this without many people seeing this done so use the tunnels."

"I will Sir. You can count on me."

Goods were bought, sold, and taken here in the main hub where a variety of vendors lined the streets. In this place the strong took from the weak and beggars sat alongside cowards hunting for the shade of the selling stands. The crowds rumbled, shouted, and screamed out prices and deals. They certainly had a way of life. It was a rough one but somehow it worked for them.

The men whisked me off, unnoticed, down a hidden path where no other people were. They took me to a door that led underground. The tunnel was mostly dark with just enough lighting to see that we were in a tunnel. It smelled like mildew and laundry that was in the wash but forgotten about for three days. Above us, I could hear the muffled footsteps of the people in the village. Being underground lowered the temperature by at least four or five degrees. This minor change made my experience considerably more bearable.

We had reached the other end of the tunnel. I could see the bright lights of the day trying to sneak in through the cracks of the doorway exit. The guards led me up a half flight of steps. The door opened and the lively colors of the light flooded in like an overflowed dam after a great storm and I was blinded for a moment.

We were outside once again. The heat in the city was like a furnace being turned up as high as it could go, inside a closed room in the middle of an August heat wave. My face was covered in sweat which stung my eyes. I grimaced but toughed it out. I had to for Caroline and Chandra.

We were behind the main strip of town. In front of me was a building that looked like a large log cabin lodge. We walked in and the guards had me wait in a small room near the main entrance. They stood outside the room like bouncers at a new and exclusive nightclub, waiting for Thorn or Raven. Or at least at the time, I had assumed this was the case.

While I was being escorted to the diminutive waiting room, Raven and Jester went to get Thorn who was at home waiting for his top men to give him a favorable report.

"Raven... Jester, I hope that you have good news for me," Thorn said.

"We learned quite a bit," Raven said. "Chandra sang to us like a bird after we brought in Liam."

"What did you learn? Is Sam here?"

"Yes, he's in Necropolis. We have him in the main hub," Raven said.

"Excellent. Did he come on his own free will?" asked Thorn.

"Not exactly. We had to make a deal with him. Sam was with Tate and while Jester and I could take him on and win, we learned more about what Sam was doing here."

"Deal? What sort of deal?"

"We told Sam that we could make arrangements to let Chandra go in exchange for him. He really wants to see his wife."

"So we have Liam and Sam then. We can work with that," Thorn said.

"Well, to get Sam to come with us without spilling any blood, we had to trade Liam," Raven explained.

"What!? We had them where we wanted them. Why would we do something like that? I should take your life force right now," Thorn threatened.

"And you would be well within your rights, Castro," Jester said, jumping in quickly. "But we were able to acquire even more interesting news about Sam. The Protectors… they think he is their chosen one."

"That's ridiculous. How could he be the chosen one? Qurina is the one. We've all seen what she can do. Raven, you know firsthand what she is capable of."

"But sir, we had to find out and Jester is right. He could be the chosen one. His power levels are off the charts."

"Is he stronger than my Qurina?" Thorn asked.

"It's hard to tell but they are both at least as strong as you are, Thorn," Raven said.

Thorn turned and ran the back of his hand over his stubble as he considered their options. "So now we trade two Protectors for one. Why should he fight for us? He has seen the Land of the Promised."

"Because he loves Caroline. I think that it's time to have her talk to him," Jester suggested.

The men formulated a plan before sending out word for Caroline to be summoned. She was in the desert using her powers to beautify the area. Despite her relative isolation, once she was told Thorn wanted to see her she quickly returned to the city and arrived at Thorn's home. She wore white flowing linen pants with a thin white tank top and tan sandals.

"Qurina, you look absolutely stunning," Jester commented as she entered the room. "How does it feel to be one of us?"

"I've always felt a connection with you Jester so I feel the same."

"You do realize that no one actually wins those initiations. Raven and I take turns and we were undefeated until last night," Jester explained.

"Well, I'd have to imagine that it's because you fight from a place of rage and hatred. I feel love coursing through my body. Don't get me wrong, you are very formidable opponents. Your hate blinds you and you only have one speed.

Love, while it can blind me at times, it keeps my mind pure. I can see things just before they happen. It creates the illusion that I am moving faster. I am just reacting sooner."

"I see that you have been meditating and studying, my star pupil," Thorn remarked.

Thorn was oddly fond of Qurina. She was the best of both worlds. She saw the struggles and the pain that it took to survive in Necropolis, yet she was able to exist as if this world was the Land of the Promised. Her belief in love had transcended its boundaries. She was a fierce fighter and had pledged herself to his people. Her faith in love was almost holy in such an unholy place. If his heart was not hardened so long ago, he may have felt guilty for deceiving her.

"Come, warrior. I have news from Sam."

"Sam! You know where he is?" Qurina cried.

She was filled with joy and excitement and gave Thorn a hug. Her spirit warmed and cooled his body at the same time. She still had that contagious spirit that I had fallen in love with. Her humble confidence always made me feel like she could do anything and because I was with her, I could do anything too.

"Yes, he is here. We found him."

"I must see him right away! Where is he?"

"Hold on Qurina, there is more. When we found him, he was fighting with the Protectors," Thorn said.

"Why would he be fighting with the Protectors? They have assimilated so many of our people."

"He believes that we are the bad ones. I cannot tell you that I am a good person. As you know, our powers come from a dark place," Thorn reminded.

"But that place exists for all of us, Thorn. Look at what you had done. Your knowledge of love and hate is why I am what I am today. You're not the bad guys. We are not the bad guys. Let me talk to him! He will listen to me! He loves me!"

Thorn ordered for me to be brought.

After the men left to retrieve me Jester told Qurina, "Understand, we had to use dampener cuffs on him because he is one of them. We had to be careful. He is unharmed …a little weak from not being able to use his abilities to maintain his strength."

"Okay." she said, hardly able to hide her excitement.

She was sitting at a small square-shaped table made of thick petrified wood with her chair facing the entrance. Thorn stood behind her in a back corner of the room. Jester stood to her left with his hand on her shoulder. Raven sat at the table to Caroline's right.

I felt nervous to see her again. The cuffs made my senses dull but they could not dampen the emotions that I felt for my soul mate. Our love was true and pure. The Great Source had given us an ability only matched by our other half. Her powers stemmed from her love for me. My powers stemmed from my undying love for her.

Caroline knew my heart and my deepest thoughts. She knew that my affection for her flowed like the Wabash River. No rock or dirt or any land mass could slow it down. Somehow we managed to find each other again. We were now in two different worlds, forbidden to interact with one another. Still, somehow, she was there. She was sitting and waiting for me on the other side of that door, which seemed to open so very slowly. I eagerly entered the room and there she was. It was hard to believe. My heart was overcome with joy and happiness. I dropped to both knees and reached out to her. My eyes filled up with tears. "Caroline? Is it really you?" I asked hoping that my eyes have not deceived me.

"Yes! Yes! It's me! Sam."

It had been so long since I'd heard her call my name that way. It was as beautiful as a bird's song on a sunny Saturday morning. She slowly stood up and began to cry tears of happiness. Her eyes were locked in on mine. My vision was a little blurry because of the tears. She walked over to me and fell to her knees. We latched on to each other as best as we could, due to the cuffs being on my wrist. She kissed me passionately.

Her soft lips brought me back to that first night we met and our wedding day. Every kiss brought me energy and a feeling of unfiltered adoration. I felt stronger and the cuffs on my wrists suddenly felt like a chain of paper clips. As easy as one could break a pencil, I snapped the chains in two. Arms free, I could finally give her a proper embrace.

"I have waited a thousand years," I whispered to her.

"You found me," she said.

We hugged each other and kissed a little longer. I did not want it to stop but the sobering moment had to come. She was here for a reason. She had chosen to be here in Necropolis City. Why would she be here? This was a place for souls that are hard-hearted and those that have malice and uncaring feelings for all things except greed and power. These people stopped at nothing to get what they wanted.

Caroline must have felt my thoughts. The moment had passed and the questions needed to be answered. I started to notice the other people in the room. I looked around and they were all staring at me as if I were a lab rat and they were scientists.

I look up at them from my kneeling position. "Hello," I said awkwardly. "I'm Sam and this is my wife Caroline…. Well, I guess you already know who she is. Uh… I …."

"Nice to meet you, Sam. I am Castro Thorn," he said in a surprisingly pleasant voice. "I believe that you have met my associates Raven and Jester."

I nodded at the two men. I'm not sure why but I felt it would have been rude if I did not exchange the pleasantry.

"I must say Sam, I have never seen anyone break those cuffs before. That was truly impressive," said Thorn.

I was unsure how to respond so I didn't. I stood back on my feet. My body had regained full strength. Thorn was exactly how I pictured him. He seemed to be in control at all times. He was playing chess with me even at that moment. Every word was calculated and constructed to solicit a response or a reaction. He was a master at reading people and emotions. This is why he was their leader.

"In all my years I have not seen love's purity displayed in such a way. I can tell that she has your heart," Thorn said.

"Yes, she does. That's why I'm here. But what confuses me is why she is here," I responded.

"Like all before her, she chose this place," Thorn said.

"You must have tricked her or something. She would never choose here." Then I looked at Caroline. "You would never choose here had you known, honey. Now, please come back with me."

"Had I known what?" Caroline asked.

"The truth!" I pleaded. "Necropolis is a place for those that are not fit for The Land of the Promised."

"Are you saying that I am not fit, Sam? I'm home and have been for almost two years. These men are my friends. I consider them family," she declared.

"Don't say that, Caroline."

"Why not? It's true. Thorn has taught me so many things about myself and Jester has been a friend, travel companion, and a protector to me. This is my home, Sam. Maybe instead of assuming that it's is all bad, you should give it a chance."

"Caroline… you have to see… Necropolis is not your home. I am your home and you are mine. Come back with me and I'll be your protector, your family, and your friend," I pleaded.

She softened. She had been expecting to find me in Necropolis for so long that it never occurred to her that I may have been in the Land of the Promised by choice.

"Sam, they must have brainwashed you somehow. There is no way you would have sided with those people when they were responsible for the suffering of so many others. How can you tell me this is right? You call yourself a Protector. Protect the right people."

"Who? These people Caroline? Do you know who they are? Have any of them told you what they did to get here? This place was created specifically because of the actions of men in this room. The people of the Land of the Promised are safe and can live the way they do because the Great Source is protecting them from Thorn. But they didn't tell you that did they?"

Caroline paused for a while after hearing my words. She was looking at the men whom she just called family. I could tell that she had not been told any of this.

"I just don't know what to believe right now," Caroline said, with her hand combing through her hair.

"*Believe me,* Caroline."

"...I love you Sam, with all my heart. You and I have a special connection. Which is why I know you are telling me your truth. The problem I have is that I've seen so much suffering here and something has to be done about it. I thought that my purpose here was to find you but I am beginning to see that I am here to find myself. This journey that we have been on has taken us to two different places. I want us to be together but I cannot go back with you, honey." Tears were streaming down her face but she was firm in her convictions. "Will you think about staying with me, here?"

At that point, I thought that I had seen as much foolishness as I had ever seen. She wanted me to stay in Necropolis. I thought about the promise that I made to her.

No matter what... How could this be? I thought to myself. My wife wants me to stay here. "But what would we do here?" I asked.

"There is much that I would love to share with you, Sam. All of my time has been spent with you as my guiding light. I could be doing anything and somehow you would creep into my thoughts. I'd wonder if you were doing the same thing as me at the same time. I am tired of wondering. I want my husband back but I cannot leave here. Give it two weeks and let's see where we are at," she offered.

I had to consider the proposal. Even though I would never have dreamed of staying in Necropolis, I was there and Caroline was clearly being deceived. I could not give up on her so quickly. I didn't have very much time but I had to make her see me for what I had become and trust that my truth was the truth.

"What do they think about it?" I asked looking at the men in the room.

"You are welcome as long as you'd like, Sam," Thorn said. "We have nothing to hide here."

"What about Chandra?" I asked.

Raved cleared his throat and answered, "We need to guarantee that you won't try anything slick while you are here so we may need to hold her a little while longer."

"No, let her go. Sam will give his word not to try anything or fight anyone here. Won't you Sam?" Caroline asked.

My eyes glanced at the men in the room but they did not raise an objection to her. I returned my gaze to her nodded my head. "But there are two more concessions, no more cuffs for me and Caroline has to come back with me for two weeks as well."

"I'm not sure that's a good idea," Raven objected.

"Your right Raven...it's a great idea!" Jester said, suddenly joining the conversation. "I would like to go with you. Can you make that happen? I've never been."

"Well, that makes two of us," Caroline said.

"I will make arrangements and I'll need to send word by way of Chandra. Would it be possible for us to speak before she leaves?" I asked.

Thorn exhaled a long sigh as he measured his response. "Raven, you will escort Sam to his partner. Make sure that their conversation is brief."

"Yes Sir," Raven replied.

Chandra was still in the same room as before. The cuffs had taken a toll on her body. She was very weak and looked frail. She refused to eat any type of food offered to her and only drank enough to stay alert. Her force didn't look very strong but I could tell that her spirit was not broken.

"What have they done to you?" I asked her. Before she could respond I turned to Raven and demanded, "Release her now!"

"Now hold on Mr. Impatient. You need to tell her the deal first."

I helped Chandra to her feet. "...Sam? How are you here? Why is he here?" Her eyes drifted back and forth between Raven and I. She seemed dazed.

"It's very complicated but Caroline is here and I have made a deal to get you, Tate, and Liam home safely," I explained.

"What kind of deal? Are you staying here? I can't let you do that Sam. These people will take your life force. You cannot trust them to keep their word!"

"I have to do this. Just have Liam and my father prepare a place for us in two weeks."

"I don't understand Sam. Are you coming back?" Chandra asked, now even more confused.

"Yes, I'll be back. Caroline and Jester will be with me. I want to prove to her that we are not the bad guys."

"How could she think that we are the bad guys? Have you seen this place?"

"I don't know but somehow she has been deceived by these guys. We have to show her the truth."

"Alright, that's enough," Raven said as he postured himself between us. "If you want to go you'd better leave now before I disobey an order and waste you myself," Raven said to Chandra.

He unchained her and they sized each other up like two prizefighters before a slugfest. Neither of them were ready to back down but the clock was ticking. Chandra had evidently regained her bearings.

"Okay, Chandra, please go now. There is much for us to do," I urged.

"There is a tunnel just to your right with guards waiting to escort you out of our lands," Raven explained.

She glared at Raven before turning and quickly walking out of the room.

Chapter 18

I Saw Her

CAROLINE GREETED ME near her sleeping quarters. She lived off a dirt road in a row of houses made of old rusted tin and dead wooden trees. Her home was at the end of the row on the right side. I was very nervous walking down the dusty path with her. She was my wife but much time had passed and it was almost like dating again. We'd take turns glancing up at each other and looking away when the other attempted eye contact. We were young and twenty-one all over again. I had so much to say but I could not figure out how to start. I was there to rescue the love of my life but she didn't need to be rescued. Perhaps it was our connection that needed to be fixed. I still felt the love and energy of a thousand suns when I was around her but it was different. We'd seen things that couldn't be unseen. Our oneness with the universe made us blind to what was right in front of us.

"I don't want to lose you, Caroline," I said.

"You won't Sam," she stopped walking and looked me in the eyes. "I've missed your face. I can't believe I am here walking with you. In my deepest hopes, I wanted to have you back with me. I prayed to God that you would be by my side again. But for a long time nothing happened." She placed her hand on my cheek and continued, "Perhaps we needed to go on this journey separately in order to feel love in its purest form. I don't know. Sam, you have all of my heart and all of me. There is no way for you to lose me. Love will guide us back together."

I smiled at her words. Her soft hands were on my cheeks and the world around me disappeared. Her touch could make me feel as though I was standing on a cloud in the sky. My feet were light. I didn't feel the ground. It was her touch that let me believe I could fly.

"You make me feel like I can do anything," I said to her.

"In this world, I am finding that there isn't much we can't do," she said with a smile.

Caroline grabbed my hand and she continued walking with me to her home.

"That's it! Right there. The one on the end," she declared.

"Wow, that's yours?" I asked in amazement.

Her home was unlike any of the others I had seen on this side of Hinterland. It was a log cabin lodge made of oak. Where the other homes had weeds and crabgrass growing she had wintergreen colored grass. There was a white picket fence that surrounded her front yard. There were small planters boxes hanging from the top of the fence, which contained yellow and white lilies, blue irises, and pink dahlias. She had a large wooden porch with two rocking chairs made of pine.

"How is all of this possible?" I asked.

"Like I said, there isn't much that we can't do here, Sam." Then she leaned over to me and kissed me on the cheek. "Come on in."

Inside was just as beautiful as the outside. She had a wood burning fireplace made of multi-colored stones. Her ceilings were vaulted. She had a loft for a bedroom which overlooked the living area. There were apple scented candles all around. They provided the lighting and set the mood for our reunion.

"I'm so floored. Your place is beautiful! I would never have expected this. How did you do it?"

"The power of thought is great here. I'm not sure how more people couldn't do it," she said in a matter of fact sort of way. "All I did was think about you and all of the charm you have inside. I know that you try to hide it from most people. You want them to see a tough macho guy, you pretend that it isn't there. But I see you, Sam. I see you for who you are and the good in your soul. It's one of the reasons that you have my heart. As I thought of you, my mind created this. I didn't know it but my spirit must have known that you would come and I needed to get things ready."

"Well, I am impressed, to say the least. This is really nice."

"It makes me happy that you like it," she said as she walked into the kitchen.

"Would you like anything? I have one of your favorite snacks."

"Which one, popcorn or you?" I asked.

"Ha-ha, Mr. Fresh. But it's not just any popcorn…" she said as she peeked her head out from the threshold of the kitchen. "It's Chicago-style gourmet popcorn."

"You do know me well."

She walked back out to the main living area with a bowl of yellow fluffy popcorn. She held the bowl in one arm like a football and grabbed my hand with her free hand. We walked over to her couch which faced the fireplace. We ate popcorn and began to fall into a familiar pattern. It had been years since this was even a possibility and now we're together watching the fire. Its flames danced around the logs like a ballerina dancing at Clowes Hall.

"And as far as the other snack, if you are lucky, that can be arranged," she whispered to me softly.

"Well here's to being lucky," I said as I raised my hand up with a pretend glass to make a toast. I inched closer to her and kissed her gently on her full lips. She let out a slight moan of approval. I began to caress her arms slowly. I felt them start to pimple up with goosebumps. She exhaled hard through her nose to avoid unlocking her lips with mine. Next, I purposefully guided her blouse away from her body and flung it to the floor. She had nothing on underneath. The hot days in Necropolis dictated that one only wears what one needs. It was like touching her for the first time on our wedding night. I stopped kissing her to gaze at her topless body. "Let me look at you. I have missed being able to gaze at your glorious frame," I said.

The light from the fire cast a perfect shadow on her flawless figure. I found myself staring at her beautiful breasts. She blushed faintly and continued kissing me.

She started to remove my shirt now. She methodically moved her hand about my body. Her hands were warm to the touch and gave me a sensation unlike anything on Earth. It felt like pure electricity and feathers all at the same time. I embraced the feeling and rode it as a surfer would a wave.

"I love you so much," I whispered.

"I love you too," was her soft reply.

We removed the rest of our clothes and made our way up to her bedroom in the loft. She slowly laid her body on top of her plush linen sheets. Caroline gestured for me to join her and our bodies merged together. We were a twisted pretzel, only able to tell where one ended and one began by the tones of our skin. We made love most of the night, re-consummating our promise to one another.

As we laid on the bed together I started to notice a change in my abilities. Our connection was back. I could sense her moods and feelings but I could not read her thoughts. She was feeling happy mostly, but there was something that she was holding back purposefully.

"Caroline, you know that I will always love you no matter what, right?"

"Of course, honey, I know you love me."

"I know that you are hiding something. I can feel it. You do trust me, don't you?"

"Of course Sam. I trust you but I...I don't think it's time for me to tell you what's on my mind."

"Honey, I trust you too. I know that you are doing what you think is right. The timing may not be good but I deserve to know what's going on with you. It will strengthen our love for one another."

"Sam, if you'll just give me some time. I promise that I'll tell you. Let's just enjoy right now and we can talk about this later."

I didn't want to let it go so easily but we were easing back into a relationship that had been severed for over four years. I had to show her trust and give her more time to let me all the way back in.

"Okay, I trust you," I said as I give her a peck on the cheek.

It was hard for me but I did trust her. I didn't want to lose her because I wasn't patient enough to allow her the time that she needed.

The first week had passed. Caroline and I spent almost all of our time together. We were like young lovers again. People in Necropolis City would stop and stare as we walked around holding hands. A public act of affection was an anomaly in a place like this. Necropolis was the Wild West with every man or woman for him or herself. One time while we strolled around the city, Caroline saw two men arguing with each other over a wild rabbit they found and killed together.

"It's mine, I saw it first," said the first man.

The second man quickly snatched the rabbit out of the other man's hand and said, "No I killed it so I get to eat it."

Caroline saw the two men and rushed over to them before I could stop her.

"What is the problem?" she asked.

"This man right here tri..." the first man started talking then he looked up and saw Caroline. "Qurina..." he said, leaving his mouth open. The other man was also staring in awe and dropped the rabbit.

"Qurina, we are sorry to bother you with such a petty dispute. We had a disagreement about who should get the rabbit." The second man said. "Will you help us resolve it?"

"I'll help you under one condition," she said. "You will agree to abide by my ruling and no one loses their life force over this disagreement."

The men both gesture in agreement.

"Did you both put forth effort in capturing this rabbit?"

"Yes, but I did the most," the first man said.

"No, I did more than him," the second man said.

"That's enough!" she commanded. "Give me the rabbit. The Great Source has created this animal. Sometimes we need to kill to survive. Other times the Source provides us a way out of taking life. It is my belief that you meeting me here today is your chance to find a way out.

This rabbit is no longer yours or his. I call upon the powers of Ekon to heal this animal."

Her hands begin to glow neon purple as a black light does. In a flash, the wild rabbit starts to kick its feet and wiggle its ears. Caroline gently patted the small creature on its head and released it.

She looked over at the men. "It is one thing to let your hate fuel your fire and help you defend this land. It is another to let it consume you. You need to find a way to control your rage and save your petty squabbles for the battle that is to come. Now, so you men don't go hungry, you will have dinner with me tonight. Come to my home before the weather breaks and the cold has consumed the land this evening."

The men were surprised at the invitation. "We are honored that you would choose us as your dinner companions," the first man said. They were not used to being treated with kindness. It was usually a liability in this place.

Up until this point, I hadn't seen her use her powers. I only knew that she had a strong force within her. I wasn't even sure if she knew. Caroline was able to waken a dead creature. I didn't know the power of love was that strong. She was clearly further along in her training than I could have fathomed. "Could Arawn have been right?" I asked myself. Her feat was no easy task. I could heal myself and others but even that took lots of energy and concentration. Caroline was special.

She looked back at me. She had a look of embarrassment and the color drained from her face.

"What's wrong?" I asked.

"Now you know," she said in a soft almost whispering tone.

"Know what? That you had abilities? I felt your energy after we made love that first night. There's nothing to be ashamed of honey."

"You knew?"

"Well, I didn't know to what extent or that you could do that, which was amazing by the way, but I knew that you had a lot of potential inside of you."

"Wait, how do you know so much about it?" she asked.

"I have a confession to make, too." My aura illuminated bright white. My eyes started to emit a clean light. I turn to her so that she could see me. "You are not the only one with abilities."

"Sam, I didn't know."

"When we are together, do you ever get a prickle in your gut?"

"Yes but…"

"That's you sensing my power levels. I can't tell to what extent your powers are but I know that they are high. It brings me joy to know that you have these abilities," I said with a smile.

"I am happy that you have powers, too. Are there a lot of people with our abilities in the Land of the Promised?" she asked.

"Actually there are only ten Protectors and there may be a few more with our gifts but they cannot harness them like we can. It takes training and a lot of meditating. By the way, why did those men call you Qurina?"

"That's a name Thorn gave me when I became a Marauder. It means great she-warrior or something like that."

"So you have had to fight before?" I asked. There was a mixture of excitement and concern in my voice.

"Yes but only once. It was part of the initiation to become one of them."

"Did you win?"

She gave me a little smirk and said nothing. She just continued walking. I caught up with her and decided not to ask again. I had concluded that she'd won.

"Who did you beat?"

"Sam, do you really want to know all of this?

"Yes!" I said with enthusiasm. "These people walk around doing their own thing until you arrive. Some of Earth's most hardened people live here and they seem to fear or respect you… or maybe a little of both. For you to have only had one fight, it must have been a big and important one. So, yes! I would like to know how you got the name Qurina and who it was that you beat to get it."

She gave a big sigh and said, "Raven, Castro Thorn's number one guy."

"What? They made you fight that guy? He's tough. From what I'd heard, he'd defeated some of our best Protectors."

"Honestly, it wasn't that big a deal. He probably took it easy on me." She gave me a shy look as if to say, *Please let's drop it now.*

I obliged and said nothing more. Defeating Raven was a big deal. He didn't strike me as the kind of person that took it easy on anyone. He'd want to be sure the ones that had his back were as tough and as aggressive as him.

Two weeks had passed and our days in this unholy city had come to an end. Necropolis was a place full of chaos and disorder. We saw many fights and Caroline broke up most of them. She was able to move about the land unchallenged. I'd see her stroll around the streets helping people. She'd offer meals to the hungry, help the wounded, and solved disputes without any major incident. Even though we were able to move freely about, I always had a sneaking suspicion that someone was watching us at all times. Whomever it was did a good job of not being detected.

Chapter 19

The Land of the Promised

I T WAS MY turn to show her the Land of the Promised. Caroline and Jester could only stay in the city for two weeks. If they had stayed any longer they would be assimilated into the Great Source. This meant they would be part of a consciousness with no thoughts of their own because they did not choose the Land of the Promised like everyone else here had done. You had to be awakened to the realities of our world and they were not. This is also why Caroline was so easily deceived by Thorn and his men.

To be awakened one must accept and forgive themselves for his or her inequities on earth. Because the Great Source is Love, he allows the individual to see and have an inordinate understanding of the universe. The awakened individual is able to view life from all perspectives. His choices are made for the greater good of all instead of what is good for him alone.

Caroline, Jester, and I were almost to the cliffs that divided

Hinterland and The Land of the Promised. As we walked Jester was working hard to cast doubt in Caroline's mind about my home.

"I don't think this place will be all they say it is, Caroline. People like to over promise and they always under deliver."

"We will see. Even Thorn talked about this place as if it were Heaven," Caroline replied.

"Yeah but Thorn isn't exactly known for being upfront and honest now is he?"

"I guess that is a good point."

"We may be leaving early if we get too bored. Just saying..."

"Okay, it's a deal. I really want Sam to come back with us after this is all said and done."

Jester shrugged. "Well, that will be up to you to change his mind Qurina."

In order to get to the top of the cliff, Caroline and Jester had to bind on to me. We were expected which made the attempt easier. Normally, a force field would block anyone from attempting to climb up the cliff. I was able to ascend to the top without climbing and my aura was on the same frequency as the force field. I could cross it without taking on damage. At the top of the cliff, Jester and Caroline had trouble breathing. Their skin emitted smoke and they gnashed their teeth because of the unbearable burning sensation they felt.

"Sam!" Caroline called.

"Don't worry, honey. Your bodies are just not used to the environment. You will adjust," I assured them. "Also, you will not be able to use your powers here, Jester. Hate is powerless in the Land of the Promised. Caroline, with some assistance you could use yours. You have not been awakened to do it on your own."

A few seconds later they did not feel the burning anymore.

"I feel strange. What is that?" Jester asked.

"It is joy or happiness," I said.

"I must say, it is a pleasant feeling."

"Yes, it does feel wonderful. Why am I feeling this way for no reason?" Caroline inquired.

"The reason is that you are in a special place. Your soul is rejoicing for it is home again," I explained. "We are almost there guys. I can't wait for you to see the Land of the Promised."

We arrived at the gates a short time later. Jester was in awe of the structure. Caroline commented on the iridescent lights. The doors had opened and my father had a surprise for Caroline and me. He was standing next to a man and a woman. They were smiling and had sincere looks on their faces.

The man was young, he looked to be in his early twenties. He was shorter than me but still tall. He was fit and had a sprinter's build. His hair was faded around the sides and the top was cut in a box shape with tight curly locks. The locks draped from the top of his hair like a weeping willow tree. His hue was light brown, almost copper toned. The young man was wearing a pair of jeans and a blue Colts T-shirt with a horseshoe on the front. The Colts were my favorite team back when I was on earth. I wondered who he could be. I did not recognize him right off but there was something conversant about him.

The woman was white and looked to be in her mid to late thirties. She was blonde with smoky grey eyes. She wore a white sundress with blue flowers that curved around her womanly figure. She was very pretty and her hair was styled in long lazy curls, purposefully shaded over her shoulders.

"Who are they?" Caroline asked me.

"The older gentleman is Gerald. He's my dad. The other two I don't really know."

We walked through the gates of the city. I introduced Caroline and Jester to my dad. Jester greeted him with a handshake and his trademarked smile. Caroline gave him a great big hug.

"I've heard so much about you Gerald," she said. "It's like I already know you."

"Sam has told me so much about you too, Caroline," my father said as he looked over to me. "You did good son."

"I'm Susan." The woman standing with Gerald said to the group. She had a slight southern accent which was only noticeable in certain words like y'all (you all) and lil' (little).

"Oh, my mother's name was Susan," Caroline remarked.

"I know." The woman smiled at her.

Caroline gave the woman a puzzled look and began to study her face. "Is that you, mom?"

"Yes, it's me. I've waited for this moment since the day you were born. It has been my dream to meet you face to face again. I got to meet you the one time. You were such a tiny lil' thing then. I held you in my arms for only five minutes before the doctors took you away from me. I didn't make it but a few hours after that. You've turned into such a beautiful woman."

"Oh, mom!" Caroline said. Her eyes were full of tears. The two women embraced warmly and held onto each other for a time.

My father waited until their embrace was complete before saying, "This is Sidney, your son."

Caroline and I looked at each other first. Our hearts were filled with instant joy. "What are you doing here?" I asked. "I thought you were going back to Earth."

"I decided not to," he said simply.

He was a handsome looking young man. A good mix of Caroline and me. He took on the form of what he would have looked like in his twenties, had he made it through the crash.

"I'd always wondered what it would be like to meet you, Sydney," Caroline said. "Why did you stay here?"

"After you had passed, I knew my family was here. I wanted to meet you and see you. I felt your love for me for four months and it was the kind of love that I felt in the Land of the Promised. There was no way I could replace that feeling had I gone down to Earth. So I decided to stay here," Sydney explained.

"Oh, my son. I wish you would have experienced life on Earth. There is pain and there is good. Sometimes there is both. It makes you appreciate and understand better," Caroline said, "But this moment would not be possible if you were not here. I would not have had the chance to meet the baby that I carried in my belly for four months."

Sydney nodded.

Caroline reached out for an embrace. He pulled us both in for a group hug. I felt so many emotions. Having my family all together made me feel stronger and more bonded with the universe. Having family is not always a blood relationship. It is a bond between the people that want to be a part of your life. The closeness of the group makes the single person stronger. The whole is greater because love is the rope that binds and connects us. Family coming together makes for an abundant power source that replenishes the sick and the weak, makes enemies tremble, and moves mountains. Nothing stands in the way of a strong family fueled by love. With my wife and my son alongside me and the Protectors, this could be our way to bring order to our world.

"Are you ready to see the sights?" I asked Caroline.

"I think so," she responded.

"I'm ready too!" Jester said, almost seeming more excited than Caroline.

Jester was normally the type that would try to scheme his way in and out of situations. He was always working an angle. In the Land of the Promised he found it difficult to resist the feelings of joy, happiness, and love. These were feelings that he had long since abandoned to become the person that put him in Necropolis. Here he felt compelled to be genuine in his thoughts and feelings. He was able to trust everyone around him. He could relax and enjoy the other side of his self.

Sydney and Susan wanted to join us and showed Caroline around. We made a plan for each of us to take a shift showing them our world. Susan took us on a bicycle ride alongside the coast of the city. It reminded me of Route 101 that stretches from Washington State to California. We coasted down hills and around corners feeling the cool breeze from the ocean flapping our clothes. The road was so smooth that it felt as though peddling was not needed. On one side of us was a wide blue ocean that had no end. On the other side were hills green from the trees and grass that painted the landscape. We pulled off the road to stop at the beach so Sydney, Jester, and I could go into the water. We splashed around and wrestled with the incoming waves while Caroline and Susan sat on the beach and talked.

"I never thought that I would ever meet you," Caroline said.

"I know sweet child but I have always been there with you," Susan responded.

"I guess in a way I'd always known that."

"I was there the first time you met Sam. You were such a cute lil' thing and he was so innocent too. Sam was smitten from the first day until now. I mean, a man that is willin' to leave paradise and go to Necropolis to bring the woman he loves back is some kinda man."

"Yes, but those people are in Necropolis because they were put there by Sam's friends," Caroline snapped.

"Oh, sweetie, please. I didn't mean anything by that. I was only saying that…"

"No, mom, that's just it. I don't need him to rescue me. I need him to love me and be with me. I want him to come back with me."

"Caroline, you need to wake up. This is where you should be. Not in some hellhole like Necropolis. Sam can set you free to this world."

"I don't want that. I am already free. I feel the love that he has for me. But he doesn't see the love that I have for the people in Necropolis. They need me there." Caroline explained.

Her mother was taken aback by her words. She placed her hands on Caroline's shoulder. "The Great Source gave us all a choice. It is for you to choose darlin' but there is great suffering that you don't have to go through if you'd only choose to stay here," Susan said, in that soft motherly way that only mothers can say things in.

"I just don't know mother. I don't know."

Susan grabbed her daughter's hand and gave it a squeeze. For the first time that she could remember Caroline felt the warmth of a mother's touch.

After swimming in the ocean we rode our bikes a little longer, enjoying the beautiful scenery as we continued down the road. Caroline continued to struggle with being in this world that was made for her. She did stop to smell the roses and enjoyed the time with her family. She looked at this trip as one would look at a vacation, but up to this point, I could tell she was still planning to go back to Necropolis.

Sydney wanted to show us a different kind of view. He waved his hand and we were in a big city with lots of people. It felt like New York without the smell. There were tall buildings that filled the skyline.

"Have you ever seen such structures?" Jester asked.

"Only on Earth but not this nice," I replied.

"Yeah but these are up close and in person. I'm a Texas boy. I'm usually accustomed to starry nights and open spaces."

"Trust me, there is plenty of that here too," I said.

We approached a stadium. It was similar to Lucas Oil Field but larger. Inside was an asphalt race track with American Muscle Cars lined up in a row. We had the stadium to ourselves.

Sydney stood in front of the vehicles with one arm behind his back and the other stretched out. "Take your pick," he said, smiling from ear to ear.

"What's going on?" Caroline asked.

"Uh, we are going to be driving these beautiful pieces of machinery?" Jester asked, eager to get in a car.

"Come on Caroline, this will be fun," I said.

"Yeah, it will because I'm going to beat you," she said, with an eyebrow raised.

"Y'all can stop worrying because y'all are gonna be eatin' my exhaust fumes," Susan said, joining in.

"Technically, there is no exhaust or pollution coming from these cars but we get what you are saying, grandma," said Sydney.

"I call the Camero!" Jester declared. His car was dark blue with a black racing stripe going down the middle from the hood to the trunk.

We all jumped into a car that we liked. I saw a mint condition red 1979 Corvette, but I thought it would look much nicer if it were jet black. I placed my hand on the roof and changed the color. The white walled tires were Goodyear and appeared to be showroom new. I opened the door and slid down into the driver's seat. With my hand on the shifter I decided to add a seventh gear to the manual transmission, figuring it would soon come in handy. I turned the key and the engine roared to life. I could feel the power of this tremendous machine as the car growled and grumbled, making a "Lug, lug, lug, lug, lug," sound as it idled.

Sydney jumped in an all-white Challenger from 2020. Susan chose a hot pink 2017 Charger. Caroline must have been feeling sentimental because she chose a 1972 Chrysler Imperial LeBaron.

"Do you remember this one, Sam?" she asked.

"Of course I do. It was my grandfather's but it looks brand new. I don't think you'll get anywhere fast in that," I said.

"I was hoping that we would go real slow as a matter of fact. Do you remember what we did in this car once?" she asked.

She smiled at me and waved me over to her car. I most certainly did. While the Corvette was a very appealing ride and a personal favorite, there was nothing hotter than my wife in that car at that moment. I turned off the Corvette, got out of my car and jumped in hers. She gave me a very steamy kiss and we got ready to ride.

Each car had an open communication system so that we could trash talk like any respectable family would do.

Sydney made the call. "We will do ten laps around the track and the winner gets to choose what's for dinner. On our marks, get set, go!"

The tires squealed and engines revved up. We flew around the track with Caroline and I in the back of the pack, with Jester, Sydney, and Susan in front.

"Wahoo! This is fun!" Jester exclaimed.

"Oh yeah, it's time to eat your grandma's dust, Sydney!" Susan shouted as she took the lead.

Caroline and I were taking it easy in last place, chatting about how much we missed and loved each other. We had no real interest in winning the race.

Then, Sydney challenged us.

"Hey, you guys in the back. Yes, you in that big boat. You might as well just quit while it doesn't look so bad," he said.

"I'll have you know that this car can really go if she wants. We are just cruising," I said.

"That old boat belongs in the water old man!" Sydney declared.

"We'll show you 'old'," I barked.

Now motivated to make something happen, I told Caroline to step on it. The car picked up speed but it was clear that it wasn't made for racing.

"I think it's time to use a little love to get this old girl to move," I said.

Caroline gave me a grin and said, "Let's do it!"

I placed my hand on hers which was on the steering wheel. Even though Jester could not use his powers because they were based on hate, Caroline was able to use hers with my help. Our auras were able to flow through the car. We were one with it now and could control the LeBaron with our powers.

"Okay, Care, let's go turbo," I said.

"You haven't called me that in a long time," she said with a smile.

"I do in my head all the time."

"Let's go win this thing!"

"One lap to go old man and you're still last. I'm back in first," Sydney reminded us.

"Not for long," Caroline said. Our car, being forced around the track by our abilities, passed Jester up first. "See 'ya old buddy," Caroline said as we passed him up. In a flash, Susan was in our rearview mirror too. "See 'ya mom."

Sydney was close to the finish line and was feeling confident. Caroline and I were hot on his trail gaining quickly.

"Here we come," I said.

We pulled up next to him for a moment, enough time for me to yell out, "See 'ya at the finish line young man!" We bolted past him as he stared back at us with wide eyes and his mouth agape.

Caroline and I crossed the finish line victorious. "Ha ha! That was awesome!" I said, pumped up from the win.

"We still make a good team don't we?" Caroline commented.

"Yes, we do." I leaned over and gave her a passionate kiss.

Everyone finished the race. Sydney placed second while Susan was third. Although Jester finished last his beaming smile as he jumped out of his car seemed to indicate it had not diminished his fun.

"That folks is how it's done," I said.

"Yeah, yeah, I was winning until you used your abilities," Sydney countered.

"That was a great idea. I had so much fun, Sydney," I said.

The entire group seemed to have the same opinion as we were all buzzing with excitement as we made our way out of the arena. We continued to walk around the busy city, admiring different works of architecture and art. Sydney and Jester lingered behind and talked about the day.

"I bet you can't do that in Necropolis," Sydney said to Jester.

"That is true. This place is far more amazing than I had ever imagined. How Thorn left this place is beyond me."

"You know that you don't have to go. You could stay here and live like this all the time. But you will have to give up your way of life. There is no cheating, stealing, backstabbing, or killing here. Only the purest of heart and the truthful can live in the Land of the Promised," Sydney explained.

"Well, that leaves me out," Jester said, sarcastically. "All I've ever known was that life. I've been lying, stealing, and stepping over dead corpses to get ahead for as long as I can remember. There's no coming back from that, my friend."

"But there is. The Great Source understands your heart. If you truly are ready to give up hate, then there is a chance for you," said Sydney.

"...I don't know..." Jester replied.

Sydney patted him on the back and simply said, "When you're ready, he will be here to accept you."

"This place is beautiful," Caroline said.

"Yes, it is," I responded.

"It's amazing how much one can imagine...all of these different structures. See over there...that is the building that inspired the leaning tower of Pisa."

"But it's not leaning," Jester said.

"You are absolutely right. But it does look like it," I responded.

I took them to the field where I first woke up in this place.

"Would you look at that?" Jester said. "I've not seen so much green grass and so many flowers in all my life. I was on Earth the last time I saw anything close to this. The colors are so much brighter here. Can you smell that sweet perfume flooding your nose? Oh man, this is heaven."

"Yes, it is Jester. Ekon created the Land of the Promised for us all. It was meant to be a special place with lots of wonders." I then looked at my wife and asked, "Caroline, what do you think?"

She seemed to be far off in her own thoughts but managed to respond after a short pause. "Oh... uh, it's... it's beautiful Sam. It reminds me of the flowers that I made in the deserts of Necropolis."

"Yeah, I guess they do but doesn't this make the desert feel like a small patch of grass?"

She looked at me as if I had just hurt her feelings. "Uh, umm... I think I'd like to go back into town now. Can you show me where I will be staying?"

"Sure, of course, honey. You'll stay with me," I said.

"Uh yes, your place then. I'd like to see that," she said, pretending to be more excited than she was.

I could tell Caroline was upset about what I had said but there seemed to be something bothering her. We'd had a great day so far. My comment about the desert was insensitive but I figured that I'd have time to make it up to her.

We took Jester to stay with Sydney. Jester was very impressed with the home that he would be staying at for the next few days. Sydney's place looked like a college boy bachelor pad paid for my rich parents. He had a large Ultra-HD projector in a room with fluffy remote controlled recliner chairs. It was the room he chose to show us first.

"This is my movie room," he said proudly.

"What do you watch here in the Land of the Promised?" Caroline asked.

"Just about whatever I want. I can catch any TV show or movie made on Earth or revisit the archives of life. Anyone that had a story on Earth has a file in the archives and most of them we are allowed to watch," Sydney explained as we walked around his large home.

As we entered a cavernous space Sydney announced, "This is my baller room. I plan on hosting a party here soon." The room was as large as half a football field and could easily hold a few thousand people. There was a DJ booth set up next to a spacious dance floor. He also had a bank of strobe lights that illuminated the room with bright, pulsating red, white, and blue lights.

We left the room, walked down a long hall, and came to what would be Jester's sleeping chamber. "Now this is what I'm talking about!" Jester shouted. His room had twenty foot high ceilings and marble floors. The bed sat in the center of the room.

"It's a double king," Sydney stated. The sheet and comforter were made from the softest cotton fields of the Land of the Promised. The windows stretched almost to the ceiling to let in as much natural light as possible and were covered by white curtains. The closet was a large walk in that was lined with different suits that covered the spectrum of colors.

"These should all fit you perfectly, Jester," Sydney said.

"Man, this place is great! Thanks, Sydney. These suits are awesome," Jester said, smiling, although it was not his usual smile. This one seemed joyful and warmer than the one he normally gave. It was probably his first genuine smile ever on this side of life. He then turned to my wife and said, "Thanks Caroline for letting me come."

"Well, it seems like you two have some relaxing to do. I'd like to show Caroline our place tonight. We will meet with you tomorrow so you can show your mom around a little more," I said.

Caroline and I departed Sydney's place and walked to my house. It looked a lot like the one we shared on Earth except the items on my "honey do" list were completed. Caroline stood facing the house and gasped. She was startled by how closely it resembled our home. It had a wraparound porch painted white like ours was. The porch included two wooden rocking chairs. We had always talked about how we would grow old and rock together for the rest of our lives. The front yard featured a mature sycamore tree, similar to the one we used to sit under and talk about the future. It was also the tree that we'd sat under when we made the decision to have a baby. I even had the scent of fresh cut grass flowing through the air. Caroline would always tell me how much she loved that smell. It reminded her of fall. "...you know the time before all of the leaves have fallen and it's about sixty-nine degrees outside. There's a cool breeze carrying the hopes that come with a New Year approaching," she'd say.

I only mostly got it but I'd pretend to totally get it.

All sorts of memories started to stream through Caroline's mind but they were not happy. Caroline recollected her first time walking into the house after losing me and the baby. When she saw the home, she saw the deep depression that she fell in because I was not there to comfort her. She didn't notice the scent of grass in the air. She did notice the tree. It was the place that she would sit in a melancholy state and also the place that she planned her suicide.

"I cannot go in there, Sam," she said as her body trembled.

"But it's our home. Don't you like it?"

"It's fine and it looks very accurate but... it's not the same. I just can't do it. Please, Sam, is there somewhere else we can stay?"

"Caroline, I don't understand. I thought that you'd like it. Give me your hand, help me understand."

She pulled away as I tried to read her feelings. "No Sam, I don't think I'm ready to share."

"What is going on Caroline?"

"I don't know, it doesn't feel right. It feels wrong. All of it feels wrong. It is too perfect."

"It's whatever you want it to be, sweetheart," I said trying to calm her down.

"Well, I don't want it to be anything. This is not my home. This is not what I want," she snapped.

I said nothing to her comment. There was only silence in the air.

"I think I should leave Sam. This is not where I am meant to be. I would love for you to come back with me but..."

"Caroline, it hasn't even been a day yet."

"Nothing will change between now and then, Sam. I have made up my mind."

I didn't realize it in that moment but Caroline was not ready to give up whatever was holding her back. Her depression had consumed her but her affection for me had saved her. Caroline felt the love of the Great Source but never accepted her place in his plan. She would have to forgive herself before she could be transformed. She was truly one of them. While she had not committed such travesties as most of the Marauders, she had done so in her own mind. Caroline had given up on life and on herself.

"I will find Jester and we will be on our way," she said, resigned to her fate.

"You don't have to do this, Caroline. Please rethink what you are about to do," I begged.

"I've thought about it but I don't see why I should stay. This place reminds me of what I am not. I was not good enough to be considered for this world upon my death on Earth. I don't think I'm good enough now."

"Baby, but you are good enough. If there was anyone here that was more deserving of being here it's you. You are good and kind and wonderful and sweet. I beg you to stay."

"I have made up my mind!" she said with finality in her voice.

I put my head in my hands in disbelief. How did I fail her? I had the love of my life in the most perfect place in the universe and still managed to mess things up. Caroline was the only person for me and she wanted to go back to a place of turmoil instead of staying in paradise. "...Okay, Caroline," I finally managed.

Feeling defeated I begrudgingly walked with Caroline through the Land of the Promised and back to Sydney's home. The stroll was silent for a long time. I didn't know what to say.

"...You know that this has nothing to do with how much I love you, right?" Caroline said, in a soft sweet voice.

"I am slightly confused by your wanting to leave so soon. It was not exactly a picnic for me living in Necropolis either but I stayed for you."

"I know Sam, but I need for you to recognize that we are in two different places in our journey. My place is with the people of Necropolis. Being here reminds me too much of home and all that I struggled with on Earth."

At that moment it occurred to me that this was her own personal hell. All of these people here were there because they deserved to be. Their acts and deeds on Earth allowed them to awaken and see the truth. Caroline's truth was rooted in her past. She could not see any further than right now because she was still asleep to the beauty and wonders of my world. I could see and feel all of the love in her heart but I had not found the key to unlocking her guilt and anguish.

"I see and I truly understand. I know that you belong here. I will find a way to make you see," I said. "They aren't expecting us until tomorrow and I don't know when we will see each other again. Will you sleep with me out here under the stars?"

She gave me a half smile for my efforts and replied, "I hadn't seen the stars in a long time, Necropolis is too cold at night to camp out."

I created a sleeping bag for two. We snuggled against each other, unsure of the next time we'd see one another again. I did not sleep at all that night. Most of my time was spent smelling my wife's golden hair. She had her usual scent. It was the smell of freshly picked flowers. The next morning we gathered our things and headed towards Sydney.

Chapter 20

Hard Goodbyes

WE REACHED SYDNEY's home to pick up Jester. He was taken aback that she was ready to go so quickly. He did not appear ready to go yet. Jester had a different look to him. It was not the freshly pressed pinstriped navy blue suit he was wearing. It was as if he'd seen or heard something for the first time.

"Is everything ok, Jester?" I asked.

He took a deep breath before he responded, "I think so." He tried to give his normal smile but it looked like it hurt for him to do it.

"What did you guys get into while we were away?" I asked, facing Sydney.

"You weren't gone long. We just took a walk into town. There were lots of people there," Sydney responded.

"Did something happen to Jester?" I asked.

"Nothing I could think of."

"What's up with you Jester?" Caroline asked.

"No, I'm fine. Why is everyone looking at me so funny? I was just surprised that you were ready to go. We are literally in paradise," Jester explained. There was definitely something going on with him but I was too concerned about how to get Caroline to awaken herself than to pry any further.

"It would be a shame for that suit to go unworn and sit here rotting away, Jester. You can have it," Sydney said.

"Oh wow, that's great. Thanks, Sydney. You have been a gracious host and I am honored that you'd want me to keep the suit. So, I will."

"Are you going to say goodbye to your mom?" I asked Caroline.

"...I don't think so. Maybe we will get a chance some other time. Will you tell her that I am sorry I did not stay longer?"

"I think you should be the one saying it but I'll do it."

With almost no delay, Sydney and I took Caroline and Jester to the outer limits of Hinterland. Jester lingered behind. I felt that he was trying to take as much in as he could before they left.

"I guess this is goodbye then," Caroline said to Sydney. She gave him a great big bear hug and kissed him on the cheek. Caroline faced me and we kissed. I looked into her soft deep blue eyes.

"This is not over yet. Our story does not end this way. We vowed forever to each other and I intend on keeping my promise to you. Together forever, in this life and the next," I said to her. I meant every word. We kissed again.

"Goodbye for now, Sam," she said in reply.

Jester shook my hand and I felt it. He did not want to go. Something did in fact occur last night and he was hiding it. He tried to pull his hand away but I wouldn't let it go.

"What are you doing, Sam?" Jester questioned.

"I know you were telling the truth about not going back," I said. My eyes begin to glow white. "If you want to stay, I can help even you."

Jester's eyes were big. He was not used to trusting people and tried to read me to see if my words were earnest.

"What must I do?" he asked almost crying.

"You have to let it all go. Castro Thorn and The Marauders can no longer be your family. The hate and deceit will have to end. You are a creation of The Great Source and it is his will that all of his children come home. Sometimes a father punishes his son for his transgressions. He must teach a harsh lesson for him to gain understanding. The bond becomes better once the message is learned. Do you understand what must be done?" I asked, still holding his hand.

"Yes," Jester replied, with a sigh of relief.

"Now tell us what happened," I command.

Jester looked around at all of us and began to tell us about last night. "Sydney had stepped away to talk with a friend. In the crowd, I saw a familiar face. It was my mother. She loved me unconditionally but I would take advantage of her at every turn. Our eyes connected and she knew it was me. My mom was a heavy set Italian woman from Napoli. She was about five feet even on a good day and she had lots of spunk. She had lost most of her accent once she moved to the United States but the more excited she got the thicker her accent. My father moved her to Texas before I was born. He died before I ever met him.

"Last night my mother called out to me, 'Anthony!' I looked away as soon as I saw that it was her. But her voice came closer, 'Anthony, it's me, your mom!' I tried to blend in with the crowd but it was too late. 'I knew you would make it here. You found a way to live a clean life,' she said as she reached to touch my shoulder.

I was almost never a nice person to my mother unless I needed something. I was her prized Anthony. When she touched my shoulder, I knew that she knew. She jumped back. This was the first time that I'd ever seen my mother look at me with disappointment. I've lied, cheated, stolen, and killed. My mother always believed in me. She came to visit me in jail and would always have a positive word for me.

"...Last night, I saw the color drain from her face. She told me, 'So, I guess you really are a jester as they say. You are a real joke. How could you possibly be here? This place is not for your kind. When I saw you, I thought you had finally been awakened and seen the truth. I thought you were forgiven but no; you are here conning someone else. Even on this side of life, you think you can fool anyone, don't you? Well, you don't fool me *Jester the Joke*.'"

"I stood there and let her tear me to pieces. She was right. I was a joke. I couldn't think of a time that I was not scheming or strategizing as I called it. I thought about my mother the entire night. Being in the Land of the Promised opened my eyes to what I always thought was a chumps dream. Heaven, I'd think, there is no such place. You take your paradise and you make it what it is. Now I see there is so much more. Oddly enough, I think I felt I was always loved by my mother. So, I kept on doing bad things. Now, I can't bear to lose her love. I have lost the hate inside of me. I will not survive in Necropolis anymore," Jester proclaimed.

"You need to tell Caroline the truth Jester and I will help you make the transition," I said.

Caroline listened to his story but had trouble believing it was that easy to become a citizen of the Land of the Promised. "Jester, what are you doing?"

"Caroline, you need to know the truth," Jester said.

"Cut the crap, Jester. I know you. I know how you are. You and I are friends and we need to get back to the others. You are one of us," Caroline demanded.

"Qurina! I cannot. They will take my life force as soon as they realize I have no more powers. There is no place for the weak in Necropolis. I will find my strength in the love of The Great Source."

"I don't believe you, man! Come on!" Caroline was getting frustrated.

"Qurina you can't go back there. We have been deceiving you this entire time. It was my idea to use you. It's what I always do. They sent me here with you to ensure that you came back. I am the one that made you believe that Sam was in Necropolis. You were never meant to know that world until I showed it to you," he confessed.

"Why are you doing this? I don't understand."

"Caroline, he's telling the truth," I said.

"You put him up to this, didn't you Sam? I told you that I have to go back but you are only concerned about keeping me here. I love you honey but the only way that we can be together is in Necropolis. Jester, you need to come with me now."

"Thorn is going to use you as a weapon to destroy the Land of the Promised!" Jester yelled.

Caroline shook her head trying to figure out Jester's angle. She concluded that he didn't have a good one. He was lost to the cause now. She turned her back to us. Her aura glowed blood purple. The chi wave around her body grew erratic. We were on the boarders of Hinterland and The Land of the Promised. She must have been able to use her powers because we were in some kind of dead zone.

"I will take your life force from you before I let you join them, Jester," she said as she turned back to face us. Her eyes were glowing as well.

Jester took a moment to grasp the enormity of her words. He made the only choice that he felt was right. "...I guess you'll have to finish me off then. I'd rather it was you."

Caroline was shocked to hear his response. She didn't want to do it but it was their way. Marauders do not back down from a challenge. She closed her hands together and pulled them apart. She now had a whip in one hand and a sword in the other. Both were illuminated by her purple glow. In that moment she was no longer Caroline; she was Qurina.

She swung the whip around and made it crack. Next, she lassoed the whip around Jester's throat and pulled him to her. Jester was strong but no match for Qurina without the power of hate to energize him.

"You don't have to do this!" I said.

Unwavering, she pulled the whip a little tighter. He was gasping for air and desperate for some kind of relief. I knew none was forthcoming. She would assimilate him if I didn't act. I knew Qurina was strong but I could never hurt her. My Caroline was in there somewhere.

My aura was aglow now. "Qurina, let him go!" I shouted.

"You stay out of this, Sam. It is our way!"

"It's not our way here," I said. I put my incandescent hands together and form my six-shooters. My goal was only to stun her. I fired two shots. She blocked one with her sword and dodged the other with a simple tuck and roll. All the while she didn't let Jester free of her anaconda-like grip on his neck. I decided to focus on the whip. With one hand I shot multiple shots in her general direction. I maneuvered close enough to Jester to reach the whip. I formed a machete in my free hand and with one downward chop sliced the whip. Jester quickly removed the remnants from around his neck, coughed, and then took a few big gulps of air.

"Please stop this madness. You're not a killer!" Sydney's voice rang out behind me.

Qurina stared at me then her son. She knew I was going to continue to protect Jester. She didn't want Sydney to see her cause any more harm today.

"Have it your way, Jester. If you want to be fooled too then go ahead. I am going home now." She turned and rushed off to Necropolis.

I watched her go. As much as I wanted to call out to her I knew it would do no good. Caroline was out of my life. I hoped it was not for good.

Jester was lying on the ground not far from me. He was finally regaining his breath. Sydney was first to get to him and helped him to his feet.

"Sorry it took me so long to jump in and help. I didn't think she had it in her," I explained.

"Oh believe you me I've seen what she can do. She could've killed me quite easily without my abilities. But she didn't. There is still hope for her."

"It comforts me to know that."

"So, am I ready for the Land of the Promised?" Jester asked.

I extended my hand and placed it on his shoulder. "The Great Source is waiting for his son to come home. The time for foolish games of treachery has passed. Let go of your evil deeds and know the true power of love. You have been forgiven. Now forgive yourself."

Jester's aura burned brightly. He began to weep tears of happiness. Real love coursed through his veins. "It's overwhelming! My spirit is so free. I feel brand new! I can't wait to see my mother so she can finally be proud of me."

With his transformation complete, his aura faded in intensity and eventually dissipated. He looked at me with a grateful smile and padded me on my arm. Jester, Sydney and I made our way back to The Land of the Promised. I was happy for Jester and felt he would be a great asset in devising a plan on how to help awaken Caroline.

❦

Qurina returned to the Main Hub of Necropolis city and proceeded directly to Thorn's house where its owner, along with Raven, were relieved to see her. It was very risky allowing her to leave. They needed to see if the risk paid off. They met in one of Thorn's private rooms. The goal was to find out if there were any weak points in the defenses of the Land of the Promised. Their best strategist was no longer with them but they weren't quite sure as to why. Qurina would have to shed light on that topic.

"Thorn, Raven," Qurina said greeting them in an almost formal manner.

"The daughter has returned to the home from wince she was born," Thorn proclaimed.

"And where is Jester?" Raven asked, acknowledging the elephant in the room.

Qurina looked straight ahead like a soldier at attention ready to explain why a comrade had gone A.W.O.L. "Tried to stop him but he wouldn't listen. I even threatened to kill him and he didn't flinch. He is with them now. Jester has turned his back on us."

"That doesn't make sense. What was in it for him to trade on us?" Raven asked.

"His mother got to him. She was there and she made him feel ashamed of who he was. Everything there is flawless. Maybe a little too perfect. They tried to trick me by showing me all of these textbook views and sunsets. That stuff isn't real. Nothing is that perfect."

"Yes I agree with you, Qurina, there is no struggle or pain there and that isn't a life that I have ever known," Raven said.

Thorn began speaking in an almost philosophical tone. "My friends, the Land of the Promised is truly a place of wonder. It is, in fact, real and as 'flawless' as you say it is. I have been there. My eyes have been opened but how does one live life without pain, strife, or struggles? How can anyone grow as a person without feeling all that the Great Source has created? He allowed me to leave the safe haven of the Land of the Promised to experience hurt and suffering. From that, I learned about anguish and determination. Many other experiences allowed me to harness the powers of hatred just as they helped you find your powers of love, Qurina. I want it all. The Protectors sentenced me to an eternity in this hell. I found a way out. We were forbidden to go past the boundaries of Hinterland. Now one of us has performed this feat and returned. Qurina, you are the key to our victory over the Protectors. They have terrorized our people for too long. We have been resilient and managed to keep fighting against great odds. Now it is our turn to make them suffer."

"How am I the key?" Qurina asked, curiously.

"You have a man on the inside," Raven announced.

"No, I told you that we lost Jester. He is on their side now."

"That may be true, but he is not the inside man that I was referring to… Sam will help us penetrate the city walls," Raven said.

"Sam? He would never let us in. He is too loyal to the Protectors."

"But he is more loyal to you," Thorn interjected.

"…I don't know guys. I'm not sure it will work. I don't know if I want to do that. Sam is a good man and…"

"Yes, a good man that has chosen the wrong side, Qurina. What about the souls here that have suffered because of the Protectors? Should we just forget that any of that happened?" Thorn asked.

"I really don't know about this. Deceiving my husband is not something that I'm going to do. I love the people of Necropolis. They are suffering because they can only see hate. I have shown some of them how to work together to get what they want. This is the work that I'll focus on. You will need to find another way," Qurina said defiantly.

Thorn scowled as he responded, "Let me tell you something,

Qurina. I made you. They are not your followers. They follow me. They will follow me over a cliff if I tell them to. You are here because it is my will. I have gone through too much for too long to be told by a love wielding whore what will happen. If you don't help me, I will destroy all of these people. Do you think they were good on Earth? No, they were the worst of the worst. The people here are mass murderers, suicide bombers, and evil dictators like me. Do you think they deserve to be happy? If I were the Great Source, I would have assimilated them long ago. But he is not me. We are the north and south poles. His way is to passively put these people in a place where no one can see them. He doesn't want to deal with the problem."

Qurina saw Thorn's true colors for the first time. "You won't hurt any of them!" she shouted.

"Oh really? Who's going to stop me?"

Qurina's eyes narrowed as her face morphed into a fierce look of determination. Her hands were clenched tightly into two fists. Her aura started to glow around her body. Her blood purple eyes stared Thorn down when she said, through gritted teeth, "I will!"

Thorn began to laugh in an amused, rolling chuckle. "You think so?…Raven."

Thorn gestured towards the door, which Raven swiftly approached and opened. Raven signaled and two guards entered the room. They were not alone. They had two captives with them. It was the two men that witnessed her bringing the rabbit back to life. They'd had dinner with us later that evening as she'd requested.

"What are they doing here?" she cried.

"They are our guests just like the other night at your place," Thorn replied.

"Why are you doing this?"

"You need to know what this world is. We are a savage bunch. The weak have no place here. They showed their weakness as soon as you showed them kindness. They can't fight for me because you reminded them of compassion. They can't defend themselves because of you. Look at them. They are sniveling idiots," Thorn growled.

The two men were on their knees huddled together, cowering up at Thorn.

"This one was once known as the DC terror for killing over twenty people in Washington DC. His partner over here was a lawyer that cheated, stole, and killed in order to win and make more money. How does that make you feel? Do you think they are worth protecting?" Thorn asked.

Qurina looked at them with sadness in her heart. She had too much love in her core to look at them as murderers. She saw helpless beings that needed forgiveness and empathy. She knew that the men had committed great sins but in her heart, she had too. She knew it was not her place to judge but it was in her place to protect the people she loved. Sydney, Susan, and I were all safe in the Land of the Promised. The people of Necropolis were not so lucky. *Only the Strong Belong* was their slogan. Qurina had an issue with that. She looked back at Thorn and answered, "Yes, they are worth protecting."

"I'm glad to hear you say that," Thorn said with a false smile. "One of them will have their journey ended today to serve as an example for you. I'll let you choose since they are 'your' people.

"Come on Thorn," Qurina pleaded.

"Raven, you choose," Thorn offered.

"That one."

"Wait!" Qurina shouted.

She was too late. Thorn placed his hand on the man Raven had pointed to and sent thousands of volts of electricity through his body. The man dropped to the ground and his body released a bright light. It was his soul. It flashed so brightly that the gloomy room lit up as though it were day. In an instant, the light was gone.

"Thorn! I will..." Qurina shouted.

"Ha, ha, ha. You don't want me to end him too?" Thorn interrupted.

Qurina was at a loss for words. She didn't want to see the other man perish. Her love was her weakness. She didn't want to betray me or any of her family. She was beginning to see what Thorn was and why I tried so hard to get her to stay with me. She also knew that she made the right decision to come back. Qurina had helped so many souls. There were thousands of vulnerable and helpless people that she would have left behind.

"I'll do it. I will find a way into the Land of the Promised," she said.

"I thought you'd see it my way."

"How do you want me to do it?" she asked.

Chapter 21

A New Quest

BACK IN THE Land of the Promised we were welcoming our newest recruit to the Protectors.

"I'm proud of you son," I said.

"Thanks, dad. I will make you proud."

"Don't do it for me, do it in service of the Great Source and all of the souls who wouldn't be here if it wasn't for a group like ours."

"I wish mom was here to share in this occasion," Sydney said.

"Agreed. I miss her a lot. She has been gone for two years now. There has to be a way for us to get her back," I said.

"Only the Great source can save her now," said Sydney.

I pause for a moment and thought about what my son had just said. The Great Source was the answer. I'd need to meet him in order to get her back. "I think you're right. I'm going to go see Liam," I said, feeling hope for the first time in months.

I found Liam in his backyard sitting on a black cast iron bench. He was gazing down into his coy fish pond, tossing food into the water and watching as his shiny orange fish scrambled for a bite. I walked towards him from his backside.

"Sam, is that you?" he asked without turning around.

"Yes, it is."

He stood up, walked around the bench, and gave me a big bear hug. It had been over two years since I last saw him or Chandra. Between saving souls in Hinterland and trying to find ways to get Caroline back, the days had flown by. Maybe some of it was the guilt I felt for convincing them to go to Necropolis in the first place.

"You look great!" I said, noticing that he was completely healed from the trip to Necropolis.

"Yes, I do feel much better. That place took a lot out of me. It is not a place that I'd want to go back to anytime soon."

"I can't blame you," I said. "Look, I've been meaning to apologize for getting you into this mess and…"

"Nonsense Sam. I knew what I was getting into, I helped build the dang place. I just got caught in the wrong place at the wrong time. We should have never split up. That was the mistake. If anything it was a tactical error and you weren't the one leading the mission."

"Either way, I feel bad especially after you all warned me. Tate was just helping out a friend."

"That's all water under the bridge now. Come have a seat and let's talk," he said, as he guided me over to the bench. Once we were seated he said, "So I heard you were able to convert one of Thorn's top men."

"Yes, but we couldn't sway Caroline."

"We both know how hard it is to change a mind that is clouded, which is why we try to save them when they are new to this world. In Hinterland it is still possible to tap into some of the good memories because they are still fresh. In Necropolis they are focused on the negatives making it harder to forgive. I liken it to PTSD, they have been at war in their minds for so long, that is all they see," Liam explained.

"I had to try."

"Yes, you did. You've already tried but… I am sensing that you are going to try again."

He was able to see right through me. He knew that I couldn't let this go. I was much stronger with my wife by my side. She made me happier than I could ever feel alone. I had to keep trying to convince her that I loved her and she could find happiness with me.

"I don't know Liam, but this is not the way things are supposed to be."

"How do you know? The Great Source works in ways that we don't always fully understand. His most confusing way is love. It makes us happy and can make us sad. Love fills your empty heart but it also makes it easily broken. We feel the loss of a loved one so deeply but we also use that same love and heal ourselves. How can that even be explained, Sam?"

"I don't know. But what you just said is the reason that I cannot stop trying to win her back. I need to meet with the Great Source. Can you help me?" I asked.

"Sam, please reconsider. It doesn't work that way. You don't just go see The Great Source. There are rules about this sort of thing."

"What do you mean, rules?"

"The Great Source is the reason that the universe is the universe. We are just a small portion of the cosmos. You are asking to see Ekon face to face. The body cannot stand the sight of the Source that creates life and existence. Even you, with your pure love flowing through you, will likely be assimilated if you meet him. It is said that the soul will not be able to contain itself. Like a magnet to metal, the soul will be attracted to the power of The Great Source."

"What do you mean, 'it is said'? You mean to tell me no one has actually seen the Great Source?" I asked, a little angry and confused.

"No, Sam. I mean the only people that have seen the Great Source face to face have not come back to tell the tale. I have been close to the Source and I have had conversations with the source and even that overwhelmed my soul. It was the scariest and most joy-filled moment of my existence. I wanted to be closer to him but my work here was not done. I can tell you that if it is ever done, I will be honored to be part of him."

"Ok, so is it a good thing or bad thing to be assimilated to the Great Source?" I asked, feeling the questions racing through my mind.

"Both. To assimilate with the Source against your will means that you had no choice and you were not fulfilled. He wants us to choose him in each level of our Journey. Would you want to eat a fruit that was not ripe? ...No, because it will be sour or bitter, hard, and dry. There is a perfect time to enjoy a fruit. It is just soft enough, sweet enough, and is full of juice. It is a marvelous taste. The Great Source wants you to be the perfect version of yourself before you join him."

"What do I need to do? I can't let her rot in that place."

"It is her choice, Sam. She wants to be there for her own reasons. I have never seen anyone, and I mean anyone besides Castro Thorn, who is Hate himself, see the Land of the Promised and leave. Even her companion Jester was unable to leave and he was one of their most deceptive and most conniving. Sam, the Source is the only way at this point but it will mean the end of your existence. You will be the bitter fruit. That is not what you want. Trust me Sam, I felt your longing when I saw you today. I didn't want to be the bearer of this news."

I was silent, listening to his words. It was tough to hear that she was the same as Castro Thorn. My Caroline was better than Thorn. I felt the love flowing through her. We have shared dreams together. I knew her. Letting things be what they were was not the choice that I wanted to make. Choice is a fluid thing. One could make the same choice multiple times and have different outcomes in different situations. On the other hand, one could choose the same thing over and over and get the same result each time. If one chooses the same thing time after time and expects a different result one is considered insane. Navigating through the choices has a great deal to do with time, space, and opportunity. I had all of the time in the universe but how long could I go on without Caroline? For all of time, she has been by my side and in my thoughts and prayers. She has been the source of my powers which allow me to help and rescue hundreds of souls each day without her being one of them. The space between us was unbearable for me. I may as well have been on a different planet because we were unable to be together in the afterlife. My choice was clear. What was less clear, however, would be Ekon's reason for allowing me to go back to the forsaken city.

With my mind made up, I looked at Liam and said, "I choose to see The Great Source face to face."

Liam nodded his head slowly. Begrudgingly he replied, "If that is your choice I will help you."

Liam took me down a cement path along the back side of his property. It led to a forest thick with trees. In some areas, the trees were so numerous a light was needed to see the way forward. The cement gave way to a dirt road and we continued following its winding curves. We arrived at a clearing and saw a building that had no business being in the middle of a forest, but here anything was possible.

The building was dome-shaped at the top, almost like an igloo. It was small, only about twelve feet high and fifteen by fifteen feet in width. The outer walls were made of concrete and painted white. The white walls had green moss growing up from the ground to just about three feet. The door to the building had a low clearance, which made me feel like I had to duck as I walked through the threshold.

Inside was a stand that sat under a bright light. At first, I thought it was a light that was created by someone but I began to realize that the light was a natural one, more like the light from the sun. I could not make out the walls because of the brightness. The stand that sat in the middle of the room was made of silver. The base of the stand was wide and stemmed upward like a wine glass. The stand extended up to just above my waistline. On the top stood a crystal that had the shape of a marque diamond. The crystal was being held up by a gold sculpted hand.

"Your only hope for survival is to power up," Liam said, resigned to the fact that I was going to do this with or without him. Like a parent that lets their teenager drink underage at home, he didn't like it but… wanted to be there to make sure that I would survive.

"Okay! How will that help?"

"I don't know but it seems like something you should do," he replied.

"Thanks," I said sarcastically.

I focused on some of my happiest memories with Caroline. And my aura started to shine as bright as the natural light in the room. I reached for the crystal and slowly placed both of my hands on it. The gold hand startled me when it grabbed my wrists. I heard a loud bang and Liam was knocked to the floor. I disappeared into the light.

Chapter 22

Mas

M Y EYES WERE open but there was only darkness around me. I must have been in some type of black hole because my aura was not able to shine. Wherever I was felt like space without stars. I had a floating sensation like my body was weightless.

I drifted in this vacuum until I noticed a faint speck of light in the distance. I veered my body in that direction. As I moved closer to the light it got bigger. I could see my hands again. The light was like a tractor beam. I felt myself being pulled into it. The closer I got to the light the faster it pulled me. I was so close to the light now that I was fully engulfed by it. All at once I hit something hard and unforgiving. It turned out that I was not being pulled by a tractor beam. It was gravity. I'd fallen to the ground on a hard rock slab.

It took me a moment to get acclimated to my surroundings. I looked around and saw that I was near the edge of a cliff. Behind me was a downward sloping grassy hill with rocky terrane. At the bottom of the hill was more of the same type of land which led to a wired fence. There were cows on that side of the fence which made me believe that it was a farm. The sky above was blue, the sun was shining brightly, and birds were soaring overhead.

I walked closer to the edge and carefully leaned over and saw that there was nothing holding up the ground I was standing on. It was floating. When I looked down the cliff I saw the night sky. The stars and the moon were under me. "What is this place?" I asked myself.

"Hey, over here!" a voice in the distance called. The voice sounded like a girl in her late teens.

I turn to see who was calling me but I didn't see anyone.

"Down here. At the bottom of the cliff!" the voice said again.

The hill was steep enough for me not to be able to see anyone but it also seemed to be the only way down so I decided to follow the voice. My footing was not firm as I made my descent to the bottom of the cliff. I looked around to find the voice but no one was in sight.

"Hello!" I called out to nothing.

"Over here, on the other side of that fence. But don't touch the wire, it's loaded with electricity and it's enough to kill you," the voice said.

"But I'm already dead," I said under my breath. I was frustrated that I still couldn't see the person talking to me. The voice seemed close enough for me to at least see them. Taking heed to what I was recently told, I got a running start and leaped over the fence. It was only waist high and took little effort. When I landed, I slipped on the grass and some cow manure and ended up flat on my back. I took a deep breath then exhaled as I stood back up from the fall. Fortunately the manure only managed to soil my shoes. As I looked around to see where the voice might be, I dragged my shoes against the grass to wipe off the manure. I still only saw cows grazing in the fenced in pasture.

"Over here. I'm right here. Don't you see me?" the voice said.

"No, I'm sorry, I don't. I only see cows."

"Yes well duh. I am a cow," the voice said.

"Oh," I said, not expecting to be talking to a cow. I walked over to a group of cows and began to search to see which one was talking to me. "Which one are you?"

"I'm the cute one with the black spots and the white coat."

"That helps," I responded, sarcastically.

I felt a nudge to my back. "Right here," the voice said.

Startled, I stepped away from the nudge and turned around to face whoever had just touched me.

"It took you long enough to find me," the cow said.

"I didn't realize I was looking for a cow. Are you... The Great Source?"

"Oh no Mas, I am Savanah the gatekeeper. I was told that you would come."

"Wait, you knew I was coming? You're the gatekeeper?"

"Well, yes Mas, I am, and you could look a little less surprised. You'd think you'd have seen a gatekeeping cow before. After all, we cows have been gatekeepers for all of eternity. There are some cultures that worship us on Earth you know," Savanah said, sounding somewhat offended at the limits of my knowledge on the lineage of cows.

"I didn't mean anything by that. It has been a befuddling trip so far and I must have missed my lessons on the importance of cows here. Can I ask why you are calling me Mas?"

"Why yes Mas, isn't that your name?"

"Well no. I'm Sam."

"Oh yes, that is right. I transpose names sometimes when I read. Sorry about that Mas... I mean Sam."

"It's okay."

"So, Sssaam, what brings you here?"

"I want to talk with the Great Source. My wife is in trouble."

"Oh, no. I don't think it's a good idea," Savanah said.

"Everyone keeps telling me that. The problem is, it's the only idea that will work. I tried doing it on my own."

"Yeah but maybe you should try harder Mas, I mean Sam."

"Savanah, I need to see him no matter the risk to myself. My wife is in danger and Castro Thorn is going to kill her or use her or I don't know what he will do but… I can't let him do it."

"You will never make it out. I've not seen anyone make it out of there except for Castro Thorn. It is said that he was pure hate and his soul never had a desire to assimilate."

"He is pure hate but my heart is full of pure love. Please help me Gate Keeper Savanah. I need to see him."

"Only the chosen one can enter and leave. I have heard of your abilities Mas but not of your victories. Show me that you are the chosen one." She lowered her head almost bowing to me.

My hands started to glow pure light. I touched her head with my hands and she was able to feel my aura energy. She saw flashes of me in Necropolis fighting and freeing souls. She saw me breaking the dampener cuffs. Finally, she saw me using my powers on Earth. It was all in slow motion as I rushed to the car to save Caroline. She saw my sacrifice in the name of love. Savanah's heart began to feel full and joyous. My hands stopped glowing. I slowly pulled away and looked at Savanah to gauge what she planned to do next.

"I don't know if you are the chosen one but you are very powerful."

A door designed like one could find on a house in the suburbs appeared out of nowhere. It was black with a red handle. A very bright light shined through the cracks of the doorway.

"The Great Source is through that door," she said.

I took a deep breath before walking forward. My heart beat faster and faster.

"Calm yourself, Sam," I said to myself. I thought of Caroline and my aura charged to full power. My eyes illuminated bright white. Reaching out for the door, I felt a spark of electricity shoot off the handle. I jumped back and paused for a beat. One more deep breath and I grab the handle. Volts of electricity surge through my body. I gave a yell in defiance to the pain that I felt. I pushed the handle down and the pain stopped.

Each time I tell the story, I feel like I am there again. I'm breathing hard and need a second to get my bearings. I looked back for Savanah. She and the other cows were gone.

"I hope you make it back." I heard her voice say faintly.

I opened the door slowly and walked through it. Once I was inside the threshold of the door, it slammed shut and disappeared. I was no longer in the pasture of grass. I heard water crashing against the shore. It smelled like salt and seawater. I was in some place that was tropical. It was full of colors. The sun was shining and the temperature felt perfect enough to swim. There was a breeze that flowed in both directions. My normal protector gear had changed to a white t-shirt and linen shorts. My shoes were now leather sandals.

All around me were palm trees and various types of flowers. It was a rainbow of colors, from whites and pinks to greens and yellows. The grass was green with soft plush blades. I could walk on it barefoot if I wanted to. I saw a never-ending ocean that met up with a sandy beach. There were two palm trees with a white hemp woven hammock strung between them. A man appeared to be in it gently swaying in the breeze.

Difficult to tell his height, especially with him lying down, but he looked to be over six feet and had a muscular silhouette. His shirt buttoned down the front and had short sleeves. His skin was dark tan or dark brown. The man wore a straw brimmed hat which covered his face.

He seemed to be sleeping. It would probably be rude to wake him especially if he was The Great Source. I walked a little closer for a better look at him. The man began to rustle around which caused the hammock to sway from side to side. He looked so relaxed in that hammock. I found myself wanting to lie down next to him and fall asleep just for a little while. The trip was long and arduous.

Although the man was a stranger, I felt the urge to call him brother and encourage him to move over to allow me some space to sleep. I was nearly there when I heard a voice that sounded like mine. It was the man in the hammock.

"Is it you, dad? I've been waiting for you," said the man in the hammock, his back now turned to me.

It startled me, to say the least, but I did feel compelled to answer him. "No, it's me… Sam… Are you The Great Source?"

The man turns to face me. As he shifted the hat fell from his face and I could see he was me. My brain was very muddled by this.

"The Great Source, me? No, are you?" The man in the hammock said.

"No, like I said. I'm Sam."

"That's strange because you look like me and we have the same name."

"How long have you been here?" I asked.

"Hard to tell. All I remember is talking to the cow outside and then coming in here for something and wanting to just sleep… What was it that I wanted?" The man asked.

"Well, I am here to find The Great Source," I said.

"Oh! Yes! The Great Source! Me too! Have you seen him? I need to talk to him about some…thing… I can't remember. Do you remember Sam?" asked the Sam in the hammock.

I take a deep breath still unsure as to what is happening but hoped this version of me would shed some light on the topic.

"About Caroline, she is in Necropolis and I need to help her find her way to The Land of the Promised."

"Oh, Yes! That's right! But first, you should sit and relax here with me. We can find what's it? Later." The other Sam said as he began to lie back down.

"No Sam, you need to get up! We can't stay here. We have to go." I plead.

"You go ahead, I'll catch up," he said, sleepily.

"No, come with me!" I said as I grab him to give him a shake. As I touch him, a vision appeared to me. I saw myself entering a tropical place and seeing the hammock. I lied down in it and fell asleep. I was asleep for three days. I'd been here for three days. "How is this possible?" I asked myself.

Was I being assimilated and didn't know it? Was my soul so at peace that staying here felt like a viable option? Somehow, something deep inside of me woke up enough. I blinked my eyes and my mind is back in the present. The vision had left me. The man in the hammock had turned into ash and blew away with the breeze. I realized that the forces of The Great Source were strong and my spirit truly wanted to be where I was. But, I had Caroline to think about. I didn't know what to do or how to gain an audience with the Great Source. I was alone in this place and unsure how to get out. I walked to the beach and stood in the wet sand where the waves meet land. I did the only thing I could think of to do. I prayed.

"Great Source, Creator of all things, Director of the Universe, and The One that is Love, please hear my cry, forgive me for my sins, and answer my prayers. I know that you have others that you must help. I ask that you do not pass me by. You are the source of my strength. The light that shines in me, on me, around me, and through me. I ask that you, the source of love that flows through my body, grant me the abilities and wisdom enough to be worthy of my request."

In that moment, I felt the ground shake and saw the waters trouble. The wind howled and the breeze grew stronger. The leaves of the palm trees danced back and forth to the beat of the rumbling ground. The sun in the sky seemed to be getting closer and brighter. I felt an intense heat followed by a cooling. The sensation of hot and cold quickened my blood. I could feel all of myself. The sun compelled me to come to it. But the thought of Caroline kept me steadfast in my spot on the beach.

The sun descended down to me. As it got closer it took the form of a man while still shining. My body began to shake. I was having a seizure. I fell to the ground and was unable to control myself. My mind, however, was stuck on Caroline. She had called me stubborn many times and this time, it was a good thing I was.

The sun walked over to me and touched my body. All at once, I could take a deep breath and my tremoring stopped. I lied there for a moment coughing and gathering myself. My breathing still labored, I looked over to the man that was the sun. He was no longer shining. The scene around me was still again. The man kneeled down next to me and placed his hand on my shoulder.

"Sam," he said in a silky smooth calming baritone voice. His eyes were a deep cold blue. They reminded me of the cool winter with freshly fallen snow on the ground. He smelled like freshly cooked chocolate chip cookies. He was very tall and had perfectly sculpted muscles. His hands were large and soft. His touch was like a mother soothing her teething baby. His skin was sun-kissed dark brown. He wore a heavenly white robe and was barefoot. He had a bald head and a full black beard with hints of white. His accent had a British tone to it. He spoke proper Queen's English.

"Sam. It is me. I am who you are looking for."

"The Great Source? It is you," I proclaim.

"Yes, but it might be easier to just call me Ekon for now."

I sat up and he helped me to my feet. He gave me a big hug. I didn't want to let go.

"Careful, Sam, that's a tight grip you have there," he said with a chuckle.

"I am so happy to see you. There is so much I want to say but…"

"Easy there Sam, we have time. Ask me and I will answer you in the best way that you could understand."

I took a deep breath and ask the first thing that came to my mind. "Why is a cow your gatekeeper?"

"Funny, that is the first question most ask me. Cows are a very sacred animal in some countries on Earth. They represent nurturing and motherhood. They are one of the noblest creatures in creation."

"Really, in what way?" I asked.

"Since the early days of man, cows have been the sacrifice men have made to honor me. Cows go to Earth understanding that they will be slaughtered in my name or eaten for the nurturing of entire civilizations. Even knowing this, they go and endure such painful conditions. I honor their generous spirit by giving them a noble place after they have made their sacrifice for the good of my people."

"I guess I never really thought about that."

"And why would you? Let's take a walk," Ekon said.

We begin to walk the edge of the beach and talked about many things. He told me that Necropolis was once part of The Land of the

Promised. That is, until he had to punish Castro Thorn and others like him. He also told me about the need for protectors and how he wanted all of his creations to live in peace in one great land.

"You are the key, Sam."

I nodded my head and said nothing else on the subject.

"Where did you come from?" I asked

"I'm from nothing," Ekon said.

"Nothing?"

"Yes, nothing is something. You first have to change how you think about the concept of nothing. There is no such thing as nothing. You give it a name of nothing but it is something. The space between you and I is something but you would call that nothing. Humans once thought the atom was the smallest thing until they discovered protons but even protons are made of something and that is made of something else and so on. I never started and I will never stop. I just am. Think of this all as a circle, it never starts it never stops. Energy is constant and takes on new forms as we progress through time," Ekon explained.

"I get it, strangely," I said, only mostly grasping the concept. "Why am I able to be in your presence? Everyone said that we never return once we are here."

"You are stronger than almost all of them. The powers of love rush through your body unlike anyone else. I am sending a direct current between us and grounding you in this place. When you touched the doorknob and survived it, we connected."

"So, I'm like a lamp and you are the electric socket?" I asked.

"Well sure that is close. But more like a set of jumper cables or an alternating current. We are the same thing which is love. You are as pure as it gets for your form. You don't remember this but you are already assimilated to me. Now you have to complete your purpose. I created you and Caroline for the same thing. To save my people. Before you two, no Protector was powerful enough to go back to Necropolis once the gates were locked."

"But she was tricked into going there. I must get her back."

"Yes, I know but you came to see me because you feel that you failed the last time. You did not fail. Caroline is following her own path. I did not intend for it to happen the way it did, but she is finding her way. You should not go there." Ekon stated.

"Yes, but we are a team. We have your pure love inside us and she thinks that the Marauders are the good guys. I need to make her see. You must let me go back to her."

"You are still looking at the world as black and white. There are so many colors built into the rainbow and incidentally, black and white are not part of it. Some of my children have been misguided and committed atrocities on Earth and here. What makes Tate ending Arawn's journey 'just' and Thorn's deeds any different? The answer is nothing. Tate was protecting my people. Thorn's intentions are noble in his own eyes. He thinks that we are wrong for not wanting strife, greed, or hate in our city. He wants me to allow that. In his mind, he is the just party. He will stop at nothing."

"Why don't you just stop him, Ekon? Can't you just go to Necropolis and assimilate him?" I asked.

"The same reason that no one returns from a visit with me. My presence will assimilate everyone before they were ready. That is not what I want. Which is another reason that I created you and your wife." Ekon explained.

"When the time comes I need to be there to awaken Caroline. I need your help to get back there."

"You do not have my permission to go back to Necropolis until Caroline invites you. Be patient Sam. All will be restored in time. Don't be surprised if you see her sooner than you think."

"It has been so long since I've seen her. I'm afraid the longer I wait the harder it will be to get her back. Will it be too late?" I asked.

"She is not lost. This is eternity so it will not be too late. Just be ready when she calls. She will be needing your help along with the Protectors. It is time for you to go now. I can feel your ability to absorb my love diminishing. Go through that door, Sam."

A doorway appeared and the door opened. It was my way back to

The Land of the Promised. I started towards the door but asked one more question: "Ekon, will the Colts win the Super Bowl ever again?"

He smiled and said, "Not until long after Tom Brady and Aaron Rogers retire."

I walked through the door and it closed behind me. It was dark again and I started to float. I felt gravity pulling me down. I brace for impact but instead, I slowed down just before hitting the ground. I landed softly on my feet. I was near the building in the woods and Liam was standing there with a surprised look on his face.

"What?" I asked.

"How did you get here so fast?" Liam asked.

"Not sure what you mean."

"You left seconds ago and I just walked out the door," he said.

"I've been gone for days. I talked to The Great Source and he told me that I would see Caroline soon."

"Well, they say that time with The Great Source isn't the same as we can comprehend. Tell me all about it," Liam said.

Chapter 23
Protecting in the Night Shift

ONE STARRY NIGHT Tate and I were patrolling the perimeters of The Land of the Promised and Hinterland when a mysteriously familiar purple light gleamed in the distance. It moved with stealthy precision. I saw it flash in and out of buildings and alleyways.

"Tate," I called in a stage whispering voice. "Look down there... do you see it?"

"Yeah," he answered as he ducked behind a large boulder and looked through night vision binoculars.

"That's Caroline, I think."

"How do you know?"

"I've never seen a glow like hers before."

"Me either. It's beautiful," Tate said.

"Watch it bub," I said jokingly.

"What? I was talking about her glow."

"Shh, did you see where she went?"

"No, you think we should go check it out?" asked Tate.

"Yeah, let's go. I'm right behind you."

We moved through Hinterland like commandos looking for Caroline. I could tell that she had been training since the last time I saw her. She was moving very quickly which made it hard to pick up her tracks. I knew we were close because I felt her energy aura. I also felt my energy increasing when I got closer to her. Most of me was excited to see her because it had been six months since Ekon had told me to wait for her invite. At one point I started to wonder if she would ever show her face to me again.

"There she is," Tate whispered.

We were behind Caroline and could see her peeking her head around the side of a hut. It was hard to forget the last time I'd seen her she was trying to kill Jester. The problem was, I really missed my wife. There was no risk that I wouldn't take to talk to her again.

"What do you want to do, Sam?"

We were ducked behind a building in a darkened area as we watched Caroline. At present we were in a solid position but approaching Caroline stealthily would be a challenge. There was an unpaved dirt alleyway which ran between two huts between us and her, then there was a clearing which would make it hard to sneak up on her.

"What do you think she is looking at?" I asked Tate.

"I don't know, could be anything."

And he was right. I needed to get closer. By charging up my aura, she would see my light. I could move quickly but not as fast as I'd need to for her not to see me. Before I could think of a way to get her attention, Tate had tossed a rock near her.

She quickly turned around and saw us standing in the darkness. Caroline darted off into the night. Her purple glow was just a blur.

"Caroline, wait!" I shouted. She did not break stride. "Dang it, Tate!"

"Sorry brother. I was trying to help."

"I know," I said with a sigh. That was my best shot to talk to her in two and a half years. I had to come up with a better plan if I had another chance. *Be patient* I reminded myself. My hope was that I'd get another chance soon.

My hope was answered as I spotted her again the very next night. Tate and I had just rescued ten souls from the clutches of the Marauders.

"The Great Source wants you to be whole again. Forgive yourself, for your sins are no longer your burdens. You will be judged only by your good deeds from this day forth. Choose the Source from where you came and reap the benefits of his greatness and love." I said as they were awakened.

I saw her from the corner of my eye. Caroline saw me freeing those people with Ekon's power flowing through me. I had Tate continue transitioning them to The Land of the Promised and I managed to slip away undetected as they all began to glow a bright light. Caroline saw them ascend to the great city. By the time she noticed that I had slipped away, I'd already doubled back and had her cornered. This time I was not concerned with her seeing my bright light. She knew that I could keep up with her had she tried to escape.

"Caroline," I said, softly. We stood in a dark alley close to the edge of the forest that lined the eastern border of Hinterland. There was little light except for the stars in the night sky and me.

"What are you doing here?" I asked.

"Why do you care, Sam? And it's Qurina, not Caroline," she said in a stubborn tone.

"Please... I don't want to fight... I... I miss you."

"Listen Sam, I have a lot to deal with right now. There are so many people depending on me. I don't have time to frolic with you in The Land of the Promised."

"I know. I just want to help."

"Trust me, you can't help me the way I would need for you to."

"What do you mean? I'd do anything for you whether you were Qurina or Caroline. Just name it."

"Helping me will be like helping Thorn. You don't need to get mixed up with that. He's my problem."

"But we are supposed to be a team. You know me. You know that I would do anything to help you. I'm sure that I can find a way to help you and not help Thorn."

"Sam, you really are the nicest, most caring, and loving person I know. Thorn wants me to do something that you would never forgive me for. I could never forgive myself for it either. But if I don't do it. He will have all of my people assimilated."

"What is it? I have been blessed with the understanding that comes with forgiveness. There is nothing you could do that would change who we are. We can figure things out together. We can free your people. I had awakened several of them when I was in Necropolis," I said.

"Not all of them want to be in The Land of the Promised. What about them?"

"What about them Qurina? I'm not getting it. They are killers and thieves. Why are they so important to you?"

"You come here preaching to me about forgiveness but all I hear from you is what they did on Earth. They are here now and all I want for them is to live without persecution. I meet them where they are. Most of them are so far gone, they have to remember what compassion is before they can think about forgiveness. I didn't know that by re-teaching them about kindness and love, they would become weaker. Now I have to protect them myself," she said urging me to understand.

I listened to her words and let them sink in. For the first time I understood her purpose for being there. They were her people. My wife was their protector. She was their warrior. She was not a damsel in distress waiting for me in the castle. Qurina was the general leading the charge of change. Ekon told me but it didn't sink in. She was serving her purpose which was to free the damned and the lost.

"I understand now, Qurina, and I want to help. What can I do?"

"Thorn wants me to find a way into The Land of the Promised. He wants to corrupt your city and anyone living in it. I need you to show me how to open the gates of the city."

"There is no way to open the gates of the city unless you have forgiven yourself and have been awakened. You wouldn't be able to do it without that."

"I don't think I can do that. They would know right away that I have changed."

"From the sound of things, you don't have a choice. Your people need you. If you awaken, you will be stronger than you are now. As strong as me possibly. We will make a plan together. You can explain that you had to make the change in order to open the gates."

"I don't know, Sam."

"I will be trusting you and you will be trusting me. It'll be just like old times," I said with a smile. "Do you think you could forgive yourself? Will you accept that The Great Source wants you to be with him?"

"I... I can't Sam. I just can't. I'm not there yet. I don't sleep. I don't think I need to forgive myself. I deserve to be in Necropolis."

"That's not true, Qurina. I know it. You have done so many good deeds on Earth and here. I mean, who fights for murderers? Your work is your proof. This is what Ekon wants from you. You deserve to be free. Let me help you."

I began to glow. "I'll show you." We linked hands. We immediately felt our love returning from what felt like so long ago. I felt her love for the people of Necropolis and she saw the depths of my love for her. I sensed her inability to forgive herself. So, I allowed her to see my visit with Ekon. She started to feel the intensity of his love. Slowly I could tell that she was giving over to The Great Source.

"I can forgive myself now," she cried.

"I know. I feel it. Your powers are great and it is time for you to be awakened from your slumber. Your work has just begun. Ekon wants you to fulfill your promise to his children. Like the bird to the sky, you belong to him. Ekon has chosen you as the warrior of Necropolis. Now, accept The Great Source and let your mind be free. See this world for what it is and make it into what it can be."

Qurina's eyes glowed blue. Her aura changed to the same color. She screamed as she looked to the sky. With her mouth wide open, a beam of light energy rushed out as high as the clouds. The light could be seen in all three cities.

"I feel it, Sam. I'm so strong. I sense the world around me. It's like I was blind and now I'm not. The weight on my shoulders is gone. I can see clearly what we must do to help the people in Necropolis."

"What's your plan?" I asked.

"Well, first we will need to get the Protectors on board."

Caroline agreed to go back to the Land of the Promised with me. Travel was much easier now that Caroline was awakened. It took almost no time to get back. I was nervous about asking them for help again due to the results of our last raid on Necropolis, but the Protectors were our only option. There was no other force in the universe that could stop Thorn but us.

Caroline and I came across Sydney and Chandra, who were patrolling the perimeter of The Lane of the Promised. They agreed to meet us when they were finished with their rounds. We decided to meet at my father's house again. His table seemed to lend itself to strategy sessions. It was also large enough to accommodate the entire group. Tate, Liam, Griffin, and two other Protectors joined this time.

Griffin started the meeting by saying, "First off, I'd like to thank you all for coming out for this meeting of the utmost importance. Thanks Gerald for letting us use your home. Let me introduce the ones you may not know, Qurina. This is Minna. She is responsible for protecting the eastern border of Hinterland. And this here is Warren. He is a rover over all of the Territories."

Minna was a tall blonde woman with medium length hair. She was over six feet tall and weighed about 230 pounds. Her face was pale from spending so much time in Hinterland with little sunlight. She would often say, "There's too much work to be done and too many souls to save to waste time cavorting in the fields of The Land of the Promised." Her voice was deep for a woman and she had a pronounced Russian accent. Her preference was being in the outdoors roughing it so she was perfect for her job. In her life on Earth, she was a forest ranger and wilderness first responder. She protected wildlife and lived with a group of bears for five years.

Warren was a hot-shot pretty boy from Australia on Earth. He was a surfing champion with washboard abs. His skin was copper toned, a product of being half Aboriginal and half Caucasian. The people of Hinterland were very familiar with him due to his constant roving. He was fast on his feet and easy on the eyes. Warren was very effective at saving souls. When he spoke, one could feel his passion and energy. People felt compelled to listen. His hair was shaved on the sides and curly on top. It was brown at the roots and yellow on the tips.

Griffin continued the introductions. "This is Tate. He's a squad leader and trainer. You know Liam. The others are fulfilling their obligations in Hinterland."

After the standard greetings, we decided to get down to business.

"Qurina, what is the situation in Necropolis? Why did you want us all here?" Griffin asked.

"My city is in trouble and I need your help. I am in the process of converting thousands of souls but it takes time."

"That's impossible. They are in Necropolis because they can't be saved," Minna interrupted.

"They are there because of their deeds on Earth. But Ekon wants them here too if they choose it," Qurina explained.

"It's true. Ekon told me himself," I declared.

"You know that you can count on me," said Tate.

"You tellin' me that this guy saw The Great Source and lived? I've seen you work mate and I know you defied odds getting into Necropolis, but seeing Ekon is not possible," Warren contested.

"Let's not get off track here guys," I said.

"The problem is, you want us to believe that these people in Necropolis are worth saving even though Chandra and Liam, two of the most powerful Protectors I know, were tortured and almost assimilated the last time any of you were there," Warren argued.

"Well yes. Look at me and know the truth brother," I said.

"No Sam, you know the truth. We have been keeping the Marauders at bay for years before you ever joined. Now we are changing all of this for her. I say we go back to the way things were. She's on her own," Minna said.

"Listen to the man!" said a gruff voice. It was Griffin.

"Sam is the chosen one. Liam took him to see Ekon. Whether you want to believe Sam or not, you'd better listen to Liam. He is wise and trustworthy. Liam, what do you think?"

He took a moment and looked around the table before speaking.

"...I have been to Necropolis. It's not a place I want to go back to. The Great Source saw it fit to spare my soul and allow me to assimilate in my own time. Sam and Qurina's quest is a noble one, fit for the believers. Those that don't believe in the cause will not survive this battle. I am sorry Sam. I can no longer protect this city. You will not be able to depend on me."

"But Liam..."

While our discussion continued we heard what sounded like a large sack of potatoes drop at my dad's front door. Then a sound that was hard to make out.

"Did you hear that?" Liam asked.

"Yeah," Warren said.

My father and I rushed to the door, which was to the right and down the hallway. He opened it. It was Chandra. She was in bad shape. It was as if she was in a fight and lost or barely escaped. I kneeled down next to her and propped her up on my knee. She was barely conscious.

"What happened Chandra?"

"It... was... a... rap..." she said, faintly.

I looked at my father to see if he understood what she meant. He shrugged his shoulders.

"What do you mean by 'rap'?" I asked.

"It was a... trap," she said, making a better attempt at it.

"What was a trap?" I asked.

"Sam, you better get in here mate!" Warren called.

"Qurina no!" Minna shouted.

I ran back to the room where everyone else was, to find Qurina with her aura at full glow. She seemed agitated and ready for a fight.

"What is going on here honey?" I asked.

Qurina was shaking her head and sarcastically chuckling, as she stood up from her seat. "Sam! I had to do it. It was the only way."

"What did you do Qurina?" I shouted.

"I did what had to be done."

"What... did... you... do...?" I asked again, this time more direct and firm.

"You people never planned to help. You saw it. They weren't going to help and they need to help!" she said.

"You can't be sure. We were still talking and the others may have been willing to support us."

"You don't get it."

"What don't I get Qurina? They are Protectors. It's what they do. It's in them to help."

"And now they will help," Qurina quickly remarked.

"There's no way we are doing anything for you now!" Minna said, defiantly.

"Stay out of this Minna. Please!" I said. "Caroline, if there is any part of you that is still in there tell me what you did!"

"I'm still Caroline, Sam, but I like Qurina better. There's no difference. We both still love you deeply. I hope that you can understand why I had to do it."

"Do what?" I asked.

"I saw Castro's true colors as soon as I got back to Necropolis. I have been planning out a way to save my people. I signaled the Marauders about our meeting. Thorn sent them to attack the Protectors in Hinterland. They knew exactly where everyone was. I've been scouting Hinterland for a little over a year now. I knew who would be where. I knew your weaknesses and that having you here along with Tate increased the chances of a successful abduction. I let you find me. You told me everything I didn't already know. I was finally able to forgive myself because I am doing Ekon's work," she explained.

"But Sydney was one of them. He was on duty tonight. How could you trap your own son?"

"I am doing this for the greater good and Sydney will be fine as long as you all help me. Thorn is planning to use the Protectors in order to stage an attack on the Land of the Promised."

"Sam, we need to figure out a plan to get our people back," Warren said.

"Oh, there will be no getting your people back without my people being saved too. We have to defeat the Marauders once and for all. Necropolis will be my problem afterward," she said.

"Don't you see, you are doing the same thing as Thorn? Ekon wants us to choose, not be forced to choose," I said.

"The Protectors don't realize it but they are supposed to protect all. Not just the ones they think deserve it. I'm helping them honor their purpose. They are meant to free my people the same as in Hinterland. You proved it when you broke the seal of the gates of Necropolis and saved the souls that were ready. I will get the others ready but they will be slaughtered as long as Thorn is in charge."

"I can't believe you," Minna said.

Qurina's eyes changed colors. They turned as yellow as the sun. She was channeling Ekon's light. His will was clear. "Minna, look at me and see that my words are earnest. You are one of the chosen. You are meant to help me free Necropolis from its captors. Free me from this debt that I owe you all. Forgive me because Ekon wants it. He wants all of his people to feel his love and power," Qurina stated, her voice sounding ominous.

Minna, along with Liam, Griffin, Warren, Tate, and myself locked into her gaze. We were all compelled by Ekon's light in Qurina to act on behalf of our friends and the people of Necropolis.

That's the thing about forgiveness. It is one thing to forgive others and another to forgive one's self. People have to first suppress their need to understand why. The "why" may never be enough. The act of forgiving requires that we trust. That is to say, we trust in the power of love and compassion. We trust that forgiveness will bring us the peace needed to continue on fulfilling our purpose in one life or the next. Qurina understood that the needs of the many should outweigh the needs of the Protectors. Our blindness to the old ways could have been our downfall. The Protectors could have been defeated. Warren, Liam, and Minna were all afraid of something. They had to forgive themselves for being fearful of what could happen to them. Selfishness had no place in this group. Qurina forced us to see what we needed to see and understood more than we knew.

Being one with the universe allows us to gain great knowledge in a short period of time but all knowledge is not known until you have reached the highest levels of understanding. Some can see their path and the path of others very clearly. Perhaps Qurina's awakening was what she needed in order to find a way to save them all someday.

Armed with our new understanding of Qurina's plan, the others rethought their decisions to help.

"I am really sorry, Qurina. I lost sight of the promises I made to The Great Source. I need to trust that he will guide me until my journey ends," Warren said, humbly.

"You're fine. There is plenty of work to do. I'm happy to have you on board," she responded.

With everyone's cooperation, we were able to devise a plan. Chandra was healed quickly and insisted on getting involved in the fight. She'd managed to escape after taking on ten Marauders. The others were captured and taken back to Necropolis and chained in dampener cuffs. I hoped we weren't too late.

Qurina had told Thorn that the Protectors were the key to moving freely back and forth through the cities. Being back in the Land of the Promised would allow her to visit her old friend Jester and ask him to assist with planning. He was a great strategist and knew the most about Necropolis. She would also need to bring Jester back with her as a gift to Thorn. He was a traitor to the cause and needed to be punished. There were a lot of lives on the line, very little room for error, and almost no time to waste. We would be entering Necropolis again, but this time with more firepower and a better plan.

Chapter 24
The Guillotine

W ITH JESTER IN tow, Qurina reached the gates of the main hub of Necropolis. Jester was wearing one of his new suits but it had been roughed up and dirtied to look as though he put up a fight. Qurina had him tied up by the neck with a thick frayed rope. She tugged him around as if he were a defiant dog that wouldn't walk on his own. The rope was uncomfortable to Jester. It scratched and scraped his skin until it turned red from irritation. Jester played the part to a "T" as they walked the streets of the city. The people booed, jeered, and spat on him. Others threw rocks and dirt. Jester snarled and growled at them for show. This caused some of them to back off for fear that he may have in fact retained his powers somehow.

The Protectors and I were already in the city, dressed in disguises to blend in with the crowds. Each of us had a role to play in this raid. We had to stop the Marauders here, otherwise they could do a great deal of damage in the Land of the Promised.

Qurina reached the guards at the gate and instructed them to let her pass. At first they declined her request. Might is all they recognized and she looked different. She powered up her aura so they knew she meant business.

"Your glow looks different," said one of the guards.

"I got stronger," Qurina responded.

He looked at her suspiciously and said, "No, you look softer... almost beatable."

Without hesitating she grabbed him by the neck and lifted him off his feet.

"Call me soft again!" she snarled.

"Qurina... he's sorry... Tell her you're sorry you idiot!" The other guard exclaimed.

"I'm s...sorry, Qurina," the airborne guard managed as he struggled for air.

"That's more like it." She returned the guard to the ground, who immediately doubled over and coughed violently as he regained his breath. She straightened her clothes then said, "Now let me through."

"Yes, ma'am," the other guard said.

The gate was quickly opened and Qurina and Jester walked to Thorn's meeting place in the center of the city. The city was abuzz with people and vendors. The crowds had gathered for a big announcement. The rumors swirled about the raid on Hinterland.

"It was easy, the Marauders nabbed them before they knew what was going on," I heard a bystander say to another man.

"Victory will be ours soon!" shouted another man within the crowd.

The Protectors and I followed Qurina, careful not to be detected. As we made our way closer to the middle of the herds of people we saw a large wooden stage. Raven and several of Thorn's top agents were standing like politicians waving to the crowds. To their left was a monstrosity of a piece of equipment.

It was a guillotine constructed in the fashion of one found in the middle ages. It was an intimidating structure made of oak wood and stained with blood. There were three circular openings in the wood, a larger one in the middle where a victim's head would pass through, along with two smaller ones on either side to lock each hand at the wrist. The structure was about fifteen feet high with two uprights, capped by a horizontal beam. Its razor blade weighed twelve pounds and was made from the same metal found on an ax. It was freshly sharpened because it would be a busy day for this barbaric apparatus. The steel was hot to the touch due to the heat of the day. Its mirror-like shine gleamed in the sunlight.

I was standing in the crowd next to Tate. He seemed to notice it too.

"If that isn't a heck of a way to go…" Tate said.

"Let's make sure no one has to worry about that today," I said.

We all wore communication devices hidden in our ears with trackers in them. Everyone was in position. Based on Jester's best guess the captured Protectors would have been in the interrogation rooms. They would also have very tight security around them. Minna, Warren, and Chandra were on rescue duty while Liam and Griffin occupied the perimeter guards. Tate and I were responsible for not letting Qurina and Jester get their heads chopped off. You know, the easy job with thousands of people watching in the daylight.

"Sam, we are in position and I have eyes on the interrogation rooms," Chandra communicated.

"Good. Let's get it started. Liam… Griffin… you're up. Remember, we don't want to draw attention to ourselves," I said.

Griffin and Liam were like old pros. They had to keep the guards busy enough that they didn't see Chandra's team searching the interrogation shacks. Liam, holding a cane and bent over like a beaten old man, slowly shuffled up to one of the perimeter guards and said, "Excuse me, sir."

"Move along old man."

"But I have something to show you," Liam replied.

"This is a restricted area. Thorn will have your head if you don't keep it moving," the guard warned.

"You are missing out," Liam said as he pulled out a pouch full of gold.

"How did an old weak man such as you get that? Give it here old man."

"You'll have to take it."

The guard grabbed Liam, cocked his arm back, and landed a crushing blow to Liam's midsection.

"Uff!" was forced out of Liam's mouth from the blow.

"Do you want some more? What did you say, old man?" the guard asked as he bent over to hear him better.

"Behind you," Liam said. He got a glimpse of Griffin but it was too late. Griffin knocked the guard out cold with one well-placed punch.

Liam and Griffin continued to clear the way for Chandra's team as they began searching the interrogation rooms for their comrades. As her team moved down the rows of small box-shaped buildings, they had to be careful not to draw attention to themselves. They picked locks slowly and with expert precision. They had very little luck with the first row of four. All but one was empty and it was a guard that had been shoved in there by Liam when they'd cleared the area.

"I got one," Minna called out on the comm.

"Who is it?" asked Chandra.

"It's Zeke and he's in bad shape." Zeke was a Protector. He died on Earth in the 1920's and was a real, "Yes, sir. No, sir." kind of guy. He was always up for a challenge and preferred a meaningful day's work over lounging around or idle time.

"Is he going to be ok?" Tate asked.

"I don't know, he's hurt badly. We need to get him out of the city and back to The Land of the Promised so he can heal faster. There's too much negative energy here for him to survive."

"Warren, you take him. Chandra and Minna, I need for you guys to find the others," Griffin ordered.

Besides Sydney, we still had to find Dennis and Tripper. Tripper had been a Protector as long as Liam and Griffin. Tripper was French. He was captured while transitioning a family of four to the Land of the Promised. He was unable to defend himself because his powers were focused on getting the family to the light.

Dennis was the last Protector before me. He was from South

Africa and worked as a missionary in Sudan. He was killed on Earth while protecting a group of school-aged boys from kidnappers. The abductors wanted to take the boys and make them fight for them instead of learning to read and write. Dennis was able to fight them off for almost sixteen hours until help came. Once the boys were safe, he'd died from multiple bullet wounds.

Chandra and Minna had completed a search of all the buildings in the area but were unsuccessful in finding their teammates. Back in the center of the city, Tate and I continued to keep an eye on things.

"What other places would they be, Qurina?" I asked over the comm.

"They could be at Thorn's home. He has a holding cell there. It's a half mile from where you all are currently. Head east and you can't miss it."

"Headed there now," Minna said.

Chandra, Liam, and Griffin joined her. They were able to slip past the guards undetected. When the group found the cell they also found Kane.

Kane was a Marauder. He was tall, grizzly, and was built like a heavyweight MMA fighter. He was known for his ruthlessness in a fight. He believed that the only fair fight is the one he'd won. When he lost, he tended to blame others for his issues. On Earth, Kane had been a New Yorker that didn't take much crap from anyone. He was brash and in your face. He lacked the courtesies of a refined gentleman and could be described as a street thug with charisma. While he would have been trouble by himself; he was not alone. Apparently Thorn was paranoid about a rescue attempt.

Chandra carefully scoped the room from an adjacent hallway. She then quietly made her way back to her comrades and quietly reported, "I count six of them. That's including Kane."

"I'll take Kane," Griffin announced. "Chandra, take the ones on the left. Minna, you take the remainders on the right. Liam, I need you to free our people."

"Are you sure you don't want my help here, Griffin. Kane is a tough character. You barely defeated him the last time you two fought," Liam said.

"But I did win, right?" Griffin said almost stubbornly.

"We need to get them out before any others come. We don't have time to fight them all." Griffin explained.

"Yes, sir," Liam said complying with his leader.

Kane was a strong warrior. His powers of hate were fueled by his greed and envy. He wanted to be the ruler of Necropolis. He coveted Castro Thorn's power. He'd challenged him several times and came close to defeating Thorn once or twice. At least that's how he told the story. Thorn kept him around as a reminder to all the others who would try to usurp him. Kane had several visible scars on his face, neck, and back as trophies for his second place finishes. Thorn made him keep his shirt off anytime he was in public so others could see his shame. Kane was a head guard but would never be a part of the elite circle of Marauders, even though he felt deserving of it. Thorn knew he couldn't be trusted. Kane would have had too much access to schemes and possibly overthrow him. The only people Kane hated more than Thorn were the Protectors. He felt they were a bunch of goodie do-gooders that kept the weak, weak.

"If you can't defend yourself then you should kill yourself," Kane would say before taking a life force. He forced the "weak" to take their own life force instead of wasting energy on them himself.

"Kane!" Griffin said as he revealed himself.

Chandra and Minna also came out from their hiding spots. Kane immediately recognized the voice and his men quickly took fighting stances.

"Griffin the Runner," Kane said.

"No one's running today, Kane."

"You coward, we were supposed to fight to the death. Is there no honor in you?"

"Like you'd know anything about honor," Griffin snapped.

"I'll honor you by taking your life force personally. How about that?"

"The Great Source will assimilate you first."

"Enough talking. Let's bully!" Kane said, enthusiastically.

The guards stepped forward to engage. Chandra close lined the first guard with her stretched out arm and used that momentum to back fist the next one. She alternated punches and kicks on each guard. Neither making as much as a scratch on her face.

Minna didn't mind taking a few punches during a fight. Each punch psyched her up even more. She growled and screamed at each of her attackers and laughed as they connected a punch or two. Minna moved into action. Her glow was white and fully charged. She formed grappling hooks with strong rope in each hand. She lassoed two of the guards on either side of her and pulled them into each other, knocking them out. The remaining guard seemed up for the challenge but was not.

He punched her in the stomach twice and aimed at her face. Minna ducked and countered with two jabs followed by an uppercut. The guard, dazed but still standing, was ripe for a final punch. Instead, she kicked him in the gut and finished him with a roundhouse kick.

Liam managed to slip behind the fighters and made it to the holding cell. He could see them all weakened by the dampener cuffs. All of them beaten and battered but still alive. They could not heal their wounds which is what endangered them the most.

Sydney was the first to notice him. He thought that maybe it was a dream.

"Liam," he said weakly.

"Sydney. Hold on. I'll get you out of this."

"Tripper is hurt very badly," Sydney said still too weak to speak up.

"What about you, Dennis?" Liam asked from the other side of the cell bars.

"I'll make it."

"Step back, I'll get you out of there."

Griffin and Kane were circling and scanning each other, both looking for an opening against the other. Kane had a red glow with a complete charge of hate in his heart. Griffin's light was reflecting white with a gray tint. He formed a medieval styled sword in one hand and a shield in the other.

"You need a shield to protect you. You're weak. I hate weak people," Kane said. He formed a Tommy gun with his powers and started shooting. Griffin held up his shield and managed to block the inundation of bullets. Kane held on to the trigger firing the bullets nonstop. He tried angling bullets by having them ricochet off walls and the floor, hoping that one would find its mark.

Griffin maneuvered around or blocked each bullet that came his way. This frustrated Kane.

"Keep running, you fraidy-cat. You run more than a dame. Hold still," Kane cried.

"Tough talk for a man with a gun. Why don't you put it down and fight me?" Griffin replied.

"I'm gonna take you out!" Kane screamed over the loud blasts of the Gun.

Griffin looked up in time enough to see Kane throw his gun down and race towards him. He braced for impact when he heard a thud followed by a sliding sound. Griffin looked over his shield and saw Kane on the ground clutching his side. Griffin saw blood dripping from Kane's body and realized that he had hit himself with one of his own bullets.

"Pathetic!" Griffin scoffed. "You made all of that noise and for what? Here you are bleeding your way to assimilation. Any last words Kane? I will make it quick for you." He dropped his sword and pulled out a knife. He kneeled down beside Kane, lifted his knife into the air, and thrusted downward at his heart. But for some reason, he stopped abruptly.

Griffin felt a cold biting chill flood through his body. His breathing hitched and he struggled harder each time he tried to inhale. He coughed up something. It was his own blood. Griffin was confused as to what had happened but familiar with the sound he heard next.

It was the shrieking noise that metal makes when being pulled from the body. Troubled to steady himself, he placed his free hand on the ground. His vision blurred for a moment. Then it focused back in. He could see Kane grinning at him. Kane was holding a long thick blade he'd formed with his powers. The knife and his hand seemed to be one, as they were both covered in blood.

Still bleeding out himself, Kane managed to say, "You can't run now."

Griffin fell over face first onto Castro Thorn's floor. The others had accomplished their missions but did not make it back in time to help their leader. They saw him fall to the floor. All of them were stunned at what they had witnessed.

"Griffin!" Chandra screamed.

His grey and white aura morphed into pure white light. The hallway was completely bright. Griffin's spirit rose up and flew into the light. The bright light disappeared and Griffin's body was gone too.

Liam walked over to Kane and saw him laughing and coughing up blood.

"Do you want some old man?" Kane growled.

"Ekon's love compels me not to end you right here and now. Knowing that my friend was fulfilling his purpose brings me joy. The Great Source would never want you. So I won't kill you," Liam said.

"But I will," Minna cried as she separated Kane's head from the rest of him with an ax that she had formed. Kane's lifeless body released its red light to The Great Source and turned to black ash.

"You didn't have to do that," Liam scolded.

"He didn't either," Minna quickly remarked.

"Qurina could have helped him," Liam said.

"Well, first we have to win this war. Without Griffin, our chances decrease. With Kane gone, our odds are more balanced again," Minna explained.

"We have to get out of here before someone sees us," Chandra reminded them.

Sydney and Dennis were able to heal quickly and stayed to fight. Liam took Tripper with him back to The Land of the Promised. He would need pure love to heal.

"Sam… we stuffed the remaining guards in Thorn's cell. Sydney and Dennis are able to stay and fight. Liam is taking Tripper back home to get treatment for his injuries. That leaves us with seven Protectors," Chandra reported over the comm.

"What about Griffin? We have him too, right?" I asked.

"… Griffin didn't make it. He's with Ekon now," she responded.

"No… I should have gone. Maybe I could have helped him," I said somberly.

"No Sam, he died so that we could keep this mission going. He was brave and the man responsible has fallen as well," Chandra said.

"Griffin would want us to finish what we started," Minna said.

"She's right," said Tate, placing his hand on my shoulder.

I looked him in the eyes and felt comforted. "Ok, let's move to phase two. They will figure out we are here soon."

Chapter 25

The Wish Keeper

RAVEN, ESCORTED BY twelve of his personal guards arrived at the holding cell to find that there was no one guarding the prisoners.

"What is this?" he asked aloud to one of his men.

"Uh, I don't know sir. I've been with you all day. Kane was responsible for the prisoners." The soldier said, hoping not to be flogged for no reason.

"Kane!!!" Raven howled.

"We're in here," a voice at the end of the hall shouted.

"The cell, sir. It came from the holding cell."

"Well, go open it and find out what is going on," Raven squawked.

His guards opened up the cell doors to find Kane's men in it.

"What is this madness?" Raven asked.

"The Protectors, sir… They came and broke them out of the prison. We weren't strong enough to stop them."

"Where is Kane?"

"He killed Griffin. Then his head was chopped off by Minna's ax." The guard replied.

"So you let Kane get killed. You're telling me that you were too weak to kill a few Protectors and we have no one to execute!"

"… But sir…"

"Don't even start with me. I should end you all right now but it is clear that war is upon us. Even you weaklings will be needed… for bait at least," Raven scoffed.

Thorn was livid about the news of the Protectors escaping but his lust for vengeance against them was temporarily on hold. For the moment, he had the opportunity to settle a score. He was in a private chamber room sitting on a wooden chair. The room was mostly empty, aside from a structure that looked fit for torture.

It laid down flat like a bed and was about three feet wide by six and a half feet long. There were chains sprawled crossways over three sections of the device. The chains were linked to wooden posts, and they were threaded through notched out holes which were attached to handle cranks. The gadget had cuffs attached to it. The cuffs were made of leather and had sharp, pointy, skin piercing spikes on the inside and outside of the cuffs.

"Jester old friend, I brought this one out just for you," Thorn said to no one in the room. He then raised his voice and called out, "Guards, send for Qurina and that traitor."

Soon Qurina and Jester were called away from the platform into Thorn's chambers. Tate and I were not able to follow them. For the time being, she would be on her own. We had to find a different way in. Qurina and Jester entered the chambers where Thorn was. He stood by the torturing apparatus ready to greet his guests.

"Qurina, you made it back and with a bonus gift," Thorn declared.

"And now that I've fulfilled my part of the bargain, I'm done. The people of this city will no longer be beaten and tortured because they are weak," Qurina demanded.

"I'm sorry sweetheart, I don't think I can uphold that part of the deal just yet."

"Why not. You have the Protectors," she said.

"Well... I don't anymore."

"What do you mean, you don't?" she asked.

"Don't play dumb with me! You and this sniveling weakling here helped them escape," Thorn snarled.

"How could that be? We have been here waiting for you. I gave you their heads on a silver platter and you somehow let them escape. Of all the idiotic..."

"Enough Qurina! I know you set this all up. I know about Griffin and I know you helped them. I know that Sam and Tate are on their way here as we speak."

Qurina was frozen from uncertainty. Thorn knew about their plan but didn't stop her. She wondered why.

"What do you want, Thorn?"

"I'm glad that you finally asked." He walked around the torture device gliding his hand over the splintery surface and said slowly, "I... want... you..."

"You know that's not going to happen," Qurina said defiantly.

"I didn't finish. I want you... on my toy. I call it the Wish Keeper. The reason I call it that is because you will wish for assimilation after I am done with you. Then your wish will be granted."

"That won't happen either," Qurina said.

"Oh, but it will Qurina. You see while you are full of love and mercy. I am full of hate and jealousy. I get what I want or no one gets what they want. Every knee will bend to me and my superiority. All of those people in the main hub will be crushed. At this very moment, my Marauders are sealing off all of the exits. The people of this city are like pigs in the slaughterhouse. Either you get on the Wish Keeper or I massacre them all," Thorn declared.

"Don't do it Qurina! Sam will be here to help us," Jester declared.

"You shut up! You miserable little worm. I will get to you in a moment," Thorn growled as he zapped Jester with a volt of electricity.

Jester fell to the hard, rough floor. He grimaced at the pain he felt. Without any powers, the shock's effectiveness was evident. He wasn't sure how many of those he could take.

Qurina began to glow as she stood between Jester and Thorn.

"Thorn, leave him alone," she commanded.

"Easy there Qurina. If anything happens to me, my men will unleash hell on your precious weaklings."

"There's no way you would do this to your own people, you need them in order to take the Land of the Promised."

"Like I said. No one gets what they want. If you don't get on, I won't need these people. If they are useless they might as well be assimilated."

"You're a snake, Castro Thorn."

"Temper, temper. You don't want to anger me. Don't think I'll do it? Do you remember your friends from dinner a few years ago? I'm not accustomed to waiting for people to make up their minds. Now... be a doll and..." Thorn didn't say anything else. He simply tapped on the Wish Keeper.

Qurina reluctantly complied. She laid on the cold wood surface as Thorn began to wrap the chains around her body. He took a great deal of pleasure in hearing her grunt when he would tighten a section just a little too much. That was how he knew it was just right for him. Qurina felt the unfriendly metal of the chain pinching and squeezing her skin. Thorn saved his favorite sensation for last. It was time for the cuff straps with the spike on the inside. They were made with the same capabilities as the dampener cuffs.

Thorn began strapping on the first cuff. Qurina not wanting to give him any more satisfaction, did not scream when the spikes pierced her skin. She gritted her teeth. The second one she could not stop from letting out a groan. The cuffs had already started to weaken her.

"Uh! Thorn, you don't have to do this," she implored.

"Yes, I do. You are a traitor and a strong one at that. I can't keep you around. The people love you too much. I need them strong and hateful if I'm going to take over The Land of the Promised. You could have been part of this but your compassion got in the way."

Thorn cranked the chains of his archaic machine.

"Uhhhh!" Qurina yelled.

"Please stop, Castro!" Jester cried.

"Didn't I tell you to close your mouth?" Thorn growled. He turned from the contraption and grabbed him by the neck. Jester attempted to pull his hand away but was not strong enough.

"I can't believe you. You gave up your abilities and for what? Look at you. You can't even defend yourself."

Jester's feet were off the ground. He kicked and struggled for air. Thorn tightened his grip. Jester flailed his arms and legs in a desperate attempt to free himself.

"You're like a cockroach on his back. You are so dependent on others for your life. Is this what you want?" Thorn threw him to the ground. "You disgust me."

Jester was relieved to be alive but knew the stakes they faced. With this in mind, he managed, "You're the soft one, Thorn."

"What did you say?"

"You heard me. You're the great Castro Thorn and here you are being merciful. That is a sign of weakness. You are afraid of Qurina which is why you want her gone."

"You little... you will be my first example. Guards! You will be taken to the guillotine. I want you to see how merciful I am."

His guards did not respond. Tate and I found a way in and took out several guards along the way. I'd heard my wife's screams and followed the sounds. Tate and I were outside the torture chamber.

"Your guards are indisposed at the moment," Tate said as we walked into the room.

"You've proven to be very crafty, Sam," Thorn said as he slowly backed away from Jester and towards Qurina.

"It's over Thorn. We've already freed the Protectors. Your men aren't here to save you. You don't have to take this any further. I will give you my word that you will not be tortured or assimilated," I said.

"But you will lock me up and throw away the key," Thorn replied.

"You will be treated fairly and humanely, which is far more than anything you've done for anyone else," Tate said.

"You think that's what I want? To be a caged bird in some cell? I thought you knew me after all these years, Tate."

"You act as though you have a choice. It's two to one and you know how powerful we are," I said.

"I think you've made the mistake in your math. As a matter of fact, you plus Tate equals zero," Thorn retorted.

"You make no sense," Tate said.

"I'm willing to bet that you will put on dampener cuffs."

"What dampener cuffs?" Tate asked.

"These," Raven said from behind us. He was standing dangling out two pairs of cuffs off his pointer finger. Raven also had two other Marauders with him.

"We can take them, Sam," Tate said. I noticed he was already glowing.

"Maybe you can. Maybe you can't. I'd rather hold the bloodshed until later. For now, put on the cuffs before I kill Qurina."

Thorn cranked the chains tighter. The weakened Qurina was unable to hold back her screams any longer. She was, however, still defiant and as stubborn as she ever was.

"Ahh! Uh! Don't... Uh! Do it. S... Ah! Sam," she managed to say between the torturous yelps.

"You know I'll do it. Tate, tell him."

"Ah!" Qurina cried again. Castro Thorn was being relentless. Qurina was bleeding from the spikes in her wrists.

"She will bleed out," Tate advised.

"Ahh! No, Sam! Don't... Ooh!" Qurina shrieked.

"Ok, Thorn you win. Just please stop."

"Are you sure?" Thorn asked as he gave another tug on the crank.

"Yes, yes please stop," I begged.

Thorn stopped the cranking. "Put on the cuffs," he commanded.

Raven flung the cuffs at us. We both put them on.

"Take them to the guillotine," Thorn said.

"Let Qurina go. You have us now," I said.

"I have no plans to let her go."

"But you said..."

"I said that I would stop inflicting pain on her. I never told you that I would set her free. She can't be trusted."

"You can't be trusted," I roared.

"Get them out!" Thorn yelled.

Chapter 26
The Challenge

TATE AND I stood on the platform where the guillotine was mounted. From up close the machine looked more gruesome and intimidating. I could see the blood stains from the others that had fallen victim to its sharp reliable edge. The guillotine had a perfect kill record. I'd hoped that somehow Tate and I would never fall prey to this soulless monster.

I felt myself getting weaker with the passing moments. It was an all too familiar feeling. Tate had never been cuffed. He was too strong. Until now he'd been the most feared Protector of us all.

The crowds booed and hissed at us. Some threw stones and other hard elements. The cuffs made us slow easy targets. Unpleasant is the nice way for me to describe the pain that overtook my body each time a rock or metal fragment hit me.

"We need to get out of here," Tate said.

"Yeah, but how?" I asked.

"Let's hope the others are able to help."

Raven and some of the other top Marauders walked out onto the platform. The crowd changed their jeers to cheers. Castro Thorn followed soon after. The sound was deafening. He was like a rock star. With just a wave of his hand the crowd went silent. Thorn gestured over to a guard and Jester was forced to the platform. The guards pushed him roughly across the stage. The people began to boo as they realized who he was. Next a bloody and beaten Qurina was pulled to the stage. The crowd fell silent. They were unsure what to think. She had been so kind and gentle to so many of them. They did not know why she would have been up there as a prisoner.

Thorn began to address the crowd. "My people, before you are traitors to Necropolis city and its citizens. These people would conspire to bring us all down and have us assimilated to The Great Source. What say you to this madness?"

"Boo! Boo!" the crowd proclaimed in unison.

"Each of these men have been found guilty of conspiring to bring down this city and its inhabitants."

"Boo!" the crowd roared again.

"I have seen fit to show no mercy for it is not our way! What say you?"

"Guillotine, guillotine, guillotine!" the crowd chanted.

I looked at Tate, Jester, and Qurina. I could see they were all unsure of what was about to happen but were ready to accept their fate. We were being cuckolded by the people and knew Thorn would assimilate all of us if it suited his agenda.

Sydney, Chandra and the others were in the crowd. They were hiding in plain sight, careful to keep on their disguises.

"What's the plan, Chandra?" Dennis asked.

"The plan is we wait until we know something about whatever is going on."

"We can't just sit here and let them execute our friends," Minna said.

"No one will be executed today, Minna. We just need to make sure that we aren't making things worse," Chandra said.

"I can hear you guys," I whispered, realizing that our comms were still working. They never checked us for hidden devices.

"Sam!"

"Yes Chandra, it's me. I'm a little weak from these cuffs. If you guys could help us get these off, I'm sure we can find a way to defeat Thorn."

"Didn't you break the chains before dad?" Sydney asked.

"Yes, but..."

"What were you doing for that to happen?"

"I... I don't know. I can't remember."

We were interrupted by Thorn talking to the crowd. "Who should be first?" Thorn asked as he moved down the row holding his hand over each of our heads.

"Jester, Jester..." one group proclaimed.

"Sam, Sam..." another group shouted.

"Kill Tate, Kill Tate!" yelled another group.

"What about her?" Thorn asked, holding his hand over Qurina's head. He was smiling and felt delighted at the crowd's responses to this point.

"Set her free!" said a voice from the crowd.

"Show her mercy!" shouted another.

"Mercy, one of us! Mercy, one of us!" the crowd began to chant.

Thorn's smile morphed to a glare. He had not anticipated the crowd reacting the way they did. He waived his hands in an attempt to get them quieted.

"No, no, no! She is a traitor, too!" he yelled.

Finally the crowd noise subsided long enough for him to explain Qurina's crimes. "She has joined forces with the Protectors. She led them here today. I found them and I captured them before they wreaked havoc on us all."

"That is not true!" Qurina interrupted.

"You shut up you traitorous witch!"

"Let her speak!" another voice shouted.

"Yeah!" shouted the crowd.

"I came here to free you all. The Land of the Promised was built for all of us. Some of you, like me, were not quite ready to accept and forgive. Ekon sent me here for you. Even Castro Thorn can come with us. There is nothing but condemnation in this place. The Source wants us to be happy and whole. I can show you the path to freedom. It is Ekon's wish that I do this for you. Thorn would have you suffering and deceived. I will show you Ekon's truth and power. I was fortunate enough to see the Land of the Promised. It is a land without limitations. Your dreams will be realized through the one that created us."

"She would have you all become pathetic and dependent. Don't you see what happened to Jester? He was one of the most powerful of my men. He was a great warrior and now look at him. He is a sniveling weakling. Because Jester is so helpless and pitiful, he will go to the guillotine first," Thorn declared.

Many in the crowd cheered but there was a small group that did not. Qurina had a faction of people that wanted to follow her. "People, he is my friend and I will not see him punished. He is here for you all too," she said.

"He is here for himself. That is who Jester is," Thorn interjected.

"You're here for yourself, Thorn. Castro Thorn is the reason for your suffering! Thorn was planning to murder you all if I had not agreed to be put in cuffs. Take a look around. His special forces have all of the exits blocked," Qurina declared to the crowd.

The people began to mumble amongst themselves. As they looked around they saw Thorn's Marauders guarding exits. A rush of mistrust for Thorn matriculated through the mass. A few would be deserters attempted to rush the exits but were beaten and whipped.

The hordes of people screamed and shouted, "Let us go! Let us out! Please don't do this. We are your people."

"Calm down. You are all safe. I want you to bear witness to the destruction of the Protectors," Thorn announced.

He signaled to a guard to put Jester in the guillotine. The guard complied by tugging on Jester's cuffs and forced him to walk over to the structure. The guard kicked him in the back of his knee to force him down to his knees. He jammed Jester's head through the large hole, locked his neck in place, and gave a nod to Thorn.

Jester did not beg or scream although he was frightened. He looked down and saw a bucket underneath him. He presumed that the bucket was there to catch his head after it was cut off. While he did not fully feel ready for assimilation he found comfort in knowing that he was on the right side for once.

Thorn raised his hand in the air to let the executioner know to drop the blade.

"Wait!" Qurina pleaded.

Thorn kept his hand in the air.

"What?" Thorn replied.

"I should go first. It was my idea to come here."

"Patience Qurina. I'll let you go next."

"But…" she began to say.

"Challenge!" I interrupted.

"What did you say?" Thorn asked.

"Challenge. I challenge you. If I win you spare Jester's life."

"What do I get if you lose? You don't have anything I want. I can just kill you."

"It is a challenge. You have to accept it. It is our way. You made it our way," Qurina said.

"A technicality. Plus he is not one of us," Thorn stated.

"But I am," said Qurina.

"So, you want to challenge me? I made you and there is no way that you could win this fight. You are too weak. Accept your fate so we can get on with it."

"You didn't make me. You helped me find who I am. Ekon's love created me and I will always be stronger than you."

Thorn was hesitant to accept the challenge because of her confidence but he knew rationally there was no way for her to win with the state she was in.

The crowd became restless at Thorn's hesitance and began to chant, "Challenge, Challenge…" over and over again.

Thorn raised his hand to signify that he was about to speak. The chants dissipated.

"I will accept her appeal. Like all of the others, she will fail to defeat me. My distain for all things is why I am so strong. Right now I am very angry at Qurina for this. She couldn't just follow my plan and do as I said. I made her one of us. I brought her in and she sat at my table. Now she has shown me a great disrespect. For that she will be punished by my hands and assimilated. If she wins she will be your new leader," Thorn decreed.

The hoard cheered and screamed. They wanted bloodshed and didn't seem to care whose it would be. Qurina seemed pleased that Thorn accepted. Raven would be the Judge of the contest. He was the only one that they both trusted to keep things as fair as a battle like this could be.

"Raven, please un-cuff me."

"That was not part of the agreement," Raven replied.

"What is this? What do you mean? How do you expect this fight to be fair?" she asked.

"You made the challenge, Qurina. This is our way. Your terms were simple. There were no specifics except that you two would fight. Besides, what fight is ever fair?"

Qurina's eyes grew wide. Her heart pumped faster. She became fearful in the moment. I could see her confidence fade. Weakened by the cuffs myself, I was unsure how to help her.

"But how did I break them last time?" I thought to myself.

Chapter 27
Finding Love's True Power

IT WAS TIME to toe the line. The battle for Necropolis would be decided by this fight. The strongest of the Protectors were all on the platform ready to be executed. Our only hope was Qurina but she was in cuffs and preparing to fight a man that wielded hate at the highest level.

Thorn stepped to the line. His aura was a deep dark merlot red. His eyes went black. He'd taken his shirt off revealing the scars from when his dad had tortured him so many years ago. He could have easily chosen not to have them in this form but he wore them like a badge of honor.

Qurina stepped to the line unsure of what would come. Her fear had left her as she thought about a verse in the bible, "Whom shall I fear?" She prayed and remembered why she was here. It was Ekon's will. She put her foot on the line drawn for her and closed her eyes.

"Open your eyes little girl. I want you to see all of this," Thorn said to Qurina.

She was surrounded by cheers and shouts but heard none of it. For her everything went silent. She opened her eyes as the first blow came crashing into her face. Qurina fell to the ground. Part of her wanted to stay there but her faith made her get back up.

"You punch like a schoolgirl," she said as she stumbled to her feet. Her mouth was bloodied and her lips were swollen from his one punch. She felt the sting but remained strong. Thorn continued to punish her body with kicks and punches, taking his time to make sure that she felt every blow.

I couldn't endure it. My wife was being beaten half to death and I was helpless to stop him. I made an attempt to help by rushing between them. Thorn easily knocked me back several feet and commanded the guards to hold me down as I watched.

"You see that, Qurina? Even Sam can't help you," Thorn said standing over her limp, beaten body. He began to laugh and kicked her again.

I continued to fight and struggle with the guards to no avail. Then I heard a voice through my comm, "Tate hold your cuffs up in the air."

It was Sydney. He was standing on a nearby roof wielding a bow and arrow. Tate was very weak but did as instructed. Like a lightning bolt from the sky, his cuffs were shattered by a direct hit from Sydney's arrow. Tate was free and immediately felt some of his strength return. Simultaneously, Minna managed to sneak onto the platform and fought the guards off me. She quickly helped me to my feet and unlocked my cuffs with a key taken from a guard.

Like Tate, I felt instantly stronger without the cuffs, although I did not feel my full strength return. I knew that Qurina couldn't hold out much longer. Thorn had been toying with her, inflicting pain but careful not to finish her off just yet. Qurina had been fighting hard to stay conscious. Her eyes were blurry and bruised. Her lip was busted. Her clothes were torn and her bruises could be seen through the holes of her ragged clothes. Some of the Marauders responded to our escape by rushing the stage. Sydney, Tate, Minna, Dennis, and Chandra fought them back. They were no match for us without the cuffs on. The Protectors fought off twenty Marauders. I saw white and red auras clashing and flashing back and forth. The white lights never relented. I went after Qurina.

"Not so fast Sam, this fight is between them," Raven declared.

"But he's going to kill her and she has those cuffs on," I said.

"She knows our ways. If you think these people will follow her after you intervene then you don't understand anything that is going on. If it is truly the will of The Great Source that she leads this city she will find a way. But I can't let you interfere, Sam."

"But look at her, she can't take much more and those cuffs are hurting her. Let me break her cuffs, Raven."

"No. You'll have to go through me if you think that's going to happen."

"Then so be it," I said. My glow burned white. I felt myself getting stronger by the second.

Raven started to glow and formed two ancient weapons called Sais. They were tri-bladed mini swords which were limited in range but maneuverable, sharp, and deadly.

"This doesn't have to happen, Raven. Just let me release her from her cuffs to make the fight fair," I implored him again.

"I gave you my answer. Now knuckle up!"

I was feeling close to full energy with my glow. Raven screamed and charged at me with his weapons. He was fast and strong but so was I. He flung one of his weapons at me. I ducked to miss it. Raven was able to connect a punch to my side. Then he tried to stab me with the other Sai. I caught his arm and followed with a head-butt. As he staggered backwards I punched him in the face. Raven was off balance. I kicked his leg up with a leg sweep and elbowed him in the sternum. Raven hit the ground so hard the platform shook.

"Help!" I heard a call. It was Jester. He was still in the Guillotine. The blade was no longer locked in place. All of the fighting and bumping on the platform had shaken the blade loose. It could fall at any time and end his life-force. I had Raven on the ground. I looked at Qurina then back a Jester. She heard him too. I hit Raven one more time to knock him out. I started toward Qurina who was on all fours coughing up blood. She held her hand out to let me know to stop.

"Save him, Sam," she commanded.

Qurina was referring to Jester. I ignored her and continued towards her.

"No! Save him, Sam!"

I stopped. She was being selfless. She would rather me save Jester, even if it meant she would be assimilated. Tate was fighting a Marauder and had launched him in the air. The Marauder hit the guillotine causing the blade to release downward. I sprinted towards the machine and leaped into the air with a flying kick. My foot smashed the blade like a glass window when it was perhaps only a foot above Jester's neck. The metal shards cascaded down the guillotine platform and stage. I quickly helped Jester out of the guillotine.

"Thank you Sam!"

"No time for that. I have to save Qurina," I replied.

"What? No, you can't. She has to figure this out on her own. The crowd needs to see her win on her own. They need to see Ekon's will being done if there is any hope of saving them," Jester explained.

"But she is going to die."

"Have a little faith, Sam. She's got him right where she wants him," he said confidently.

Jester was right. I was not showing faith. I stood in the presence of The Great Source and he told me what was going to happen. I'd forgotten that it was his will. I thought it was up to me to save her. But it was up to her to save herself. My job was to give her my love and support.

I rushed over near Qurina. Raven had come to and started to remember where he was. "You!" he said to me.

"Relax, I won't interfere." The other Protectors hurried to assist me after subduing The Marauders. "Wait guys, she needs to do this herself," I said.

Castro Thorn was still winning the fight. He spat on and taunted her. Thorn looked back at the crowd of watchers. "Look at her. She was once a warrior and one of the strongest among us. Now she is a fool on the ground waiting for me to end her misery. Should I kill her now? Has she been punished enough?"

"Finish her!" a man yelled. Most of the others cheered. It appeared the crowd would get their bloodshed for the day. Their allegiance seemed to shift easily to whomever was the winner. They were a very fickle group of souls.

"Come on Qurina get up!" I shouted.

Her body was worn and battered. She didn't have much left in her. Qurina and I connected eyes for a moment. I saw a spark left in her. I had to help her ignite it into a flame. I had to believe that some part of my wife was still there.

"Caroline! Don't leave me now. We promised each other. In this life and the next. It is the next life. It's our time. I need you to get up like the warrior that you are and find your way back to me. These people need you even if they don't realize it. I need you. Even Thorn needs you."

"Shut up Sam. You're too late," Thorn said with electric volts sparking from his hands. He was ready to send her to assimilation. He kneeled to the ground and whispered in her ear. Finally, he placed his hand on her to send volts swimming through her veins.

But... nothing happened. He tried again with the same result. The people in the crowd fell silent again. They were not sure what was going on. Thorn stood and stepped backwards with a look of bewilderment.

A laugh came from Qurina. "Thorn, you have lost. You are now rendered powerless and the weakest of us all. You had your chance and it is over. Give up now or you will feel my real powers," Qurina said as she stood to her feet.

"This can't be!" Thorn exclaimed. He attempted to punch Qurina in the face. She caught his fist and easily pushed it away.

"It will be, Thorn," Qurina said.

"Never!" He shot a volt of lightening at her.

Qurina waived her cuffed hands and the lightening vanished.

He slowly backed away from her.

"How did you? I don't understand. Your cuffs, they are still on!"

"Yes but Sam helped me realize that Ekon's love is the most powerful force known to us. These cuffs dampen my ability to feel love. But I don't just feel it. I know that I am loved. I have faith in love and its powers to prevail against all things, including hate."

She broke the chains and began to glow powder blue.

Thorn felt something that he hadn't known since the days his father had beaten him. It was fear taking over his body. He turned and ran across the stage but the crowd blocked his escape. "Let me out of here. I'm Castro Thorn. You can't do this to me. Raven, old friend. Help me!"

"Sorry Thorn, it's not our way," Raven said somberly. He knew that his actions were equal to betraying his only friend but he was bound by the rules he was charged to enforce.

The hoard grabbed Thorn and pulled him down from the stage. As he struggled against vengeful hands his hair was tugged and his pants were ripped. They began to scratch and strike him. Thorn fell to the ground and was swallowed up by them.

"Turn him loose!" Qurina demanded in a stern and sturdy voice. In that instant, the crowd listened as she commanded and backed away from him. Thorn was lying on the ground weeping. Qurina stepped down from the platform and grabbed his hand. "Before you tried to electrocute me, you whispered in my ear. Tell them what you said to me, Thorn."

"I…I said, nnn… no mercy."

"That's right, no mercy! Unlike you, I know that mercy is not a weakness but a powerful tool. I will not assimilate you. You aren't ready for that. You may never be."

"If you show me mercy Qurina, I will not repay you in kind when given the chance."

"Oh, don't worry Thorn. I will not give you the chance," Qurina responded.

Her hand glowed. She placed it on his forehead. Thorn began to scream and then fell silent. His eyes glazed over. He was awake but did not seem to be present. He wasn't dead but I also wouldn't call him alive.

"Take him to one of the cells. He won't be able to hurt anyone anymore," Qurina said to two men in the crowd that she trusted. The men had to drag Thorn by the arms because of his catatonic state. He didn't seem to be aware of anything going on around him.

"What about him, Qurina?" Sydney said, referring to Raven.

"Well… that depends on him," she replied.

"Qurina, I have been Thorn's friend and most loyal servant for as long as I can remember. We have committed many wrongs together. Today, I saw something I had never before thought was possible. You beat Thorn without throwing a punch. Thorn created our rules and I enforced them. I can abide by our way and follow you. I don't think that I am ready to accept Ekon's love but I will honor the laws of this city."

"But can we trust him? He will try to help Thorn as soon as he gets a chance," Minna said.

"Thorn is all but gone. There is nothing to help. If he decides to terrorize my people he will have to deal with the Protectors." Turning to Raven, Qurina said, "I accept your explanation. I'm sure that in your own time you will understand the powers of love just like Jester. I also think it is time that you all call me Caroline again. Qurina is no longer needed. Caroline is the gentle part of my soul and I will need her to finish the task that I started."

Caroline was now facing the crowd and said, "People of Necropolis. Ekon has chosen me to lead you to his promised land. This journey starts today. We must first heal our hearts. The city will also heal. Your pain and suffering will end soon. You will all be forgiven in time. I can show you how."

Upon hearing this declaration, the people cheered and cried joyful tears.

Epilogue

OUR WAY OF life changed after Caroline's victory. The Protectors were no longer focused on Hinterland only. There were people like Sydney who followed in Caroline's footsteps. He became her right hand man. She taught him all that she knew about being a Marauder. He gained a sense of pride understanding both cultures. He learned they were not all bad. Most of them were misguided and needed to see that things could be better.

Jester is working on his powers of love now that he is reunited with his mother. Because he had already harnessed the powers of hate, he had an idea of how to tap into his abilities. I have been training him and he has shown promise.

Necropolis is more like an outreach center now. Those once considered lost still have a chance to be citizens of the Land of the Promised. Tate and Dennis lead a monthly trip into the Land of the Promised for those that are curious about the other side. Caroline says that those that visit the Land of the Promised have a higher conversion rate and find it easier to forgive themselves.

Liam finally reached the highest level of enlightenment. Yet he had decided not to assimilate with the Great Source. His knowledge has been useful here in the Land of the Promised. We find that most of the answers we seek can be found through Liam instead of risking our life forces attempting to visit Ekon.

After the great battle, Chandra decided to take a leave of absence from the Protectors. She believes that Raven will find a way to undo what Caroline did to Castro Thorn. Chandra said that she couldn't rest easy knowing that he is not completely assimilated. She was last seen in a deep wooded forest training and meditating. Chandra did vow to rejoin the group if her special skill set was ever needed.

Tate was given a promotion as the new leader of the Protectors. He only lasted a few months before he realized he was more suited for saving souls and "kicking rogue Marauder butt." He gave the position to Tripper, who has been doing a great job in Griffin's place. Tate and I continue to train together and are still considered to be the strongest of the Protectors.

The other Protectors still patrol Hinterland. Warren and Minna find fulfillment in saving the souls of there. When they come across a difficult soul, they usually work with Caroline to find different ways of converting them. The next life is close to harmonious again. Ekon must be proud of his creations.

As for Raven, he visits his longtime friend Castro Thorn at least once a week. He talks to him about his week or the challenges of his day. While Thorn does not respond, Raven knows that he is in there somewhere. He hasn't given up hope that Castro will regain consciousness. Raven is careful in his actions and assists Caroline in any issues she has. His favorite part of his new role is keeping the new souls of Necropolis in line.

Sometime after the battle with Thorn I met Caroline at her request. Caroline was mostly healed from her fight with Castro Thorn. We sat on her couch to discuss our future together.

"What do you think, Sam?"

"About what?" I said.

"About us."

"I think that I love you. In this life, we are bound by nothing but our own minds."

"That sounds great but how is this going to work? I have to be here in Necropolis. My work is here," Caroline explained.

"I know and I would never stop you from doing Ekon's will."

"Your work is in Hinterland," she said.

"Yes, it is. But with Thorn gone, we can see each other as often as we want, right?"

"It's not that simple Sam."

"Why not? I don't understand."

"These people still have their way. It has been like this for a long time. I have a daunting task ahead of me. There will still be those that will resist like Raven did. It won't be safe for you all of the time," she explained.

"I know, but for you, I will take that chance." I leaned in close, kissed her on the lips, and said, "I love you always."

She responded, "In this life and the next."

The End

CPSIA information can be obtained
at www.ICGtesting.com
Printed in the USA
LVHW090727081019
633401LV00004BB/468/P